PRAISE FOR AMANDA LAMB

Amanda Lamb has crafted a compelling story... Maddie is definitely not dead last but out front, unearthing clues to the unfolding mystery. Keep digging, Maddie. Keep writing, Amanda!

–Scott Mason, author and Emmy-award-winning journalist

Amanda has a gift of taking the reader on a journey of intrigue, laughter, and insight into what can be the wonderful and troubling world of journalism. She opens the mind with a laser beam shot of reality and we are better for it.

–David Crabtree, award-winning television anchor and journalist.

I love the way Amanda Lamb plunges into a powerful plot and takes readers for a riveting ride! *Dead Last* kept me glued to the pages... The writing is crisp and clean. The story is compelling. There's an authenticity in Amanda's prose thanks, in part, to the author's background as a top-notch television journalist covering crime stories. What an awesome debut as a novelist!

–Bill Leslie, former news anchor for NBC affiliate WRAL-TV

Amanda Lamb weaves together an intriguing mystery with a behind-the-scenes look at TV news in her debut novel, *Dead Last*. With 25 years of crime reporting, Lamb spins an authentic, compelling story about a reporter who finds herself in the midst of solving a murder. Readers will love the colorful characters & personal insights that make this mystery a must-read.

–Sharon O'Donnell, author and award-winning columnist

DEAD LAST

a Maddie Arnette novel

DEAD LAST

a Maddie Arnette novel

AMANDA LAMB

Durham, NC

Dead Last
Amanda Lamb
www.alambauthor.com
books@lightmessages.com

Published 2020, by Light Messages
www.lightmessages.com
Durham, NC 27713 USA
SAN: 920-9298

Paperback ISBN: 978-1-61153-342-2
Ebook ISBN: 978-1-61153-329-3
Library of Congress Control Number: 2020931336

This book is dedicated to the real Maddie.
I miss you every single day...

1

THE RACE

As I CLIMBED THE HILL to the eleven-mile marker, I started feeling light-headed. The combination of needing something to boost my electrolytes and the midmorning heat was making my head throb. It was in the low fifties at the start of the race, but the early spring temperatures had quickly nudged their way into the seventies, making me deeply regret my decision not to wear shorts. I knew better.

I was lost in my personal reverie of heat exhaustion and the craving for Gatorade, when I noticed a commotion in front of me. A woman was falling. It looked like she was going down in slow motion, her arms and legs floating through the air in cartoon-like gestures that were unlikely to break her fall, in my split-second opinion. She hit the ground multiple times on her way down—knee, elbow, knee, elbow, forehead. In my head, a crescendo of symphony music narrated her fall. It escalated as she descended toward the unforgiving pavement.

It took a few seconds for me to grasp what was happening.

I was just a few feet away from where the woman's body lay sprawled out on the ground, a mass of bloody, tangled limbs. I had a choice—stop and help her, or move right and keep running, pretending like I didn't see her. I only had a moment to wrestle with my conscience. I had been training for this half-marathon for months. It was my first long race since my husband, Adam, died, and I was running in his honor. Around my neck I wore the pendant he had given me on our fifth anniversary, a straight golden arrow. He would want me to finish. But wouldn't he also want me to stop and help this woman?

I debated both scenarios. After all, what could I really do? I didn't have any medical training. I didn't even remember how to do CPR. I had no skills that qualified me to assist. Yet I knew in my heart that I was trying to justify my desire to keep running and temper my guilt. At that moment, my hand instinctively went to my throat and I touched the smooth, flat arrow. Despite the heat radiating from my skin, it felt cool to my touch.

"You're straight as an arrow, a straight shooter," Adam used to say to me. I stopped so quickly that I had to steady myself to keep from tripping and falling on top of the injured woman.

I wasn't the only person who stopped. The next few minutes were a dizzying combination of people screaming, running, and yelling into their cell phones, calling for help.

"There's a woman who fell. She's hurt badly. I don't know. We're running the road race. I think it's around mile eleven. I'm not from here. I don't know the roads," a middle-aged man in a white tank top that was stuck to his chest with sweat yelled into his phone. He switched hands and wiped his other palm on his red athletic shorts. "Does anybody know what road we're on?"

People yelled out where they thought we were.

"Williams Boulevard?"

"Near downtown."

Another woman said she would drop a pin and send it to 911. She was intensely scrolling through her phone and staring at the screen, wide-eyed. Another man ran across the street to a corner to get a better look at the street sign.

The injured woman had rolled onto her back and was moaning now, her limbs shaking uncontrollably. Blood thick with pieces of black asphalt chunks trickled from cuts on her limbs and forehead. At least she was conscious. That was the only good thing I could think of as I surveyed her injuries. The situation looked terrible in my non-medical opinion.

"Park Street, we're on Park Street," the sweaty man finally yelled into the phone after the man who had run across the street to look at the sign returned and confirmed the location. As he spoke to the 911 operator, he stared nervously at the woman on the ground.

I did the only thing I could think of. I got down on the ground next to the woman and knelt on the pavement beside her. I gently cradled her fingertips on the hand closest to me and leaned in close to speak to her as other runners, with towels and water bottles, gathered around to clean her wounds. The road scraped uncomfortably against my knees as I angled to get a better position where she could hear me.

"It's going to be okay. We'll get you help. I promise. Help is on the way," I said quietly, but firmly in her ear, glancing up at the man who was on the phone with 911. He nodded at me to let me know I was telling the truth. I could see a group of paramedics elbowing through the crowd of confused runners. Many of the racers were wearing headphones and were in their own little worlds, just like I had been seconds before this woman fell in front of me. It was clear many of them didn't understand what was happening, because they hadn't seen it happen. They were caught up in the race fog, the zone where all that mattered was pushing through the next two miles to the finish line. Instead of parting to let the paramedics pass, some of them looked annoyed by the interruption until they noticed the woman on the ground. Then they parted like the Red Sea, giving the emergency responders an even wider berth than they needed.

"No," the woman said to me, in between moans. "No, it's not."

"Not what?" I asked gently amidst the swirling chaos.

"Not going to be okay." The woman struggled to push the words out of her mouth, bordered by a protruding bottom lip which was swollen to twice the size of a normal lip. I tried not to look alarmed as I concentrated instead on making eye contact with her beneath her fluttering eyelids.

"Sure, it is," I said, with forced cheerfulness, wondering if the woman had broken bones. I assumed she was delirious with pain and didn't really know what she was saying. She probably wouldn't even remember this conversation.

"This wasn't an accident. My husband is trying to kill me." The woman whimpered and closed her eyes. "I think he may have poisoned me," she whispered. Her face went slack and her limbs stopped twitching. She was unconscious, and I felt my body being pushed aside by the paramedics. Hands were on my waist and shoulders, shoving me out of the way.

"Ma'am, you need to move aside," said a young blue-gloved paramedic in a crisp white uniform with one end of a stretcher in his hands, as he hip-checked me so he could pass.

I stepped back. Even though my skin was still red and glistening with sweat from the run, I shivered as a chill passed through my body. I was a journalist. People told me things all the time. Crazy things. Very little ruffled me. But in this moment, I wasn't a television reporter, I was just another runner. Why was this woman telling me something so outrageous? What did she expect me to do with this information? Should I go to the police?

I stood there, motionless, in the middle of the field of runners moving around me in every direction. Despite my stillness, my brain was moving faster than their feet.

I watched helplessly as four paramedics worked on the woman. There were flashes of color all around her—blue gloved hands flying, white towels covered in red blood stains. I wasn't sure what I should be doing. I didn't know the woman. My job was done. I had comforted her until help arrived. Still, something kept me there. I wanted to call someone for her, but I had no idea who to call. I certainly couldn't call her husband, given what she had just told me.

After a few minutes of checking vital signs, putting an oxygen mask on her face, and dressing her wounds, the emergency workers hoisted her onto the white canvas stretcher. A female paramedic ran alongside the stretcher holding the mini-oxygen tank that was attached to a mask on the woman's face. Two men on either end of the stretcher gripped the metal handles and rushed her into the back of an ambulance waiting a few feet away. The fourth paramedic ran ahead to open the wide panel doors of the vehicle. The runners parted instinctively to let the stretcher through, their eyes darted away. They avoided looking directly at the woman. I suspected they averted their gazes out of pity, respect, or fear of what they might see.

As the ambulance pulled away, the handful of us who had stopped to help were now left standing there in the middle of the road among a few discarded blue latex gloves and dirty towels. We were strangers who'd stopped to help another stranger. After an awkward moment, the group disbanded, shaking their heads, giving cursory waves, and either walking away or jogging back into the crowd. It was almost as if we felt too guilty resuming the run after what we had witnessed. But what choice did we have? We had to cross the finish line one way or the other.

Suddenly, a warm gusty breeze spun a piece of paper into the air and dropped it at the toe of my right sneaker. I shuffled closer to step on it and stop it from taking off again. I reached down and gingerly pulled it from beneath the front of my shoe, trying not to rip it. It was a race bib that was stained with what appeared to be a fresh spray of blood. I assumed it belonged to the woman who fell. Safety pins dangled from the corners of the number attached to torn white pieces of her shirt that still clung to them. The paramedics must have ripped the bib off while they were treating her. There were large black numbers across the front and the runner's name. 5556, Suzanne Parker.

I turned the paper over and examined it. There was handwritten information on printed lines on the back that are used to identify someone in case of an emergency. I reminded myself that I always failed to fill out the back of my bib as instructed. This was a wake-up call for me not to forget again.

Suzanne had written her age, 37; her address, 217 Sylvan Lane, Oak City; her phone number and her emergency contact person. It read: Tanner/husband and included his cell phone number next to it.

Why in the world would she put her husband as her emergency contact person if she thought he was trying to kill her? Everything about the situation screamed: "stay away." This wasn't my job anymore. I had given up crime reporting after Adam died. My heart wasn't in it anymore. After watching someone I loved wither away, the last thing I wanted to do was go to blood-spattered crime scenes and look at gruesome autopsy photos. Stepping back was the best thing I ever did for my sanity and for my family's well-being. My twins, Blake and Miranda, were now my number one priority. They needed me to be strong. I could never fill the void that losing their father left in their lives, but I owed it to them to try and love them enough for both of us.

Feature reporting was a big departure from the dark alleys, jails, and courtrooms where I'd honed my skills as a young journalist on the crime beat. But it was time for a change. When my manager came to me after I'd returned from family medical leave and asked me what would make me happy, I jokingly said, "Animal stories!"

Apparently as my boss was pondering my off-the-cuff remark, our marketing department had uncovered new research that showed the top trending stories on social media were stories about animals. Hence my new franchise was born: *Amazing Animal Tales*, often referred to by more sarcastic members of the newsroom as "Amazing Animal Tails." Yet they marveled at my ability to constantly come up with content to fill the tongue-and-cheek segment. There was no shortage of three-legged dogs named Tripod that had survived horrific accidents; cats that had crisscrossed the country, only to find their way home again years later; escaped emus that terrorized small towns; dogs rescuing kids who'd fallen down wells; blind horses that could traverse obstacle courses; and dolphins that could read humans' minds.

As I held the race bib, its bloody tattered edges fluttering in the wind, I decided I was not going in search of Suzanne Parker and her paranoid murder accusations. I was not going to rush to the hospital to see if she was still alive and pick her brain for more information. I was done with that life. I had spent years lurking around shadowy corners and fielding calls and text messages from dark people. I had finally clawed my way back into the light after Adam's death, and I didn't want anything to take that away from me, not even a woman who might really need my help.

As I sat in the backseat of the Uber headed toward Chester

Hospital, I told myself I was just going to check on Suzanne. I was not going there to get involved in any drama. I was a single mother now to two ten-year-olds. I needed to focus any my spare energy I could muster on them.

I felt it was only natural for me to want to see if Suzanne was okay. It was, after all, a traumatic experience to see someone fall like that. It was the right thing to do—I would just check on her to make sure she was okay, and then I would be on my way. I might not even talk to her. I might just ask someone in the emergency room what her condition was.

I had her name, and I could have called the hospital saying I was from the TV station, and asked for a condition update. So that I was sitting in the back of an Uber on my way to the hospital, while my fellow runners were taking photos with their medals and having a beer, was proof that I was already in too deep.

I just couldn't get her out of my mind. Not only the fall, but her chilling words: *My husband is trying to kill me*. She'd said them with conviction. They were hard to ignore and impossible to forget.

What if she was right and she was poisoned, and didn't survive? Wouldn't it then be my responsibility to tell the police what she had told me? I tried to push the frightening thought out of my head. Step one, find Suzanne.

I was thankful I had brought my phone with me during the race to listen to music because I could call an Uber. I had planned to meet friends at the beer tent at the end of the race, but I texted them that something came up and I had to leave. We rode together, started the race together, and then each ran at our own pace. Normally I would have been one of the first in our group to finish, but not this time. Given what had happened, finishing the race strong wasn't exactly my priority.

I half-heartedly ran the last two miles because I figured it would be easier to get an Uber downtown, where the race party was underway, than to try and cut over on some random street and get one. When I crossed the finish line and heard the electronic sensor *ding*. I didn't even look up to see my time on the large digital billboard. I knew I was probably one of the last finishers.

There were only a handful of spectators still milling around. Most people were in the food and drink area, enjoying a well-deserved snack. I quickly exited the racer's chute after a young female volunteer handed me my medal, with a big "Congratulations!" She clearly felt sorry for me because of my abysmal finish. I could see the pity in her eyes. I grabbed a bottle of water from the near-empty cooler and headed to the nearest street corner to call a myopic Uber.

One thing I didn't think of was how cold I might be after the race. Once you sweat and then cool off, it's hard to shake the chill. Even with leggings on, my exposed skin was covered with goosebumps. I wrapped my arms around my body to stay warm. The Uber driver's air condition wasn't helping any. I glanced at my phone to see what her name was.

"Kia, do you mind turning the air down a bit?"

"Sure." She chuckled. "But my name isn't Kia. It's Robin."

"Says right here, *Kia Soul*," I said, holding up my phone screen over the seat for her to see.

"Honey, that's the car I'm driving. A Kia Soul." She laughed, and I joined her, embarrassed and tickled by my mistake, happy for the distraction.

"It would be a pretty good name, you have to admit," I said after catching my breath.

"I might use it." She winked at me in her rearview mirror.

The moment of levity almost made me forget the seriousness of my mission—finding out if the woman who fell in front of me was still alive. The fall came rushing back to me, like I was replaying a piece of news footage, over and over, on my laptop. Only this time I couldn't slow it down or rewind it to study the intricacies of the moment. I could clearly picture Suzanne going down, her body parts hitting the pavement in a frightening series of split-second blows divided only by the symphony music in my head.

As a regular runner, I was no stranger to falls. One summer I slid on a sandy patch on a cement boardwalk at the beach and fell hard, first onto the pavement, and then into the coarse seagrass in the dunes. Like Suzanne, I bloodied my shoulders, elbows and knees. For the rest of the summer I wore large pieces of gauze secured by white medical tape to protect my wounds from the sun. I wasn't seriously injured, but my pride ached a little, especially when people asked me how I had gotten hurt. I wanted so much to have a better story.

So it was possible that Suzanne had simply lost her footing. It happens all the time with runners, especially if they're tired.

I thanked Robin and jumped out of her Kia Soul, chuckling when I said her correct name. She had dropped me at the curb in front of the emergency room doors. I looked down and realized I still had my bib number pinned to my shirt. I started to unpin it, and then decided it didn't matter. Nobody in an emergency room was going to pay any attention to me or what I was wearing. In my experience, most people in emergency rooms were focused on their own personal crises. I was always myopic when I took Adam to the hospital for emergency transfusions of platelets.

There was the time when the scrubs-clad, Puka-shell-wearing, Starbuck's-coffee-drinking, gelled-hair male nurse asked me flippantly what Adam's *concerns* were. At the time, Adam was leaning awkwardly to the side in the wheelchair, with a knit cap covering his bald head and a red fleece blanket wrapped around him from his mid-torso down to his ankles. I was always worried about him being cold and his temperature was one of the few things I could control.

"His concerns?" I said as I sensed my face morphing into an

open display of anger. "He's dying. He has a brain tumor. And without a transfusion, it's doubtful he'll make it through the night. Do those qualify as *concerns?*"

Without looking up, the nurse typed something into his computer and told us to take a seat. I ignored his request, and stood there right in front of his desk, staring at him. All I wanted was for Adam to be able to lie down while he waited for the transfusion, instead of sitting on his painful bed sores in the wheelchair. The staredown worked. We got into an exam room in just twelve minutes. Of course, he didn't get the transfusion for six more hours, but at least he was comfortable while he waited.

So on this day, as I exited the Uber and went through the revolving door into the emergency room and the rush of cold air inside hit me, I was right back in that moment with Adam. I even peered across the room at the front desk, looking for Mr. Puka Shell. This time I was met by an affable, middle-aged nurse. She stood up and guided me with her hand on my shoulder behind the desk and through the double doors.

"We're so glad you're here. She's been waiting for you. She told us to bring you right back when you got here." The nurse pushed me through the door marked *Staff Only,* into the treatment area.

"You must be...I'm not...it's just..." I was thinking Suzanne must have told them she had a friend racing with her, and the hospital staff assumed it was me because of the number pinned to my shirt. I shut up and decided this was most likely the only way I would get back there to see her considering I wasn't family, and if her friend hadn't arrived Yet she needed someone with her. At least, that's what I told myself in order to silence my inner voice that knew I was breaking all sorts of medical privacy rules by allowing the ruse to continue.

"She took a bad fall, and she's pretty bruised up," the nurse said. "Still waiting on results on the concussion and toxicology.

Checking to see if she has any medication in her system that could have contributed to her accident," the nurse rattled on. "Do you know if she was taking any prescription medication? Her race bib, where people generally include that information, must have come off when they were working on her, because it wasn't on her when she came in. She hasn't been able to help us with much. She's loopy from the pain meds we gave her."

The nurse was speaking so fast, I was pretty sure there had been a pot of coffee that she had just drained in the break room. I couldn't shoehorn one word into her monologue.

I suddenly realized that Suzanne must have identified the person she was waiting for as a relative, someone who would be allowed to have her medical information. Otherwise, the nurse would never be telling me all this. I dared not interrupt her for fear of blowing my cover.

The nurse was a perky, blond woman in scrubs, with a friendly but tired round face that didn't match the intensity of her chatter. She pulled back a white curtain to let me pass into the treatment area, and then drew it closed behind me. Suzanne was hooked up to several machines with wires and tubes dangling from a medal stand next to the bed. Her hands and forehead were wrapped in blood-soaked gauze bandages. Her long dark hair was stiff and matted on the pillow beneath her. As soon as I slid into the green recliner next to the bed, her eyes shot open and she looked directly at me, parting her swollen lips slightly.

Here it is, I thought. The jig is up. Here is the moment she tells the nurse I am not the person she was waiting for, she rings her call bell, and I promptly get evicted from the treatment area. And maybe even worse than that, they call hospital security and tell them I'm a journalist who lied about my identity to get into a patient's room.

"Sis, I'm so glad you're finally here," she said just above a whisper, with a weak smile. She looked in the direction of the perky-but-tired nurse who now appeared to be deep into writing down some information from one of the bedside machines, on a chart attached to a clipboard.

I sat stunned, trying to process what was happening. My first assumption was that she was delusional from the fall and the drugs and really thought I was her sister. My second guess was that somehow this woman knew exactly who I was and wanted to make sure I was allowed into her room. But how could she have possibly known I would come?

We sat in silence for a few seconds. I took a deep breath and decided I would give this bizarre scenario a few minutes to play out. I told myself I could leave at any moment. I didn't owe this woman anything. I just came to make sure she was going to be okay. I was not here to complicate my life.

A minute later, perky-but-tired nurse opened the curtain so she could step out, and then pulled it closed behind her, leaving us alone. I sat there staring at this strange injured woman, wondering how I had fallen into another rabbit hole.

I was still and quiet for a moment as I tried to gather my thoughts and assess the situation. Maybe Suzanne had a head injury and was confused about who I was? If that was the case, it might be medically unadvisable for me to say anything to upset her. So I waited for her to speak again, my back rigid in the chair as I shivered when I remembered how cold I was.

"You can call me Suzanne, but you probably already know my name, because you're here," she said with a sluggishness in her voice, like she was struggling to speak through her swollen lips. The painkillers were also probably contributing to her slurred, labored speech.

She parted her lips and tried to give me a toothy grin. It made her look a little bit crazy. She winced in pain, but at the same time tried to hold her lips rigid like she was posing for a photograph. Was it a wicked smile? I didn't know this woman, but this definitely wasn't the tender, my-sister-is-here smile she had given me when the nurse was in the room with us.

"I knew you would come," she said, without slurring this time, turning her head slowly on the pillow to look directly at me. I looked around the room for a moment, wondering if the voice had come from somewhere else, because it was so clear this time.

"Look." I shifted uncomfortably in the green leather chair, trying to pull it away from the bed to put some distance between us. "I think there's some kind of misunderstanding. I'm not—"

"Not my sister. Of course you're not. You didn't really think I thought you were? I just said that so they would let you back here." She closed her eyes as if our conversation was requiring too much energy. Then she chuckled a little like someone losing her mind.

"I was running the race. I was right behind you when you fell, and I just stayed with you until help arrived."

"I know, and thank you, thank you so much. So scared." She opened her eyes wide and stared at a spot on the ceiling. "You don't even know. I didn't totally realize what was going on, then suddenly *I did*. Everything went gray, fuzzy, started to fall, couldn't stop myself. Legs felt like jelly." She waved her bandaged hand to a hidden melody, above the blanket like a conductor in front of an invisible orchestra.

A red oxygen monitor was clipped to her middle finger and protruded through a hole cut through the thick layer of white tape on her bandaged hand.

"So how did you know I would come?"

"Because of what I told you," she said matter-of-factly turning away from the ceiling to look at me again, this time with her deep brown expressionless eyes. I couldn't read them, they were so dark.

"I haven't told anyone else my suspicions. Only you. You were the first one, the only one. Before, I was afraid to say it out loud. But now it's out. When I said it to you it was like a huge weight lifted off me to know that someone else knows. I know it sounds crazy, a woman you don't know telling you this unbelievable thing, this horror story. It even sounds crazy to me now as I talk about it. But maybe I am a little crazy after everything he's put me through."

Everything this woman was telling me seemed sincere. But it still was not making sense. What did she expect me to do about it?

"I was so dizzy. I run all the time, and I've never felt like that before. Think he definitely put something in my water, maybe not enough of something to kill me, but enough to mess me up, make me collapse, to hurt me in little ways," she said, breathlessly, and then started hacking like she might be coughing up a lung.

"Do you want me to call the nurse?" I got to my feet, my gaze darting at the monitors around the bed, not knowing what I was looking at or for. I must have blocked all the medical knowledge I'd gained during Adam's many stays at the hospital. I couldn't remember what was what, yet the sounds—the beeps, the whooshing of the machines, were all too familiar.

"No, I'm fine," she said, between gritted teeth, and clearing her throat. "Just water, please."

I started to hand her the Styrofoam cup filled with ice water on the bedside table. A straw was suspended by a thick chunk of shaved ice in the middle of the cup. As I waited for her to take it from me, I realized the bandages wrapped clumsily around her hands wouldn't allow her to grasp anything, so I lifted the straw gingerly to her red swollen lips and let her take a few sips. When she stopped drinking, I pulled the cup away and set it back down on the table. It seemed like an intimate gesture to share with someone I didn't know. Many times I had helped Adam take sips of water in a hospital bed, but she was a stranger.

"Thank you. Whatever he gave me dried my mouth out. Like cotton. Awful."

"Your husband?" I asked, confused, not sure if she was talking about what the doctor gave her in the emergency room, or the poison she allegedly got from her husband.

"Yes, he put something in my water bottles. I know it. Well, suspect it. I found them filled on the counter early this morning, with a note that said, *Run hard*. Not his style. He's not thoughtful like that. Not sure why I didn't pour them out right away. Should have known. He's a doctor. He would know just how to do something like this."

Suzanne closed her eyes as if what she'd just told me sapped her last bit of energy. Within seconds, her breathing took on the regular cadence of a person in a deep sleep. I turned to see the nurse peeking from behind the curtain.

"She may be out for a good long while. She was hysterical when she got here. Like I told you, we gave her something for the pain and something to make her less anxious. It might make her sleepy." The nurse busied herself with the various machines again. "She'll be getting a room as soon as a bed becomes available. She'll need to stay here at least tonight to make sure she has no serious injuries. Plus, there may be some stiches needed, and I'm afraid she's got broken ribs. Unfortunately, not much you can do about that. Just got to wait and let them heal. She's very lucky, considering the spill she took. That's why I don't run. It's too dangerous." She chuckled and a winked, smoothing down her scrubs over her curvy figure.

I smiled at her joke and nodded, trying to be polite. I was still too confused about who I was supposed to be and what I had just learned to even come up with an appropriate response. I moved away from the bed and offered the nurse a half-hearted wave as I ducked out of the room, into the hallway. It was a mistake to come here. The last thing I wanted to do was get mixed up in someone's marital strife.

At the same time, I felt sorry for Suzanne. She seemed desperate, but what she was telling me also seemed insane—that she had been poisoned but was able to run eleven miles before collapsing. And even if her husband really was trying to kill her, she needed help from the police, not from a local television reporter who did stories on pot-bellied pigs.

I looked for the closest exit sign and bolted toward it. It was part anxiety and part cold that made me run so fast. But even as I was escaping the gray halls of the hospital where I had spent so many unhappy moments with Adam, I had a feeling I was not done with this place or with Suzanne.

2

BUSINESS AS USUAL

I ASKED FOR THIS, I reminded myself as I listened to the voicemail from my assignment editor telling me what my story was going to be that day.

"Maddie, this is an amazing story. You are going to absolutely love this one," Janie gushed. "Call me back."

Janie Paige thought everything was *amazing* when she pitched stories for my animal beat. While I appreciated her passion, I also knew that behind her enthusiasm was yet another pet tale that was probably going to be not-so-amazing. I would just have to create some magic and make chicken salad out of whatever was thrown at me. I kept telling myself that at least I wasn't on my way to a crime scene where someone had cut up a body with a chain saw, put it in a cooler, and dumped it in alligator-infested waters after first trying to burn it with lighter fluid, in a metal trashcan. That was one of my cases the previous year.

"Okay, so what's this amazing story?" I asked Janie, trying

to match her excitement, born in equal parts from her youth and her exhaustingly positive personality. I had her on speaker phone while I did planks in my den. My arms and legs trembled as I rounded the two-minute corner.

Janie said in a rush of words without breaths. "So a woman leaves the room for a minute while her baby is in the high-chair eating breakfast. The family's parrot, Puffin, is in a cage nearby chattering away, because they talk a lot, right? They mimic what people say," I nodded my head even though she couldn't see me through the phone. I glanced at my sports watch as it counted down my three-minute plank. My whole body was shaking now, but I refused to quit.

"So kid picks up a grape, it goes down the wrong pipe, gets stuck in her throat. She's choking. Bird starts screaming, 'Mama, the baby. 911. Mama, the baby. 911!' Woman comes running back into the room, does the Heimlich thingy-ma-bob on the kid, out pops the grape. The parrot saved the kid's life. Isn't that amazing?"

I collapse on the white fluffy rug beneath me, face-planting in the soft curly shag. I picture my interview with the tearful mother bouncing her chubby, adorable baby on her knee while Puffin preens over her shoulder in the background, playing the reluctant hero. I want to stay here, buried in my rug, and hang up the phone. But I know I can't do that. I force myself out of my prone position, into child's pose and turn my head to the side so I can respond to Janie without being muffled by the carpet.

"Wow, Janie. That is something. How do you find these stories?" My voice was part incredulous, part sarcastic. Janie didn't seem to notice.

"I know, right? I get so many emails about these animal stories, it blows my mind. I wade through them until I find a home run like this one. I mean, we can't do dogs finding kids trapped in sink holes every single day. Got to branch out. This one is the bomb."

I couldn't disagree with her on either front. Our viewers did seem to love a good animal-hero story. Whenever I previewed my stories on Twitter, Facebook or Instagram, I got hundreds, sometimes thousands of likes, comments, and shares. When I used to cover crime, I was lucky to get a couple dozen interactions on a post about a murder investigation or a trial. Because social media engagement was quickly becoming an important part of how my company measured the value of its on-air talent, the more interesting my stories were to the social media audience, the more positive feedback I got from my managers.

When I reached ten thousand followers on Twitter, I got the following email from one of my supervisors: *Congratulations on reaching this fantastic milestone!* I read it twice to make sure he was talking about Twitter.

I pictured myself taking a quick video with my phone or doing a Facebook Live, panning from the cherubic baby to the heroic bird, and posting it with a cute caption like *You won't believe this story. He's more than just a pet. He's a lifesaver.* It was guaranteed to get me a couple of thousand interactions online from dedicated fans. I was in. I pushed myself up to a standing position so I could stretch.

"Just give me the address and tell Buster I will meet him there."

"Yes, the mom and the baby and Puffin are available at eleven o'clock, which is perfect because Buster needs to work with Virginia at the state legislature after your shoot."

"He's not going to like that, pulling double duty." I lunged with one leg and stretched the other calf. She already knew this about Buster Patton, my regular photographer, how he hated to be pulled in multiple directions in one day.

"I know, but we're short today, and Dex told me there were no other options." She was referring to our surly assignment manager. Dex Hunt was surly mainly because he had to figure out how to staff a newsroom to fill more than ten hours of news programming a day from 4:30 a.m. through 11:30 p.m., with about half the number of people he needed.

Dex was a retired Army captain. Sometimes his assignments felt like military orders with no room for interpretation or negotiation. In this case I decided it was Buster's battle to fight, not mine.

I got the parrot-woman's address from Janie and mapped it on my phone. It was only about twenty minutes away, which meant I had plenty of time to get ready. The twins had already left for school via carpool. The rare mornings when I didn't have to rush to school and then rush to an assignment felt like a gift. Just having five extra minutes to drink my first cup of coffee without it becoming lukewarm while I raced around the house looking for book bags, jackets, and shoes, made a major difference in my demeanor. I cherished my time with my kids, but since Adam died, the mundane tasks of everyday life, without his help and support, sometimes seemed insurmountable.

As I backed out of my driveway, a steaming travel mug of coffee wafting its delicious scent from my cupholder, my phone rang. I looked down at the screen on my armrest, which showed the number was *an unidentified caller*, which meant the person was not one of the twenty thousand or so contacts already programmed into my phone. Usually I would let these unknown calls go to voicemail, but for some reason I hit the answer button.

"Maddie Arnette," I said, in my professional, no-nonsense voice, which I reserved for business calls. It was a mixture of "How can I help you?" combined with a healthy dose of "I don't have a lot of time. Get to the point, please."

"Oh, thank God I got you, Maddie. It's Suzanne Parker. Suzanne from the race. I have to see you. He's crazy, seriously.

You have to help me." Her voice pleaded just above a whisper. I quickly scanned my brain, trying to remember if I had told her my name at the hospital. I guess I did. But how did she have my cell number? I didn't remember giving it to her.

"Slow down, okay? What's going on? Where are you? Are you still in the hospital?"

"Yes," Suzanne said, in a raspy whisper, "but I'm in the stairwell."

"In the stairwell? What in the world are you doing there?" I swerved to avoid a moped that was traveling at about half the posted speed limit. I was so distracted that I decided to pull over into a drugstore parking lot while we talked. Puffin would have to wait.

"I was lying in bed, you know, just dozing, when I looked up and saw him wandering around outside my room. He had flowers. Can you believe that? Brought me goddamn flowers after he'd tried to kill me. Was so scared. Started shaking, couldn't stop. Somehow, don't know how, I pretended to be asleep. Closed my eyes, made my breathing very slow. He tiptoed into the room. Thought for sure he was going to strangle me. I kept one eye open a crack so I could see where he was the whole time. I was ready to scream if he touched me. And just when I thought something bad was going to happen, he stopped about a foot from my bed and left the flowers on the table next to me. Must have gotten spooked by a nurse or something and rushed out of the room. Didn't see him go, but I heard him bump into the table and knock it into the wall. When I heard the door close, I snuck out into the hallway, made sure he was gone, and ducked into the stairwell to call you. I was so afraid he might come back."

I was having a hard time hearing Suzanne. It sounded like she was cupping her hands around the phone. I knew I should just tell her that I was busy, that I was on my way to an assignment, and that she should call hospital security if she was truly afraid. But before I could stop myself, I was offering to help. My conscience wouldn't allow me to take the risk of not believing her the way my mother's friends had not believed her when she told them about my father. My mother's story was always the thing that turned me from a journalist into a bleeding heart in situations like this. I couldn't let Suzanne's story end the same way as my mother's story did.

"Do you want me to call someone, hospital security, the police?" I whispered, for no apparent reason since I was sitting alone in my car.

"No! No police. He's really connected. If I report him without proof that's he done something wrong, he'll just make my life more miserable."

"Well, you can't stay in the stairwell all day. He's probably gone by now. Why don't you stay on the phone with me and walk back out into the hallway and see if it's clear. If he's there, let me know. A doctor is not going to be stupid enough to do something to you in a hospital where there are witnesses."

"Ok," Suzanne replied, in a shaky voice.

I could hear the whoosh of a door, and then a cacophony of hospital background noise—people talking, buzzers and alarms going off, metal carts rolling by on the linoleum floor.

"I don't see him," Suzanne said, in a normal voice that startled me because it was so much louder than the muffled whisper she had been using. "I think he's gone."

"Good. Go back to your room and get some rest. You need to focus on recuperating so you can go home."

"That's the last place I want to go," Suzanne said, above the rustle of what sounded like her sheets as she was apparently climbing back into bed. *Good girl*, I thought to myself.

"What I want is for you to believe me," Suzanne whined, sounding more like a little girl than a grown woman. "Can't you come back to the hospital so I can tell you the whole story."

"Suzanne, I'm at work. Besides, I'm sure you have a lot of friends and relatives who know you much better than I do. They would be the best sounding board for what you're dealing with."

"I do. But I need someone neutral to help me sort this thing out. Everyone loves Tanner. His patients love him, even my friends and family love him. So I can't talk to them about it. They're biased. He's a great actor. He's got everyone fooled. He pretends to be this great guy. But he has a dark side to him...." It got so quiet I wondered if she had gone back into the stairwell.

"Talk about what?" I heard a strange male voice, in the background.

"Nothing," I heard Suzanne say. "Nothing at all, Tanner." I couldn't help but wonder how much of our conversation he had heard and what the repercussions might be for her. But it was too late to ask. The line went dead.

I threw the car in reverse so hard it felt like it jumped off the ground. I tried to calm myself down, to tell myself that Suzanne's phone probably died, that she was fine, and that Tanner couldn't do anything to her in a public place like a hospital. He wouldn't be that stupid.

I hit Buster's number on the touch screen in my car and waited several rings for him to pick up.

"Buster, I need you to do me a favor. I need you to interview this parrot lady without me. I'll meet you back at the office later to log the tape and write the story."

"You know Dex doesn't like it when we do it that way. He wants to see you talking to the woman on camera. He wants long two-shots of you guys walking together and talking about the baby-saving-parrot," Buster said, with more than a dash of sarcasm.

"I know. I promise this is the last time. Something came up. Something important," I sped east on the highway, toward the hospital.

"Something always comes up," he said in his most critical voice, but then softened.

He had given me my fair share of passes since Adam died, but I was concerned my credit in the good karma bank was about to dry up.

"Okay, but you owe me. These people can be so hokey. I'm not good with hokey." He gave a grunt and a laugh that made me feel that I had at least one fire under control.

As I got closer to Chester Hospital, I told myself that I had to be calm. I had to make Tanner think Suzanne and I were old friends and I was just coming to check in on her. I couldn't let him suspect that she had told me anything about what was going on between them.

I parked in the hospital garage and headed across the breezeway toward the patients' rooms. I wondered what kind of doctor Tanner was. I knew some doctors could be arrogant, afflicted with the God complex, but arrogance alone didn't make someone an attempted murderer. And bringing flowers to the bedside of the woman you just tried to kill seemed like a major contradiction.

As I approached Suzanne's room, I noticed the door was ajar just a crack. I started to push it open, and then decided against it. I didn't want this man to think I was in a hurry to get into the room, so I knocked first.

"Suzanne, hey there, it's Maddie. Can I come in?"

"Maddie?"

"Yes, I won't stay long. Just wanted to check in on you."

I pushed the door open a little wider only to see her lying quietly in her bed. The gauze on her wounds looked fresh, and her skin was regaining some color. She was curled up on her side, facing the door in a fetal position, with the covers bunched up in between her balled, bandaged hands. Her eyes were closed, but her lids flapped like butterfly wings at the sound of me coming into the room. Looking at her in this state, I couldn't imagine her having been out of bed just fifteen minutes prior when we were on the phone together. I wondered if she was acting so fragile because Tanner was still in the hospital, and she didn't want him to know she was getting better.

"Maddie, you came." She uncurled of one of her balled hands and reaching out in my direction. "You really came." A weak smile spread across her face. It looked as if it might be painful for her jaw. She winced.

"Yes, I had to make sure you were okay. Are you okay? Is he gone?" I whispered for fear he might still be within earshot. I was starting to wonder if Tanner had ever really been there, or if Suzanne had told me that just to get me to the hospital.

"He left. I told him I was too tired to visit with him. He told me he'd be back tomorrow, that they would probably release me then, and he would take me home." She squeezed my hand as tight as she could through the bandages and looked at me with wide, frightened eyes. "I won't go with him. I won't."

"Suzanne, do you have anyone you can stay with? A friend or relative? I'm sure they will believe you if you tell them what's going on."

"There's no one, no one I can trust." Her voice filled with tears.

There was a knock at the door and a young nurse came in and explained that she needed to take Suzanne's vital signs. She was petite and in pink scrubs, with her brown hair pulled back in a tight ponytail. She checked Suzanne's pulse and temperature and then readjusted her bandages, occasionally glancing at her clipboard, which lay on the end of the bed. I sat silently in the chair next to the bed, feeling awkward about having this nurse perform intimate duties while I was in the room with a woman I barely knew.

"You're almost done with this antibiotic. Not sure if the doctor ordered another bag. I'll check." The no-nonsense nurse picked up a bag from the IV pole and held it up to the light to look at the tiny puddle of gold liquid that remained in the bottom.

My eyes trailed from the bag down the plastic tube to Suzanne's arm, where presumably a needle was stuck in a vein beneath several pieces of white tape that held it in place.

How had she gone into the stairwell if she was attached to this IV? Sure, you could walk down the hall rolling the tall metal IV stand, but it was unlikely in her condition that she could have done this, let alone opened a door and taken it into a stairwell. Again, I wondered if her cries for help were just aimed at getting me to come. After all, she was obviously lonely and scared.

Everything inside of me was screaming that I needed to leave again, to run away from this situation, but something else much more powerful was tugging at me to stay. If what she was telling me was true, she might end up dead. I couldn't risk that. When I closed my eyes, I pictured my mother covered in blood from a gunshot wound. I was never sure if it was a true memory, or if it was a picture I made up, cobbled together from what others had told me and from various media accounts I had read online over the years.

"Suzanne, are you sure you're telling me everything? Was Tanner really here?" I scanned the room for clues.

"Yes, he was here. He was sitting right where you are, just before you got here. He's gone now," she said, groggily, closing her eyes. She emphasized the word *gone*.

I wanted to believe her, but something other than the logistics of moving with the IV was bothering me about her story. I looked at the bedside table—*no flowers.* She'd specifically told me that Tanner had left her flowers next to her bed. I wasn't going to make a big scene, but I was starting to feel like I had been played, and I needed to leave quickly before I said something to this woman that I might regret.

"Suzanne, I should be at work. I've really got to go back to the office."

I stood up and practically ran to the door without looking back to see her reaction. I was so single-minded I didn't see the nurse returning to the room with a large vase of flowers in her hands. I almost ran right into her, but instead moved to my right to let her pass with a whispered "excuse me." As I stepped into the hallway, I could hear the nurse's voice in the distance behind me.

"Miss Parker, I found a vase to put your pretty flowers in from your husband. I'll put them on the windowsill right next to your cards so you can see them."

Puffin's owner, Penelope Bunch, said directly to the camera. "And then I heard a screech. Not his normal screech, but a high-pitched screech. Almost human-like. And that's when I knew something was really wrong. Am I looking at the right place? I know you said to look at the chair to the right of the camera and pretend someone is interviewing me, but I keep looking into the camera. I can't help it. Sorry, do we need to do that again?"

"No, it's fine. Don't worry about it. So what happened next?" Buster's disembodied voice came from somewhere off-camera.

I could tell by his lilt that he was annoyed with the woman and simply wanted her to get on with her story.

As I stared at my computer screen, headphones blocking out the newsroom noise, and logged the interview for the bird-saves-baby-from-choking story, all I could think about was Suzanne. What was really going on with her? I had googled her name and discovered she was a public relations executive who specialized in crisis management. She had a local office, but according to her website, her clients—some major corporations and high-profile people—were from all over the country.

She was heralded for rehabilitating the image of a bigtime CEO in California who got his secretary pregnant and then fired her after she refused to have an abortion. Suzanne framed it that the young woman had trapped him and was just after his money. She said he'd never asked the woman to have an abortion because he was Catholic and wouldn't have done that. Suzanne said the secretary made up this allegation after he refused to give in to her blackmail demands.

Suzanne also represented a company that had discovered e coli at forty-five of its restaurants across the country, which ultimately led to all 675 of its franchisees dumping a week's supply of meat. The company lost millions of dollars, but with Suzanne's help, they saved their business from going under by being transparent about the problem and promising the highest possible standards of food safety going forward. She said it would be like an airport after a terrorist attack—the safest place in the world to eat.

I was sincerely impressed with her credentials and couldn't imagine how her husband had turned this pit bull of a businesswoman into the scared patient who cowered in a stairwell at Chester Hospital. But I also knew that education and wealth didn't insulate you from domestic violence.

I also checked her Facebook page, but her account was set to private. Only one stunning profile picture appeared on the screen. It was hard to believe it was the same woman. Her perfectly coiffed, long dark hair framed her heart-shaped face accented by rosebud-shaped red lips, long black lashes, and penetrating brown eyes. She was giving the camera a coy sideways glance.

When I googled Dr. Tanner Parker, I found nothing. The only thing I could imagine was that he may have a different last name than his wife, which wouldn't be unusual for a professional couple. I tried searching doctors by first name only, but was rewarded with hundreds of random results that led me nowhere. I made a mental note to ask Suzanne what his last name was, and then I chastised myself. I had already decided *not* to go any deeper into Suzanne's drama, but I couldn't help myself. I wore the memory of my mother's death like a heavy coat that sometimes suffocated my better judgment.

"How does it look?" a voice said, from behind me. I could see Buster looming at the corner of my desk, in my peripheral vision.

"Looks good. Sorry again that you had to shoot it alone. Like I said, there's something I've kind of gotten wrapped up in. Not sure what the deal is yet. Trying my best to walk away."

"Heard that one before." Buster chuckled then opened my top desk drawer to the right of the computer and grabbed a jar of peanuts, opened it and helped himself to a handful. "Maddie, don't take on something else. I know you. Remember why you walked away from the dark side in the first place. Adam would want you to work on being as stress-free as possible so you can concentrate on the kids. Got to go. Heading out to the legislature with Virginia."

I couldn't see his eye roll as he turned and walked away, but I knew there was one. Buster was unusually calm despite the disruption in his day. He was also being uncharacteristically sensitive about my delicate balancing act between sanity and going over the edge. He had witnessed my downward spiral in the months following Adam's death, and I think he was ready for me to crawl out of the dark hole and re-enter the world of the living again.

I was now alone in the crowded newsroom with my

headphones isolating me from the white noise. I started thinking about what Buster had said about Adam. He was right. Adam had begged me to get off the crime beat years before he even got sick. He had watched me every single day as the job depleted my energy and robbed my soul of positive karma. It was like I was walking around with PTSD that flared up with each brutal crime I covered.

Taking care of Adam was the turning point in my career. His death stripped me of any desire to cover other people's tragedies. The last thing I wanted to do was knock on another door of the parents of a dead child. But was feature reporting really the answer? Did it give me the intensity that my personality thrived on? I hadn't examined this question. It was as if I was afraid to think about it. I had once been in the middle of the fire. Now I was so far away from the fire I couldn't even see it.

I felt Suzanne's story tugging at me, the mystery of it, the familiarity of a puzzle begging to be solved. As much as I was trying to keep it at bay, I couldn't ignore it.

The truth was I had been running away my entire life, way before Adam's death, since the day Roger killed my mother.

3

TOES IN

I NERVOUSLY STIRRED the foaming milk in the top of my latte, dissolving the artistic heart the barista had made on the surface. It was just a meeting, I told myself. I wasn't committing to anything. I didn't hear from Suzanne after I left the hospital that day. I didn't hear from her the next day or the day after that. I assumed we were done, that whatever strange, brief relationship had developed between us out of her trauma was over, and that we were both moving on. I was relieved.

Three days after Suzanne was released from Chester Hospital, she called. I was on my way to an early dentist appointment and told her I only had a small window of time to talk. I had saved her number in my phone so I would have the option of screening her calls in the future. I picked up this time because I felt like it was best that we have a clean break.

"So Maddie, I'm back in the house. I didn't know what else to do. It's ironic that I help people deal with crises for a living, yet I can't solve my own crisis." She punctuated her sentence with an uncomfortable laugh that trailed off into silence.

Suzanne went on to tell me that if she left, Tanner would surely kill her because he wasn't about to fight her for custody of their fourteen-year-old son, Winston, or pay her alimony. She said he was cheap and possessive of his son. She also told me he had a mean streak that no one else ever saw but her.

"You need to call the police," I told her again. "You need to get a domestic violence protective order." I heard my words coming out as hollow promises of safety. I knew from experience that neither the police, nor a restraining order could protect someone when an abuser was determined to harm.

Suzanne said she knew if she reported her suspicions about Tanner, she would come across to the family court judge as a hysterical woman, someone unfit to have custody of her son. He was a doctor with an impeccable reputation as a strong, stable medical professional in the community and she was a crisis-management public relations hack with a reputation for hyperbole.

By the end of our conversation, I had agreed to meet Suzanne for coffee so we could continue talking through this in person. Everything in my gut told me not to do it, but it wasn't the first time I had ignored my gut.

When she walked into the coffee shop, I couldn't believe this was the same woman I had seen in in the hospital. She looked exactly like her pulled-together self in her Facebook profile picture. Her long black, sleek hair fell halfway down her back and cascaded over the front of her shoulders. Her snug, red wrap dress fit her curves impeccably. She strode across the restaurant in black patent stiletto heels. When I wore high heels, I looked like I was walking on a high wire between two skyscrapers. She looked like she was walking on the red carpet at Fashion Week in Paris.

Across Suzanne's left arm was a black cashmere wrap. Over

her other arm was a large silver bag that looked like it was big enough to fit a small car. Her outfit was punctuated by a statement piece, a massive black braided rope necklace that looked like it must weigh fifty pounds.

"Hope I'm not late, Maddie," Suzanne said with what appeared to be a freshly lipsticked smile. Her pale skin was flawless. Her long, black eyelashes looked like something out of a mascara advertisement. They had to be extensions, I thought. She glanced down at her phone in her hand. "Just seven minutes," she said to no one in particular referencing her tardiness.

"No worries. How are you, Suzanne? How are you feeling? You look great!"

"Still tired. A few knots on my head, and those darn scrapes on my knees are taking forever to heal. Otherwise, pretty good. They found nothing in my system in the first toxicology screen, but I told them I wanted a full in-depth panel done. That takes about sixty days, and they're making me pay for it out of my own pocket. Insurance won't cover it because it's not deemed medically necessary." Suzanne waved her hand in the air as if to say, *jerks.* "But I need to know what I am up against. Sneaky bastard. I'm still convinced there was something in my water. I didn't just fall for no reason."

"So you're home. Is that a good idea? I mean, do you feel safe?"

"No, it's not a good idea, Maddie, but I don't have any other good ideas right now. He's acting all sweet. But I know he's full of crap. I found something in his phone that I think may explain some things."

Suzanne slid her phone across the table so it was facing me. She hit the picture icon and pulled up a screenshot of a text. It read *See you at noon. Can't wait*. It was followed by three heart emojis and signed *G6*.

"Well, that could be an affair, no doubt. It is suspicious,

but we don't know anything for sure. And Suzanne, in my experience, there are plenty of men who cheat on their wives, but that doesn't mean they're killers."

"True, but you don't know Tanner. He's an all-in or all-out kind of guy. When I first met him, he was in medical school. He was engaged to this little mousy thing. They had even put down a deposit at the country club for their wedding reception. He dropped her in a nanosecond when he decided he wasn't into her anymore and would rather be with me. He did it the day the wedding invitations were postmarked. That should have been a big red flag for me. But I was in love, or lust, or some youthful combination of the two, and I couldn't see it. But now I do. If he's done with me, he's done with me."

If Tanner really was a complete narcissist in the way Suzanne was describing him, maybe he was capable of harming her. What if I had the power to stop that from happening? What if someone had helped my mother get away from Roger? Would she still be alive? I didn't want to live in the land of *what if* anymore.

"Suzanne, what can I do to help?" I heard the words tumble out of my mouth, like it was an out-of-body experience. I was hovering above the table, looking down at myself with this woman getting ready to say *yes* to something that would most certainly take me down a complicated path.

"I knew you were the right person to talk to." Suzanne reached across the table with both hands and grasped my right hand firmly, not letting go. It was uncomfortable to be touched by this woman I barely knew.

"I know you're a reporter. I recognized you the minute I saw you standing over me that day of the race, when I was lying there battered and bruised in the street. Later when I thought about it, I decided it must be a sign, having you come into my life in that way, in that very moment when I really needed someone with a clear head like yours."

"I wondered how you knew my name, how you got my cell phone number."

"I called the station and Janie gave it to me. She's so sweet. I told her I was an old friend of yours and was in town for a few days and absolutely *needed* to connect with you."

Janie. Of course. I should have known. I made a mental note to talk to her yet again about giving out my cell phone number to random people who called the news desk.

"But Suzanne, you know I don't do crime reporting anymore. I'm a feature reporter. I basically cover lost cats and dogs that rescue people from wells." I gave a nervous laugh. I still didn't believe this nonsense was really my job.

"Maddie, I get it. I'm not talking about a story. I'm talking about my life. You *were* a crime reporter, so you have the skills to help me investigate this situation on the down-low so I can figure out what I'm dealing with and get out safely."

"Suzanne, I'd be glad to help in any way I can, but why not hire a private investigator, someone more qualified than me to help you unravel this situation? You need someone who can help you gather real evidence that will help you in family court with your son's custody situation."

Suzanne rolled right over my suggestion, like she didn't hear me.

"Like an idiot, I ignored my mother's sage advice. She's a lawyer. Against her advice I co-mingled our finances a few years after we were married. He sees everything I do, from a financial standpoint. I can't buy a goddamn pair of shoes without him knowing. He really doesn't care about things like shoes, but I'm pretty sure he would notice me paying for the services of a PI."

I shook my head and stirred my coffee that was now lukewarm. I heard Buster's voice in my head telling me not to dip my feet in the pool any deeper than they already were, to just get up and walk away. But then I pictured my beautiful mother, a woman I never really got a chance to know. I thought about Winston, a little boy who could possibly be in danger, and I knew I had no choice but to help Suzanne.

"I'll do it. Where do we start?"

"How about we find out who G6 is?"

No good reporter gets scoops from public sources. Sure, there are things you need to check in order to get the basic details for your story—court records, arrest records, search warrants. But the real meat comes from insiders who trust you enough to share information with you confidentially. For me, that person was Kojak.

He was an old-school cop with a cropped beard and not a lick of hair on his head. He always wore wire-framed glasses perched on the tip of his nose. I suspected that he didn't really need them to see as much as he thought he did, but he kept them there, balanced on the end of his nose just in case. Because he was a detective, he dressed in plain clothes, but his badge and service revolver were always on the left side of his belt just beneath the flap of his jacket, where he could reach them quickly.

Sometimes, for fun, I would ask him to open his jacket just so I could see the badge, like they did on the crime show dramas on television. This usually caused both of us to deteriorate into guttural laughter.

"How do I know you're a real cop?" I would say.

"Take a look at this, ma'am. Does this look real to you?" He would respond haughtily.

"Actually, it kind of looks like the badge my photographer got at Target when he dressed up like a cop last Halloween." I snickered.

Kojak's real name was Tommy Flick, but because of his bald head and his proclivity for Tootsie Pops ever since he quit smoking, everyone who knew him well called him Kojak in honor of his namesake, the popular television detective from the 1970s.

Most of the time, we spoke by phone instead of in-person. Even though Oak City was growing exponentially, it still had a small-town feel, and a crime reporter eating lunch with a detective on a regular basis would surely create talk. He didn't tell me everything, but he never lied to me. Most importantly, he warned me when I was going down the wrong path and told me to keep going when I was on the right one.

"So she thinks he might kill her, but she won't go to the police?" Kojak said when I told him about Suzanne. I had started from the beginning, from the race until my most recent interaction with her at the coffee shop. While I relayed the story to him over the phone, I could see my face in the giant mirror above my couch as I paced, full of nervous energy, around my living room.

"What do *you* think?" Kojak said.

I knew he sensed something off in the tone of my voice. He knew me that well.

"I don't know. It's hard to tell if she's yanking my chain because she's lonely and needs a friend, *or* if she's just a little bit nuts, *or* if she's really scared and telling me the truth. But she does seem credible to me. I don't want to take a chance if she is telling me the truth and might be in real danger."

"I understand," Kojak replied sympathetically, his skepticism temporarily displaced. He was one of the few people other than Adam who knew about my mother. One day, in an emotional moment, I slipped up and told him the story when we were talking about domestic violence case. It only happened one time, and we never talked about it again after that. I knew this was because Kojak respected my privacy and didn't want to pry.

Right now I sensed that my mother's story was the elephant

in the middle of our conversation. His voice shifted from the normal hard edge as he teetered on to something softer. "So what do you need from me?"

"I just need to know what's really going on with this guy, her husband. Is he really a bad dude? Is he having an affair, beating her, plotting to kill her? Is he a sociopath who plays the good doctor during the day and then comes up with ways to murder his wife at night? Or is he just a run-of-the-mill bad husband, and she's a paranoid woman who believes he's trying to kill her? "

"Wow, that's a long list, kid," Kojak said with endearment. Even though I was not much younger than he was, he always called me *kid*. I think it had a lot more to do with my level of enthusiasm and his perception of me as sometimes being naïve than it did with my age. There weren't many people I would let me call that, but he was an exception to many of my rules.

"Not really. Just need you to run him down. See what you can find out about him. You're *so* good at that type of thing."

"Okay. Flattery will get you just about anything you want. You know that." He chuckled. "Name, age, place of employment?"

"Tanner, probably late thirties, doctor."

"Tanner is the last name?"

"Actually, first. His wife's name is Suzanne Parker, but I'm pretty sure they don't have the same last name. Not sure where he works or what kind of a doctor he is."

"Wow, that's pretty specific. I'll just Google that crap and I'm sure I will come up with something right away." He snorted sarcastically. "Can't you get a little more out of this chick? Would sure make it a whole lot easier to get the goods on this guy if we had a better starting point."

"I know it's not a lot to go on, but it's all I've got. I'll try to get more out of her. I'm sure she will tell me whatever I want to know about him. I've just kind of been hanging back and not asking too many questions because I was trying not to get involved. But here I am—*involved.*"

"Okay. For you, kid, and you only, I'll check him out. But I'm not making any promises. You're not giving me a whole lot to work with here."

"I know, but if anybody can figure something out, you can. I mean, how many Tanners can there be in Oak City? Oh, and there is one more thing. He might be having an affair with a woman who calls herself *G6*, like the jet plane."

"Well, that certainly narrows it down. I'll just post something on Facebook about that and see if one of my friends can round her up. What kind of a woman calls herself G6 anyway?"

"Well, it's a jet, right? So someone fast, intense?"

"That was a rhetorical question. I know exactly what kind of a woman calls herself that."

I pictured his smirk over the phone, his glasses dipping precariously close to the end of his nose, about to fall off. I turned and caught a glimpse of my face in the mirror and couldn't help but smile myself.

"Maddie, this one has your name all over it!" Janie perched her hands on her tiny hips in a confident posture. Her Airpods were half-cocked as one bulged out over the top of her right ear and protruded through the mass of tight, blond curls that framed her thin, freckled face. Sometimes she wore a full headset with two earpieces and a tiny microphone that made her look like she should be in a control tower landing planes.

"What if I told you a man was saved from a potentially killer shark, by a school of dolphins?" Janie's dark brown eyes got wider and her hands flew from her hips like she might be trying to swat away a fly or do some wild interpretive dance to music that only she could hear.

"Wow," I said, hardly able to hide my disinterest.

"So it happened in Florida, but the guy lives here in Oak City. And here's the absolute best part." She stopped and looked around the busy newsroom, where no one was paying any attention to us, yet she acted like she had a secret just for me and leaned in closer. "He's got frigging video of the whole damn thing. He was wearing a GoPro. So all you have to do is interview the dude and get his video, and voila, add water and stir, and you've got an amazing story!"

There is was again, that word, *amazing*. For once I wanted Janie to bring me a story and be honest with me and say, *This story sucks, but we're going to do it anyway. So good luck with it. Do the best you can.*

These days if anyone had video of something dramatic, it was automatically a story. It didn't matter what the quality of the video was or what it was about. If it was sensational, we wanted it. Facebook and Twitter videos often became stories that took precedence over real news coverage.

I always tried to do the best I could with whatever story I was assigned. It was in my DNA. But some stories were harder than others for me to make relevant and interesting. Sometimes a hamburger was just a hamburger, and it was never going to be a steak. But at least we had video of the dolphins. That was something. Janie was right about that. People would watch an hour of a shark trying to crash through a school of dolphins to get to a man before they would watch a boring, but important, story about the school board or health care.

I had hoped to have an easy day, a mindless story that I could put together with minimal effort so I might squeeze in another visit with Suzanne and get some more information out of her. After all, what in the world did she expect me to do without Tanner's last name or the name of his medical practice? How was I supposed to find out anything about this man if she wouldn't give me any real information to go on?

To be fair, I hadn't asked the right questions. Suzanne was so focused on G6 in our last meeting that I forgot my journalist hat and left the coffee shop with only a handful of details about Tanner. It wasn't like me to be so careless, but when I was with Suzanne I wasn't a reporter. I wasn't sure exactly who I was.

"Okay, so you're set up with shark guy at one o'clock. He thought we might buy this video from him, but I explained to him that local news organizations don't buy stories, that we're not like the tabloid shows that pay people for stuff. I think he's cool with just giving it to us now."

"You think he's cool with it?" I sounded more incredulous than I intended. I knew it wasn't Janie's fault, but I really didn't want to go all the way to this guy's house only to discover he had sold the footage to TMZ and our story was dead in the water, pardon the pun.

"No, I am sure. I'm sure of it." She sounded like she was trying to convince herself. "He's cool. He wants to do the interview with you, *you specifically*. He's a big fan."

"Amazing," I quipped.

Big fan was a euphemism we used for people who were starstruck by local TV personalities. Given that Channel 8 had always been a powerhouse news organization in the community, with a dedicated following, there were many viewers who grew up watching the station and felt like the reporters and anchors were part of their family. In short, this often helped us get interviews.

As soon as Janie rounded the corner away from my cubicle, I decided I was going to call Suzanne and lay it on the line. I was going to tell her I needed more information, that I couldn't help her unravel her situation without it. I was going to be clear this time. I would put my journalist hat on and demand what I needed in order to help her. Just as I was running the dialogue for the call in my head, my phone rang.

"Kid, it's me," Kojak bellowed, in a scratchy voice, sounding like he had just coughed up a lung. I knew it was him because his profile picture of a smirking face with a lollipop dangling from his lips popped up on my screen.

"Hey, you. I was just about to call my friend and prod her for some more information you might be able to use in your search."

"Well, I got something. I found G6."

"No way. That was fast. How in the world?"

"Well, I started thinking that had to be a hooker name. I mean, come on. Who refers to herself as a G6 but a hooker? So I asked my buddies in vice, and they were like, 'Oh yeah, we know her. She works at a restaurant on the southeast side, Mexican joint. She's real pretty and real popular.' Apparently she's out of the business now, recently retired, but everyone still knows her by that nickname."

"What's the name of the restaurant?"

"It's called La Fiesta. A hole-in-the-wall joint, but great food. Lot of cops eat there. That's probably why she never got busted. My guess is that she had a quid pro quo deal. They get good lunches, maybe a little street intel on drug dealers and such. She stays out of the slammer."

"And maybe a little something else?"

"Nope, not going there. She's no street hooker. She's one of those chicks that advertised on a website. They pretend to be a lonely suburban soccer mom, and then the guys get hooked after one meeting with her and are forced into coughing up five hundred dollars for a brief roll in the hay in a cheap motel room. I'm telling you, there are a lot of idiots who fall for that crap. Seriously, a beautiful brunette minivan-driving soccer mom wants to hook up with your pasty, white, fat, middle-aged ass? You got to be kidding me. How dumb can these guys be? Women don't need to go on a website to find sex. If they're on a site like that, they're *selling* something."

Kojak had a tendency to sound-off on lofty platitudes, like he was giving a monologue as the star of his very own crime drama. While I agreed with many of his tirades, I didn't have the time or patience to deal with this one right now. But I knew enough to humor him until he got to his point.

"I get it. But in many cases there's a pimp, a ringleader, someone who is taking the money from these women as soon as they make it. They're not doing it willingly. No one chooses that life. It's called human trafficking. Ever hear of it?"

"Yes, smart ass. All I'm saying is the johns are the worst part of the equation. Without the demand, the sex trade would not exist. I'm not criticizing the women who do it."

"I hear you. Okay, well I've got to go because I have to interview a guy who almost got killed by a shark, but was saved by dolphins, and then I will head over to the restaurant to check her out."

"I can't believe you gave up the glory of autopsies and gunpowder residue for that shit. You're wasting your talent."

"No, I'm preserving my sanity."

"Maybe. But then why can't you walk away from this lady and her crazy story?"

"I just want to help her. That's all." It irked me sometimes that he knew me so well.

"A likely story. Call me when you're ready to go to the restaurant. I'll go with you. She runs with a pretty rough crowd. Don't think you should go alone. If she figures out you're spying on her, her cohorts won't be happy. She's got some brothers who have spent plenty of time behind bars. They're the kind of people who cut people's fingers off when they owe them money and don't pay."

"No way. I need to do this alone," I said. And I meant it.

When I first met Hal the shark guy I was pretty sure that

despite what Janie had told me, his motivation for doing the interview was money. It was my job to sell him on the idea that fame in his hometown was much more valuable than the few thousand dollars that some tabloid show might pay him.

"Hal, it's a pleasure to meet you. Wow, what an experience you had. Lucky to be alive. I know our viewers are going to be amazed by your story."

Hal ushered Buster and me into his house and motioned for us to sit on a big comfortable brown couch in his large spartan den. Buster left the camera equipment in the car until we knew for sure if Hal was going to play ball.

"Oh, you want to talk to me *on camera?*" the interview subject often asked. "I thought this was going to be in the newspaper."

On one occasion, a pizza delivery woman who was robbed at gunpoint and ironically had a large tattoo above her breasts that read *Unbreakable*, called the newsroom to tell them I had tricked her into doing an interview.

"Was there a large camera there, and were you wearing a microphone, ma'am?" Janie asked the woman.

The answer, of course, was *yes*, but the woman still insisted she didn't know she was being interviewed on TV. She also said we had promised to crop out the tattoo from our shot, which would have been impossible considering its placement. The interview aired, tattoo and all. She ended the phone conversation with Janie by referring to me as a scrawny little white bitch.

Like the pizza delivery lady, I was sure Hal knew exactly why we were there and what our intentions were.

"You know, I've been thinking about it, and while I love your station, I'm not sure this is the way I want to go," Hal said hesitantly. I tried not to let my face reveal my disappointment. Now I was going to have to grovel. I spent far too much time in my job operating in what I called *desperation mode*. I was often desperate for an interview, yet I couldn't let the person I was trying to get on camera see my desperation. It was exhausting.

"I grew up watching you guys. Used to sit with my dad at night while he watched the eleven o'clock news. He drank a beer, smoked a cigar, and always had a stack of three Oreos. If I was real quiet and didn't tell Mama about the beer or the cigar, he'd let me have one of those Oreos." He shook his head as if he were right there in that moment, curled up in the chair with his father's arms around him, puffs of cigar smoke swirling above his head, licking the silky white cream from chocolate cookies.

Hal, a lanky, leathered man in his early forties, wore a sleeveless shirt and cut-off faded jeans. The jagged edges of the material skimmed his tanned shoulders. The pale blue shirt was faded by years of wear and bore a pink palm tree logo. I could just make out the faint peeling outline of a surfer beneath the tree, riding the crest of a wave. Just above Hal's mop of sandy blond hair, to the right, was a photo on a wooden shelf of Hal, a woman in a flowered turtleneck dress, and a baby in full football regalia. The baby wore a black and blue sweatshirt and knit hat bearing the logo of the Carolina Panthers.

"See, your little guy is a Panthers' fan?" I pointed at the photo.

"He's ten now. Loves football. Absolutely loves it."

"Is he a surfer like his dad?" I took a stab, assuming from his look and the shirt, that's how he wound up in a circle of dolphins fending off a shark.

"Little scared of the water still, believe it or not, given how crazy his old man is about it. I've tried, believe me, I have. Got him a longboard. Even took him to a surf camp one summer. Didn't stick. Didn't like how the waves crashed over his board while he was trying to get out past the break."

I could feel Hal's resolve melting. We had gone off-topic,

away from his reluctance and toward something relatable—children. Once I became a mother I discovered that talking about children was the great equalizer. No matter how different I was from the person I was interviewing, that we were both parents gave us common ground.

"Bet he's proud of you though. Surfing huge waves, way out there where the sharks are. Not a big fan of sharks, myself."

"Yes, he thinks it's pretty cool that his old man is a surfer," Hal said, with a spreading grin.

"Well, the great thing about talking to us is that we're going to give you plenty of time to tell your story, unlike a tabloid show that just wants your video and not your story. They'd show like fifteen seconds of it and move on to the Hollywood celebrity moment of the day. We'll give you a chance to tell your story step-by-step. Tell us exactly what happened, what you were thinking when you were out there. If your son was proud of you before, imagine how he will feel after seeing you on the eleven o'clock news—the same news you watched with your dad at his age."

I was proud of myself for bringing it full circle. I was telling the truth about how we would couch the story, versus how a national show with no local connection would tell the story. Was I massaging him to try and get him to talk to me instead of taking the paying gig? Absolutely. Was it unethical? Not at all. It was unethical to pay people for a news story, not to convince them to do it for free.

"You're right. I'll do it. Get the camera." Hal stood up and shook my hand as if we were about to sign a multi-million-dollar contract. Buster was already out the door before Hal was on his feet, heading to the car to get the gear. He knew as well as I did that people were fickle and could change their minds about an interview in just a few seconds.

"Amazing, Hal. That's great news," I said, relieved as we shared a firm handshake.

Maybe Janie was right. Maybe it really was about finding something amazing in every single story.

~

La Fiesta was one of those restaurants that was hard to classify. It was certainly a Mexican-themed venue, as the name revealed, but there were also large stuffed llamas in a cage near the entrance, with a sign that read *Don't feed the animals!* Piñatas and traditional wide-brimmed velvet hats with gold and silver embroidery adorned the walls. Dusty multi-colored crepe paper streamers hung from the ceiling looking like remnants of an ancient birthday party that someone forgot to remove.

Kojak told me G6's real name was Maria Lopez, and that she was the main hostess and cashier at the restaurant, which belonged to her family. When I first walked inside, it was so packed I couldn't see anyone who matched Maria's description. A young Hispanic girl with dark hair in long braids that went halfway down her back met me at the hostess stand. She was wearing heavy black eye makeup and large, dangly silver hoops. Despite her attempt at looking older, I doubted she could be more than fourteen years old. She showed me to a small corner table and handed me a worn plastic menu, its edges frayed and peeling back. The surface of the table was wet, having just been wiped down, and crumbs of tortilla chips littered the floor beneath the table, a sign that the pace of their lunch rush was so frantic they'd had little time to clean up in between customers.

The energy of the restaurant was upbeat and warm. Men in work boots, wearing paint-splattered pants and shirts with their names on them crowded around bowls of chips and salsa, laughing, talking, and dipping. Waitresses edged around the tight spaced tables, holding brightly colored trays of hot food above their heads. Beneath the din of chatter and dirty dishes clattering into the busboy's bin, was the subtle beat of Mariachi band music playing through the overhead speakers.

I peered over the top of the menu and scanned the restaurant for a woman fitting Maria's description. After surveying the busy room several times, I finally spotted what I thought might be the top of her head behind the cash register at the far end of the room. Her hair was dark and sleek and hung in a side ponytail across her right shoulder. A long line of customers waiting to pay obscured my view of her, but I caught glimpses of the woman's pleasant round face and her eyes adorned in the jet-black eyeliner that came out at the corners like wings. It was a look a lot of women favored these days, but like most new fashion trends, I was still on the fence about it. Yet she wore it well. She paired it with bright red lipstick on her plump limps that parted in a half-smile when a customer would speak with her at the counter. It struck me that with the exception of her olive complexion, she looked a lot like a younger version of Suzanne. Maybe that's what Tanner found attractive about her. I was sure, based on the description Kojak gave me, that it was Maria.

There were too many people around Maria for me to approach her, so I decided to order some lunch and observe. I also needed more time to formulate a plan. What would I say if I got a chance to speak with her? Would I ask her outright if she knew Tanner? That would be way out of left field. I couldn't imagine that conversation going well.

One thing I knew for sure, the food had to be good based on the number of people crowded around tiny tables covering every square inch of the room.

After a young, hurried male waiter with a stressed smile, dressed in a white button-down shirt, black pants, and a red vest took my order, I began scrolling through my emails while I waited for my food. Almost instantly, my phone rang. I quickly silenced the ringer, although the restaurant was so loud I was pretty sure it wasn't disturbing anyone. It was the twins' school calling.

"Hello," I answered nervously, always expecting the worst when school called.

A call from school usually meant someone was sick and needed to be picked up.

"Mom, it's a real emergency," my son, Blake, bellowed over the phone, tears in his voice.

"Sweetie, what is it?"

"Mom, I left my gym clothes at home!" he said, with an end of the world tone.

"Honey, it's okay. Just borrow someone else's who has P.E. another period. Or just explain it to your teacher and wear what you have on." As soon as the words came out of my mouth, I knew I had said the wrong thing. Blake was my anxious child and a rule follower. He was not about to tell his teacher he forgot his gym clothes, or borrow some smelly clothes from another boy.

"Mom, you don't understand. This is very important. I'll be in so much trouble if I don't have them!"

This would have been the typical situation that Adam would have handled. He would have left work, located the gym clothes in the laundry or in Blake's room, under my direction, and taken them to school after saying to me, "Just tell me what I need to do," knowing that I didn't have that kind of flexibility in my job. But Adam was gone now and it was my problem to solve alone.

"Buddy, Mom's at work."

"Seriously, Mom, you just don't get it, do you? This is non-negligible."

I chuckled inside, realizing he meant to say negotiable.

"Okay, I'll have to go to the house and get them, and then I will head your way. I'm about twenty minutes from the house, so it will take a little while," I said, infused with as much cheerfulness as I could muster, given that I was on a stakeout of sorts that I was about to ditch.

"Thanks, Mom. You're the best."

I was still smiling when I hung up, feeling like Superwoman. It felt good to be needed again. Adam had needed me so much when he was sick that I felt a huge void when he died. What was I supposed to do with all those hours that I had spent changing bed pans and cutting food into tiny bits and measuring out and recording endless doses of medicine in a little notebook? It felt good to be able to help again, even if it was just something small like bringing Blake's gym clothes to school.

My encounter with Maria would have to wait. I threw a ten-dollar bill on the table for the quesadilla that I would not get the chance to eat and grabbed my purse. As I turned toward the door, I glanced back for a moment and noticed the line at the counter was almost gone. The lunch rush was finally dying down. I watched as Maria walked to the end of the counter and stacked the waiters' paid tickets in a basket. As she stepped out from the behind the counter, I could see her for the first time from head to toe.

Maria Lopez was pregnant. Very pregnant.

4

SEEKING BALANCE

WHEN ADAM WAS ALIVE, he made it possible for me to balance work and home life because he was an equal participant in the child rearing. What he sometimes lacked in domestic abilities, he more than made up for in the father department. There was never a time when he said something wasn't his job or responsibility. He didn't always do things the way I did them, but that was okay. Often, with a little hindsight, I realized his way was better.

As a single parent, my son needed me to at least attempt something that passed for balance, but I was having trouble focusing on the task at hand. As I pulled onto the highway from the on-ramp, I kept seeing the image of a pregnant Maria Lopez in my head. Was it Tanner's baby? Did Suzanne know she was pregnant? I was so deep in thought that I barely missed being sideswiped by a tractor trailer careening into my lane without his turn signal. It jolted me back to reality. I jerked the wheel sharply to the left to avoid a collision. Luckily, the next lane over was clear as I swerved into it, both hands firmly gripping the steering wheel. I slowed down and caught my breath. My children had already lost one parent. They didn't need to lose the other one.

By the time I stopped by the house, found the gym clothes in the clean laundry basket at the foot of my bed, and got to school, I had regained my composure. Maria Lopez was filed in the back of my brain for another day while I vowed to concentrate on my anxious little boy.

When I got to the school office, Blake was sitting on the well-worn blue sofa in the lobby, nervously twitching his nose. It was an involuntary movement I was sure he wasn't even aware of. It had started shortly after Adam passed away. It was not noticeable unless you knew Blake and were watching him closely. But it was the kind of thing a mother noticed, a brief, almost undetectable departure from normality. I dropped the plastic grocery bag carrying the clothes, onto the couch and took Blake's sandy-haired little head and pulled it into my stomach. He buried his head in me and wrapped his arms tightly around my waist. This was not about gym clothes.

"Hey, buddy, why don't we skip the rest of the day together, play hooky. We can go do something special, just you and me. No work, no school. Maybe get some pizza and see that movie you've been wanting to see. The one your sister refuses to see so we can never go," I whispered, to the top of my son's head, which was still buried in my abdomen, but I knew he could hear me because I felt him nod.

I heard a muffled "okay" from my stomach. I unwound his little arms and held onto his tiny balled up hands, bringing him to his feet. He was small for his age, smaller than his sister, even though they were twins. This was sometimes embarrassing for him when people asked who was older. I could see now that his eyes were red from crying.

"June." I turned to the school secretary. "I think Blake is a little under the weather. I'm going to take him out for the rest of the day. Can you let his teachers know?"

June was an older, affable woman with a round face framed by a sprig of black and gray curls. She always wore her glasses attached to a colorful, frayed woven lariat around her neck, something I was sure a student must have made for her.

"I sure will, Maddie. You take care, Blake. Hope you feel better." She glanced over my shoulder to my son who nodded bashfully at her kindness. "I will sign him out." She waved, already reaching for the spiral-bound sign-out notebook, with a pen in her hand.

The truth was that June, and everyone else at Porter's Elementary School, knew what Blake and Miranda had been through. As a result, we got extra compassion points from the school staff when Blake had his little breakdowns.

While I had tried to shield them from their father's illness as much as I could, it was impossible for them not to be a part of it, given that I chose to do hospice care at home. It was important for Adam to spend his last days in his own home, surrounded by the people he loved and not in a hospital. It was also important for me to be his primary caretaker, and not a nurse he didn't know. But the downside was that the children were at a tender age and were exposed to the grim realities of dying. At the same time, they were also exposed to an army of friends and relatives who helped their dad leave the world with grace and dignity. I firmly believed that the positive life lessons my kids learned throughout the experience far outweighed the bad.

Blake was my sensitive child. Miranda was as tough as nails. Nothing appeared to disturb her, on the surface. But I knew better. Since her father's death, she was quick to anger, quick to argue, and never initiated a hug or an *I love you*. I suspected beneath her tough exterior was an insecure little girl who needed her mother now just as much as Blake did. She just didn't know how to show it. She was trying to put on a brave face, but I wanted her to know that it was okay not to be strong sometimes.

My two children could not be more different, and if I hadn't seen them born several minutes apart, I would not have believed they shared a womb, let alone the same DNA.

"Mom, thanks for picking me up," Blake said, with a piece of gooey cheese from the piping-hot pizza dangling from his chin. "I know you were working. I'm sorry to make you leave work. I hope you don't get in trouble with your boss."

Blake had an unusual level of empathy for a child his age. But it was also this sensitivity that made him sad about so many things, things he could not control—an older lady struggling to navigate stairs at the mall, a bald girl in an advertisement for a children's cancer foundation, his father's labored breathing shortly before his death.

"You know what, I am not the least bit worried about getting in trouble at work. You and your sister are number one." Before Adam's death I had been so wrapped up in work that I didn't always prioritize my children the way that I should have. Everything was different now, and so was I.

"Thanks, Mom." Blake flashed a gap-toothed smile and took a big swig of his guilty pleasure, a large Coke, something I allowed only on special occasions. Lately, I had relaxed the rules so much that *special occasions* were becoming a daily occurrence.

I put my hand over Blake's and closed my eyes for a moment. I expected to see Adam's smiling face, praising me for my newfound dedication to being present and engaged with my children. But instead all I saw was a pregnant Maria Lopez looking at me from across the restaurant. In my daydream, she was baiting me, challenging me to uncover the truth.

I opened my eyes and looked at Blake, who was practically jumping out of his seat he was so wired by his multiple refills of Coke. He hadn't even noticed my mental departure. I wondered where Superwoman was supposed to get her energy from.

~

I hadn't run much since the race. After watching what happened to Suzanne, I wasn't inspired to get out there. I was still going to classes at the gym and doing yoga at home, but none of this gave me the same euphoric high that running did. Running was my sanity, my peace, my church when nothing else could heal me.

My sneakers lay in a pile of shoes by the front door. I noticed them as I passed the pile, their blue shiny material and pink swooshes peeking out, begging me to slip them on and get back on the road. Sometimes I thought about them being in the middle of the pile, squished in between one of Miranda's sandals with a broken strap and an old flip-flop of Blake's, and I would have a mini panic attack and feel the need to rescue them. Yet every time I even thought about putting them on, I pictured Suzanne in slow motion hitting the pavement with every part of her body.

Even though it had only been a few days since we had coffee, I felt a rush of guilt for not calling and checking up on her. To be fair, she had not called me either. The more hours that passed without any contact with her, the freer I felt from the whole crazy situation. The part of me that wanted to help her was overcome by the part of me that was afraid of getting too involved. Yet I couldn't stop thinking about my mother, about how things might have been different for us if she had been able to reach out to someone. Of course, I was only a small child when she was killed, barely a witness. There was nothing I could have done to help her. Maybe now was my second chance.

It was springtime, and the weather was close to perfect.

The sky was Carolina blue. There was a light balmy breeze and a lush canopy of green everywhere you looked. It was like everything grew overnight, sprouted from winter's bare tree limbs and brown grass into this magical display. It was the kind of day that begged you to come outside and play. Having grown up in New Jersey, where one gray day turned into another for several months every year, I appreciated the mild southern climate with its opulent display of spring.

The kids were at school, and I only had a few hours before I was scheduled to shoot a story. I decided, for my sanity, I *needed* to take a run. Just like that, all the reasons I had for not running melted away. I sat on the cool hardwood floor in my hallway and slipped on my right shoe. It felt comfortable and familiar. Just as I was pulling on the left shoe, my phone rang.

"Maddie, I haven't heard from you in a couple of days," Suzanne whispered. "I was worried. You haven't given up on helping me, have you? I'm in the grocery store near your house and I thought maybe we could grab a cup of coffee."

My mind raced. How did she know where I lived? Had I told her? I must have. But I didn't remember telling her. I was protective of my family's privacy and safety. I was silent as I chewed on this bit.

"Actually, I am just getting ready to go for a run. I do want to talk to you though, Suzanne. I have some new information to share with you. But I feel like I really need some more information from you about your husband and your situation before we move forward." There, I said it, the thing I needed to say to her the most. I was proud of myself for standing up for what I needed. Kojak would be proud, too.

"Wow, that's so crazy. I just happen to be in my running clothes, too. I was going to go later, after shopping. Why don't I just join you and then we can chat while we run?"

"Are you sure that's a good idea? I mean, it's only been a few days since you left the hospital. Are you sure you're fully healed?" I had flash of all the blood on the pavement coming from her knees, her elbows, her head, matted in her hair. It seemed too soon for her to be exercising again, let alone running.

"You know, I feel great. Not sure if it's the painkillers or what. But other than a few bumps and bruises, I'm good to go. Give me your address and I'll meet you."

I panicked. I wasn't about to give Suzanne my address. What if she really was in danger and she came to my home and her husband followed her? I couldn't risk that. Innocent people were killed all the time getting in the middle of domestic violence situations.

"I'm already in the car, heading to the park around the corner," I lied. "There's a greenway there, a couple miles long, very scenic. I'll text you the address when I park."

"Perfect. I'll see you there."

As soon as I hung up, I regretted my decision to share my peaceful running time with Suzanne. I did my best brainstorming when I ran solo. At the same time, I needed to get to the bottom of what was really going on with her. Maybe running with Suzanne wasn't such a bad idea. Exercise was a type of truth serum, all that blood rushing to your brain. It was hard to lie when your heart was racing and you had sweat running down your back.

Suzanne looked completely different in her running clothes than she had on the day of the race. Granted, my first introduction to her was when she was writhing in pain on the ground, covered in blood. Today she looked like a model from one of the posters on the stalls in the bathroom at the gym that encouraged you to *Do it all* and *Be Fierce*. She wore a snug bright yellow sleeveless spandex tank top, tight black running shorts, and a black Nike baseball hat. Her hair was pulled back in a sleek ponytail protruding through the hole in the back of the cap. She had on a running belt with two small bottles of water attached, and bright pink sneakers. I was amazed that she was dressed head-to-toe in running gear to go grocery shopping. Sometimes I slept in my running clothes, clean ones of course, thinking it would increase my chances of getting up and doing it. Clearly Suzanne meant business when she grocery shopped in her running clothes.

With the exception of some small white bandages on her shoulders, elbows, and knees, you wouldn't know that she had recently taken a serious fall.

"It's so good to be running again, you have no idea." Suzanne walked over to my car from where I assumed she had parked, about three spaces away. I couldn't tell which of the cars she came from. I wondered if she had abandoned an entire cart of items in the store to meet me. Again this woman seemed desperate for companionship, *my companionship* in particular.

Suzanne leaned in to give me a side hug, something I wasn't sure I wanted to accept given the unusual nature of our relationship. I succumbed, awkwardly, acknowledging her gesture by lightly wrapping my left arm around her waist for a split second. I knew she needed a friend, but I just wasn't sure I wanted to be that friend.

"I was so bored and frustrated. As soon as the doctor cleared me to run, I practically raced out the door so I could get home and put my sneakers on. Luckily I didn't have any broken ribs. Honestly I don't know how people cope without exercise. I would have to be on some serious medication without it." Suzanne gave a light chuckle, as if her fall was just a little bump in the road and not a possible attempted murder.

"I hear you." I tried to assess where she was coming from. Despite her cavalier talk, she seemed nervous. She was tightening her ponytail holder every few seconds while we stretched on the wooden rail of a fence at the edge of the park, wrapping and twisting the band around several more times, and then pulling on her hair to make sure it was secure. She wore no jewelry except for a simple brushed platinum and diamond band on her wedding ring finger. It was impossible to miss—thick band with specks of diamonds in a crisscross pattern across the surface. She noticed me looking at it.

"Is that your wedding ring?"

"Yes. We had them designed to look exactly alike. His is bigger and thicker of course, more manly, but it also has small diamond crisscrosses in it. We saw something similar on a billboard in the Miami airport just after we got engaged and decided to work with a jeweler to create them. They cost a small fortune. Very romantic at the time. Not so much now. But I'm still wearing it. Don't want to set him off."

I soaked up this information. Tanner was a man who wore a specially handcrafted matching wedding ring along with his wife. How did he go from this to possibly being a killer?

"He never takes his off, not even to sleep, except for surgery, of course. And even then, he's got a little crystal dish by the sink at his surgery suite in his office where he places the ring and then puts it right back on afterwards. At least that's what his nurse, Julie, told me. Sweet gesture for such a creep, don't you think? He's super-paranoid about someone taking, it for some reason. Says it's the symbol of our union for life, no matter what."

I didn't know what to think. The more Suzanne revealed to me about this man, the more confused I became. Cherishing his wedding ring didn't sound like something a man who was cheating on his wife would do. Yet I had covered enough domestic violence murders to know that people often did things to make themselves look like devoted spouses when they were just the opposite. Plus, people weren't black and white. They were gray. It was possible for him to have an affair and still want to control his wife.

After a quick stretch, Suzanne and I started down the paved greenway and headed toward the lake at the center of the park that had a nice running trail around it. We passed a dog walker and a cyclist, but otherwise the path was deserted. Turtles sunned themselves on exposed rocks in the brackish lake which was badly in need of a good rain to fill it. Herons perched in muddy bogs like sentinels keeping watch over the peaceful spot. It was a hidden gem in the middle of bustling suburbia.

"You don't run here by yourself, do you?" Suzanne sounded spooked as she surveyed the desolate path. "It's a little isolated for my taste, though very pretty, very serene. I guess it's okay as long as you're with someone."

I was a cautious runner, always choosing public spaces when I was alone. Frankly, I didn't want a lesson in running safety from Suzanne. I wanted to get down to business, to blurt out the questions that I had been storing since the moment I met her. She was acting like we were two longtime girlfriends getting together for a workout, but the truth was I barely knew her. I couldn't figure out why she felt this intimate connection with me. The only thing I could imagine was that because we shared a traumatic moment together, it bonded together us in a weird way.

"Have you ever known someone who was the victim of domestic violence? I don't mean in a story you've covered, but actually *known* someone personally, like a friend or a relative?"

It felt like we were reversing roles, that she was the reporter interviewing me. I could feel tears stinging my eyes. I blinked hard to keep them from spilling down my face. I was not ready to share my anger and grief over losing my mother, with a stranger. It always amazed me how quickly I could summon the pain by just thinking about her. I remembered more about how my mother made me feel than about what we did together. Thoughts of her evoked a deeply warm feeling sprinkled with slivers of memories—like standing in my crib after a nap, seeing her arms outstretched coming toward me. I could feel her hands, with her long, thin fingers braiding my hair. I could see her kneeling to gently fasten the big white buttons on my blue wool coat.

As Suzanne and I plodded down the path, hearing nothing but our heavy breathing and the rhythmic cadence of our sneakers striking the pavement, I felt my resolve beginning to crack. *Why not tell her my story?* I had learned to keep it hidden for so many years. It was a story that scared people. It made them wonder about me, look at me differently. Because I didn't want to deal with that kind of intense scrutiny, I had kept it locked away. But keeping it private for so many years was exhausting. In a way, I was living a lie, lying to the people I was closest to—my friends, my co-workers, my children. Sure, it was lying by omission, but because they didn't know the single most transforming event that had shaped my life, they didn't really know me.

"I do know someone," I said, after what seemed like a long period of silence as we crested the hill on the far side of the lake. "My mother."

Suzanne grabbed my forearm with her sweaty palm. At first I thought it was a gesture of compassion for what I had just told her, for what I was about to tell her. But I was wrong. I turned and looked at her face and realized she was scared.

"Did you see him?"

"See who?" I replied, confused. I had been about to bear my soul to her, to tell her my deepest secret, and her question caught me completely off guard.

"Tanner. I think he's following me, following *us.* I saw someone, someone in the woods back there. Just off the path. Oh, my God, he's really lost it. We have to get out of here. I can't believe I put you in this position."

Suzanne was now clutching my arm with a vice grip and

pulling me along the trail so fast I thought I might trip and fall. I hadn't seen anyone in the woods, but I wasn't looking either. As we got to the top of the hill, there was another offshoot of the trail that led away from the lake. I pulled my arm away from her and motioned for her to follow me. She followed but continued looking over her shoulder every few seconds. We sprinted toward a cluster of office buildings, and then slowed and started fast-walking toward a set of glass doors at the edge of a low brick building.

"I can't believe I put you in this situation, Maddie." Tears were streaming down her face. "I should never have come here. I put you in danger."

She was scaring me, which didn't happen very often. She pushed me through the glass doors of the closest office building, and then leaned against the brick wall just inside the doorway. She was hyperventilating, and I thought she might be getting ready to pass out as she leaned over and steadied herself by placing her palms on her bent knees. I put my hands gently on her shoulders.

As I comforted her, I was beating myself up for being so self-absorbed in my own personal drama that I wasn't paying attention to what was going on around me. That wasn't like me. I had been so focused on thinking about my mother that I could have easily missed someone lurking in the woods, especially someone who was trying to hide. One thing was clear, whether or not Tanner really was here—she *believed* he was.

As Suzanne leaned over, the black elastic band holding her ponytail snapped and dropped to the floor. Her thick, dark hair cascaded across her shoulders and fell into her face. I pulled off a sturdy hairband I kept on my wrist and handed it to her. It was bright pink and emblazoned with purple smiley faces that looked like emojis. Miranda had given it to me for good luck when she was just five and I was running my first race. Since that day, I always wore it when I ran. Suzanne took the hairband, stood, and re-fastened her hair into a secure ponytail.

"It's okay, Suzanne." I glanced through the glass door of the office building into the mostly empty parking lot. "There's no one out there. You're okay." I decided she had imagined the whole thing.

I put my hands on her shoulders and looked into her eyes to get her to focus on what I was saying. Instead, she looked right through me, focusing on something just above my head through the glass doors. I turned to follow her gaze and saw a red car circling the parking lot and then leaving. It had a personalized license plate on the back that read *TJP*.

"See," Suzanne was standing straight and looking at me. She was calm again, her tone serious and cold. "He's never going to let me go. I'll never be able to outrun him."

5

PACING

"It's the cutest thing you've ever seen," Janie said without taking a breath. "I'll send you the photo of the horse and the goat curled up together. It's been shared, like, a billion times on Facebook!"

My mind used to freeze when the words Facebook or Twitter were used in the context of a news story, but I had finally made peace with it. Social media *was* news for an entire generation. We had to meet the people where they were spending their time, rather than force them to accept a more traditional, and some would say antiquated, way of delivering news.

Facebook was my hunting ground for my beat. Animal stories were social gold. That's where I got most of my ideas. And because most people on social media loved animal stories, they also loved me. After years of letting soul-depleting comments under my crime stories allow me to doubt the goodness in humanity, my new beat helped to restore my faith in mankind. I didn't realize how poisonous the negativity was until I was free of it.

"Great. And the horse is here? Is he here in town?"

"Well, not exactly. It's a little bit of a drive, but not too far." I could hear her banging on her computer keyboard in the background.

"It's a farm, obviously, about, let me see...looks like it's in Tindall County. About an hour and ten minutes. Not too far. Do you want to meet Buster there, or ride together?"

I tried to concentrate on what Janie was telling me, but all I could see when I closed my eyes was the terrified look on Suzanne's face when she thought Tanner was following us. I still hadn't figured out what was really going on between them, but she was genuinely afraid of him.

Once again, I urged her to call the police. I also gave her a contact name and number for an advocate at the local domestic violence shelter, someone who could better counsel her on the steps she needed to take to get out safely. But she insisted that Tanner would take their son, Winston, out of the country if he got wind that she was trying to leave him. She said he had done several tours with a nonprofit group that used volunteer doctors to help treat people in foreign countries in small villages where healthcare was nonexistent. She said he would know how to disappear. Then she would have no legal recourse.

The image of a doctor who volunteered to treat low-income people in foreign countries, once again, didn't gel with the persona of a cold-blooded killer. I knew some people were good at compartmentalizing their various layers. Tanner could possibly be a well-respected doctor, a philanthropist, *and* a violent, controlling husband.

One thing that continued to bother me was the "P" on the *TJP* license plate that Suzanne and I saw on the car darting out of the parking lot after our run. I searched *Tanner Parker*,

Tanner J. Parker, and *TJ Parker*, through multiple sites and got no results. Clearly he must have a different last name which also happened to start with "P."

I wanted to confirm his last name with Suzanne the day we ran together, but she was so upset, it was all I could do to get her into my car and take her home. We both agreed she was way too rattled to drive and that she would pick up her car later at the park.

When I pulled up to her house, I was not surprised to see a lush green manicured lawn and a garden flanked by a large white brick home. It wasn't over-the-top, but just fancy enough to make it clear that they were comfortable financially. I knew the house was most likely worth more than a million dollars based on its location, despite its modest exterior. Black shutters and a peaked roof above an expansive wraparound front porch complete with ceiling fans and large potted ferns gave it a regal look. I was reminded that beautiful houses had the power to hide the lives crumbling inside.

"Thanks so much for the ride," Suzanne said, with a catch in her voice as she slid out of the car, looking disheveled. Her formerly sleek ponytail was askew despite the pink hairband I had lent her, and her tank top was stained with sweat and slightly rumpled. I couldn't get over how much she had deteriorated between now and the moment I saw her get out of her car in the parking lot. Or had I seen her get out of a car? Suddenly, I was doubting my own memory.

"Maddie, did you hear me? Do we have a bad connection?"

My reverie about Suzanne vanished as soon as I heard Janie's question pulling me back into the present.

"Yes, sorry. Off on a mind-tangent. You know how my monkey brain works, hopping from branch to branch, one idea to the next."

"You? Never! Imagine that."

"Anyway, yes, I'll meet Buster at the station in a little while."

"Awesome."

I rolled my eyes through the phone. I was pretty sure she could see me.

"How was your night?" I asked Buster, as we drove on a winding country road to the farm in Tindall County.

"Good. Didn't do much. Just a soccer game in the rain. Super-fun. Can't believe they didn't call it."

Buster's son, Noah, with his partner, Hugh, was adopted from a woman in Idaho. They hooked up with an agency that specialized in pairing same-sex couples with pregnant women interested in putting their children up for adoption. While Buster made a modest living as a television photographer, Hugh was a bigwig at a local technology company, who traveled around the world and made an impressive salary. They lived in downtown Oak City in a fabulous new townhouse development and had a rooftop deck. It was in a gentrified neighborhood full of coffee houses, breweries, artistic boutiques and organic grocery stores. And while the location fit Hugh perfectly, Buster felt a like a square peg in a round hole. He was more of a good old boy than a young, rich hipster. He didn't know what quinoa was or how to pronounce it, and he preferred Kentucky Fried Chicken to kale.

Because Hugh traveled all the time, Buster was practically a single parent to Noah. Hence, he attended soccer games alone in the rain.

"How about you?" he said.

"Not much, just the usual. Blake had piano lessons and Miranda had a tennis match at school."

I wanted so much to tell Buster all about Suzanne, but he wasn't exactly great at keeping secrets. I also knew what he would tell me—that I should just let it go, that I had enough on my plate without adding this woman's drama to it.

Before I had a chance to decide whether to fill him in, my phone rang.

"Hey, kid," Kojak greeted me. "Just checking in to see if you ever found out anything out about the G6 chick?"

"I did. I went there. I saw her, but didn't get a chance talk to her. I had to leave. Emergency at school." I glanced at Buster to make sure he wasn't paying attention. Thankfully, he was fussing with the GPS on his phone. He spent a lot of time ignoring me when he was laser-focused on a task.

"Well?"

"She was very pretty. In fact she looks a lot like a younger version Suzanne. But here's the kicker. She's pregnant. Very pregnant. Like ready to pop pregnant."

As I waited for Kojak to respond, I looked over at Buster, who was now staring at me, wide-eyed. The word "pregnant" had wrestled his attention away from the GPS.

"Who is pregnant?" he mouthed. I knew he wasn't going to let this go now. When Buster wanted to know something, he could be very persistent.

"Kojak, let me call you back, okay?"

I hung up and looked at Buster, who was looking back at the road, shaking his head.

"What in the hell are you involved in now? Didn't I tell you to stick with hairless cats and runaway emus. That's safe. I can just tell you got yourself into some waist-deep shit right now. I can see it all over your face. Raw shit. No lie. Just look in the mirror."

I glanced in the side mirror, half expecting to see my face smeared with cow dung.

"Okay, I'll tell you the entire story. But you've got to swear not to mention this to anyone." As I said this, my stomach was clenching, knowing his idea of keeping a secret was not posting it on Facebook.

"Promise." He winked and tapped the steering wheel along to the beat of the music.

"No, I'm serious this time. Remember when you told that woman what I said about her chapped lips in her Facebook picture? About how she was in desperate need of Carmex? It was supposed to be a private, little joke between me and you, but then we met her and you couldn't help yourself. You told her. Remember how well that went over? I will never forget the awful look on her face. I thought she was going to cry. I felt horrible. I wanted to turn around and run out of her house."

"I can't believe you don't trust me." He took his hands off the wheel and swerved a bit for effect. He grinned like the hustler he was. Instead of money, he hustled for gossip.

"It's not about trust. It's about your lack of filter. You need to know when it's okay to share something, and when it's not. So to be clear, this story, it's not okay to share."

"Okay, never mind. I don't want to know."

And that's when I told him everything.

~

"My boy used to help me out on the farm, but the crack done got a hold of him," said the woman in the wheelchair, gesturing past her long gray braid to the expansive rolling green hills that surrounded her ramshackle farmhouse. "Now Brady, my nephew, he runs it. His horse, Peekaboo, he's the one curled up with the goat. Cutest damn thing I ever seen."

Marjorie's mangled toes wrapped around the foot pedals of her wheelchair. Her tanned, weathered hands were balled up into tight fists resting on her lap. Brady had wheeled her out to speak with us on the crumbling front porch of the house. The barely erect banisters were covered in peeling yellow paint. Flecks of it were spread across the uneven wooden floorboards. The rickety steps were held together by rusty nails that protruded in every direction after what I assumed were many years of quick fixes. A thin piece of lattice covered the underneath portion of the elevated porch, but in between the spaces you could see trash piled high—rusty coffee cans, old twisted pipes, threadbare pieces of material, cardboard boxes. I couldn't help but wonder if they simply pulled the lattice back, dumped their debris, and called it a day.

While Marjorie was tickled that Peekaboo's love affair with the goat had gotten the attention of the news, Brady clearly didn't share her affinity for the media. He glared at us beneath the brim of his dirty gray baseball hat. Thick chunks of black hair peeked out from beneath the cap. His face was pocked from acne, and spiderweb-like red lines framed his nose and spread out across his cheeks like a road map. It was hard to tell his age, but I put him in his early forties. He wore a flannel button-down over a white t-shirt, and baggy jeans with mud stains from his knees to his ankles, held up by a brown leather belt cinched around his waist and fastened with a large silver belt buckle.

After he deposited his aunt on the front porch and locked the wheels on her chair so it wouldn't roll across the uneven boards, he turned and went back inside without a word.

I had met a lot of Marjories and Bradys in my job—*characters.* I was fascinated by them. It was one of the best perks of journalism, meeting interesting people I would never normally cross paths with.

"Mazie, that's Brady's daughter. She the one who put the story on the Internet. You know kids, they're good with those computers. One time my Internet broke, and Mazie fixed it. She's at the community college, studying to be a nurse. So proud of her. First grand-niece to get herself schooling. Ain't that right, Brady?" she screeched through the screen door, which looked like it might be hanging on by one or two screws at the most. I could hear a blaring television playing a sporting event from somewhere deep inside the house. The crowd roared intermittently. Brady didn't answer.

I tried to pay attention to the woman's story, but I kept getting distracted thinking about Suzanne. It infuriated me the way her situation had highjacked my thoughts in the short time I had known her. I had always been good at triaging. Normally I could focus one hundred percent of my attention on the story at hand and mentally file away other issues to be dealt with at a later time. This was different. I was different. I realized I hadn't ever really dealt with my mother's death, and now this woman's crisis was becoming my path to facing those unresolved feelings.

"Princess, the goat, that's what we named her, Princess. Well, her mama died in childbirth. And they get real attached to whoever feeds them. At first it was Brady, but he ain't got no damn patience for little creatures. Never did like kittens or puppies. Not mean or anything, just got no softness in his heart, if you know what I mean," Marjorie twanged, snapping me back into the present. "Not that he hasn't had his troubles with the law. He surely has. But he wouldn't hurt an animal or a child, no matter what that woman said about him. But that was a long time ago."

Marjorie's voice became like white noise. I caught a word here and there in between my jumbled thoughts. I made a mental note to get Brady's last name and check his criminal record. I didn't want to get burned by doing a cute animal love story, only to find out the owner was a hardened criminal.

"Mazie took on Princess." Marjorie took a rare breath. It dawned on me that for an infirm-looking woman confined to a wheelchair, she sure did have a lot of energy, and probably a lot of good stories.

I thought about how close I had come to telling Suzanne *my* story, the story of my mother. Other than Kojak and Adam, no one in my re-invented life in North Carolina knew about my past. The people in the small town in New Jersey where I grew up knew the truth, but that's why I left and never went back. I shed my past—changed my name, cut ties with everyone I knew, and started over. Every once in a long while, someone from the past would find me on Facebook. I ignored their friend requests and then blocked them so they couldn't communicate with me further. As far as I was concerned, my life started with Adam, Miranda, and Blake. *Before* didn't exist.

I didn't tell Adam the whole story right away. It came out in bits and pieces. But when I finally unburdened myself and told him the entire truth, he was so understanding. I didn't expect him to be judgmental. Adam wasn't like that. But I did expect that he might be afraid to get involved with someone like me.

I told him the full version of my story the night before we got engaged. I knew it was about to happen. We had traveled to this beautiful resort in the mountains for a long weekend. At the time, we were living in Washington, D.C. I was interning at a local news station, fresh out of graduate school, trying to land a job. Adam was working on the Hill for a congressman from Virginia, where he grew up. We flew from D.C. to Asheville, North Carolina, and strangely, he decided to carry-on a duffel bag instead of checking it. After seeing his death grip on the bag, I figured out that there was something inside he was afraid to part with. And I was right. It was a diamond ring.

My intuition told me he was going to propose on the trip. I couldn't let him attach himself to someone who was so broken, without giving him all the information he needed to make a sound decision. This way he could always back out. It was important for me to give Adam a way out. But he didn't take it.

Instead, he listened and pulled me in for a hug. "You never cease to amaze me. Thank you for sharing that part of your life with me."

The next night at dinner, after a toast to our vacation, with two glasses of chilled Pinot Grigio, he slid out from the table, got down on one knee, and took my hand. "Will you share the rest of your life with me?"

The other people in the restaurant turned to watch, and let out a thunderous cheer when I nodded through my tears—tears for the proposal, tears for Adam's understanding, tears for my mother.

"Peekaboo has been Mazie's horse since she was big enough to ride. She used to climb up on a box to get on him. So naturally, when Mazie started feeding Princess, Peekaboo got a little jealous," I snapped back into the moment and realized I had been letting her talk without interruption for at least ten minutes. This made me cringe thinking about having to go back and listen to the entire interview again at the station. I always tried to keep my interviews short, asking only the questions I needed to elicit just enough sound on tape for the story. I kept copious notes so I could quickly find the exact quote I needed. Today was not going to be that kind of day.

"Marjorie, so basically the two animals started interacting through Mazie? And they made a love connection?"

"Well, sugar, I'll get to that." She sounded disgruntled by my effort to speed things up, "but we're not quite there yet."

Oh, we're there, Marjorie, we're there. But I couldn't say that out loud. I knew I had to let her get to the point in her own time. I just hoped it would be soon.

6

UNSPOOLING

"Bat-shit crazy." Buster grinned as we pulled out of Marjorie's driveway. "Where in the hell does Janie find these kooks?"

"Facebook," I said, without looking up from my iPad. I was trying to catch up on dozens of emails I had received while knee-deep in Marjorie's vortex and my own distracted thoughts. "She wasn't that bad. Just a country gal."

"Seriously, that's some kind of crazy. And she's the main event in our story," he said, hands off the steering wheel, palms in the air.

"When has that ever stopped us from putting someone on TV?"

"True that." Buster shook his head vigorously like he was trying to erase the memory of the last forty-five minutes. "And that dude, Brady. Man, he was like someone who crawled out of a cave. I thought he just might come back out to the porch with a shotgun and blow us both away. Kept hearing the theme song to *Deliverance* in my head." Buster hummed a few bars of the banjo ditty.

I popped Brady's full name into my state prison records app and looked him up while Buster continued to pontificate. He was not one to shy away from a soapbox.

"I bet he's hiding. Bet Brady's not even his real name."

Over the years, Buster and I had interviewed our fair share of characters. We had knocked on the doors of drug dealers, killers, prostitutes, you name it. We'd traveled dirt roads to trailer doors guarded by angry dogs on chains. We had taken cover when we interviewed gang members. We'd hiked deep into the woods to interview homeless people in tent cities. We'd talked to drunk people, people on drugs, people with no teeth, people with no clothes. And they all had a story. And yes, sometimes they were a little bit crazy. I learned there were fifty shades of crazy, and we got to meet a new kind almost every single day. My job was a lot of things, but it was never dull.

"It's not as bad as I thought it was," I said, after scrolling through Brady's record. "Mostly misdemeanors, petty larceny, simple assault, possession—just pot, a couple DWIs. Oh, there's also one indecent exposure. Probably peeing while drunk on a public street. He didn't strike me as a pervert."

"Speaking of crazy, let's get back to the lady who claims her husband is trying to kill her, but won't go to the police" Buster pursed his lips as he spoke.

"I really don't think she's crazy, but I don't know exactly what she is, to be honest. There are just some things about her story that don't add up. But on the other hand, I'm afraid not to believe her. I don't want something bad to happen to her, something I may be able to prevent."

"If she's truly afraid for her life, why is she screwing around with you? Why isn't she banging on the door of the police department asking for help? Doesn't make any sense."

"True. I agree, but it's not a typical situation. She wants

proof before she accuses him of something outright."

"Then why not hire a private investigator? That's what everyone does when they suspect their spouse of cheating. They don't latch on to a local news reporter and hope she can crack the case like it's some new series on Netflix. Seriously, I think this lady has been watching way too many movies or true crime shows."

"Their money is co-mingled. He would find out if she hired a private investigator to check him out."

"Come on, you tell me a big-wig public relations diva like this woman doesn't know how to siphon some funds out of her joint account and use it for whatever she wants? I think this lady is full of shit, and you're buying it. I don't think you should be so quick to help her. What is it about *her* that makes you want to jump right back into this world of murder and mayhem that you swore off when Adam died?"

As much as I hated to admit it, Buster was right. Most of the time I was pretty good at parsing good people from people who meant harm to me, but Adam's death had stripped me of this ability. I was constantly second-guessing my judgment.

"Hello, anybody in there? Are you listening to me?" Buster reached over and rapped on my head with his knuckles.

"Yes, I'm listening. I'm just taking a moment to think about what you said. You're right. There's a possibility Suzanne could be playing me. But you didn't see how scared she was in the hospital, how terrified she was when she thought Tanner was following us during our run. I think she is telling me the truth. But I do need to figure out exactly what's going on with her. As soon as we get back into town, I'm going to call her and tell her I need to meet with her immediately.

"Not so fast, sweetheart. First things first. What's for lunch?"

I wasn't sure what I remembered, what came from what

other people, and what came from newspaper clippings I read when I was older. I knew there was a lot of blood. The only time I saw blood before that was when I fell on the black asphalt playground at preschool and scraped my knee. So I just assumed my mother had a bad cut. But when I shook her, she didn't wake up. I remembered that clearly. I thought she was sleeping, but everything looked funny. Her hair was matted, thick with blood, and her eyes were partially open. She didn't look like my mother. Something was very wrong. I was too young to understand that a single bullet had caused all that damage.

I walked around her, poking her with my little fingers—on her shoulder, on her back, on her leg, on her feet—hoping she would wake up. She was always very ticklish, but when I tickled her feet nothing happened.

"Mommy," I whispered, so I wouldn't startle her. But she didn't respond.

"Mommy," I said a little louder, rounding her body again, my tiny hands making a trail on the stained hardwood floors that lined our hallway, as I crawled around her. That, I learned about later from the news reports.

"Mommy," I yelled. Nothing.

The next thing I remembered, I was in my father's arms. I don't know how much time had passed, but I knew I was safe and that everything was going to be okay.

~

I couldn't let what happened to my mother happen to Suzanne. That was the bottom line. Even though I didn't know her well, I felt that we had crossed paths for a reason, and that I owed her my attention and my help. If I didn't at least try to help her, and something bad happened, I would never forgive myself. I decided it was time to tell Suzanne about Maria Lopez, about her pregnancy. Maria being pregnant didn't mean she was carrying Tanner's baby, but it sure raised red flags. If it was Tanner's baby and he was in love with her, then maybe he did have a reason to want Suzanne out of the picture. But it all seemed so surreal, like the plot of a bad television movie. Didn't people get divorced anymore? It was a question I asked every time I covered a domestic violence murder.

I stirred my yogurt mindlessly as I listened to Marjorie's interview on my headphones at my desk in the middle of the newsroom and tried to block out the ambient noise around me—two people laughing in the cubicle to my left, the printer chugging away to my right, an anchor and a photographer shooting a segment to promote the evening news, a few feet in front of me. A newsroom was a living, breathing thing, like a tornado constantly swirling around you. Your choices were to stay out of its way by hiding in some distant conference room, or to allow yourself to get swept up in it. A good newsroom gossip session could derail the best journalists on deadline.

Regardless of the volume of my headphones, I could still hear someone talking about why she was going gluten-free, someone else on the phone "...not a story we would ever cover under any circumstances," and another person screaming across the newsroom about a Tweet from our competitor regarding a parking deck collapse.

I closed my laptop, coiled up my headphones and grabbed my purse, and decided it was time to pay Maria Lopez another visit. This time I intended to speak with her. I had no idea what I was going to say, but I believed she was the key to unraveling this entire mess. Maybe her relationship with Tanner was innocent, and maybe Suzanne was paranoid.

When I pulled up to the restaurant, it was closed. There

was a sign on a white piece of paper handwritten in Sharpie, that said, *Closed due to a funeral.* I decided to leave my business card for Maria, with a note on the back asking her to call me. I realized this was risky. She would wonder why a local television reporter was paying her a visit. But she would also be curious, and that might be just enough to prompt her to call me like so many people had done over the years after finding my business card stuck in their doors with no explanation. I learned early on that the less I said in my note, the better the chance people would call me because they just couldn't help themselves; they had to know why I was at their door.

I sat there for a few minutes in front of the building, in my car, waiting to see if someone might come to the door and retrieve the card. Kojak told me there was an apartment in the back, behind the restaurant, where some of the family members lived. Through the thin venetian blinds, I could see a faint light coming from somewhere beyond the cash register.

While I waited, I decided to rummage through my mail on the passenger seat of my car, untouched for three days. My constant need to triage in between the fire drills that had become my life meant the mail was a low priority. I paid most of my bills online, and no one wrote letters anymore. It was basically all junk mail. There was the usual assortment of catalogs—Adam's fault, as he was a champion shopper who signed up for every store credit card just to get discounts and coupons. There were also several bills that I would pay online later, a reminder for a dental appointment for the twins, and a long white envelope with my address written in big block letters in blue ink.

Every time I got a letter from Roger, I threw it in a big box at the back of my closet, with all the other letters he had sent me over the years. I never opened one of them. Just seeing his handwriting on the envelope gave me a sick feeling in the pit of my stomach. The return address was unmistakable—Penn Grove State Correctional Institution in Inverness, Pennsylvania. A maximum-security prison in the middle of the nowhere. He had moved around over the years, like most inmates, but spent most of his time at Penn Grove. I imagined that was because he was always getting into trouble—making shanks out of toothbrushes, smoking pot smuggled into the prison, talking back to the correctional officers, sexual activity with other inmates. You name it, Roger did it. All I had to do was look at his list of infractions on the Pennsylvania Department of Corrections' website to see his latest transgressions. Roger's list made it even easier for me to hate him, and gave me one more reason not to read his letters.

Even though we lived in New Jersey, the crime had taken place at my mother's parents' farmhouse house in Pennsylvania. We were visiting them at the time, or maybe we were running away from Roger. I wasn't told exactly why we were there. In a way, it was good that it happened there, because many of the gory details never made it to my small New Jersey town. Sure, there was gossip. People whispered when I came into the grocery store with my paternal grandmother, Belle, who raised me back in the town where I had once shared a house with my parents.

My mom's parents had been too old and dealing with too many health problems at the time to take on a three-year-old. My maternal grandfather, Bubby, had lung cancer, and my maternal grandmother, Nana, had diabetes. Despite Roger's conviction, my grandparents loved and trusted Belle, who was a widow with a healthy bank account and the energy to handle a small child.

Back in New Jersey with Belle, people thought I didn't notice them talking about me when she let go of my hand to let me peruse the candy aisle while she browsed in the produce section at the grocery store. Their voices were low, hushed, and conspiratorial. I heard them all right, but I tried to ignore them.

"That's her," they would say. "That's the little girl whose father killed her mother. Awful, just awful. Poor thing."

By the time I was about ten, the whispers had subsided. There were plenty of other things to gossip about—the choir director and the minister getting caught having sex in the baptismal tub; Grizzly Hutchins, who owned a popular local country bar, dressing as a woman at an Atlantic City casino; the high school secretary, Dobie Benson, embezzling $27,000 from the cafeteria and buying herself an inground pool. The long list trumped an old murder in Pennsylvania.

Roger had been locked up close to thirty-four years now and had exhausted every legal remedy possible that could get him released. A few years prior, a group of law students at a university in Philadelphia agreed to look at his case and see if there was anything left to appeal. Nothing had come of it. I imagined eager, over-worked students sitting on the floor of a conference room with Roger's files spread across the floor, poring over every detail as they drank coffee and debated the evidence. I also imagined their thrill and then disappointment when they visited with him in prison and discovered he wasn't the monster they had pictured at all, but an ordinary old white man who had aged drastically in prison.

I knew this because I occasionally looked up his identification picture on the state prison website. It was retaken annually, and if you could have lined up his photos side-by-side, you would see a dramatic change in his face between years ten and seventeen. In my opinion, that's when he lost hope, gave up and got old.

I had visited Roger when I was a little girl. It was an arrangement the family court had worked out with Belle. She would take me to see Roger once every three or four months.

I remembered we would sit on uncomfortable orange plastic chairs in a loud, drafty room. I would sit across from Roger, and he would hold my hand. Belle would always slip something to him beneath the table in a plastic bag, that he would then in turn hand to me on top of the table as if he had gotten me a gift. It was always something small, a trinket—candy, a tiny stuffed animal, a miniature slinky, a colorful bouncy ball, a mini-kaleidoscope. I knew Belle had brought the gift for me, but I always tried to pretend I was surprised and thankful. This made Roger happy, and at that time I was still interested in making him happy.

I didn't really know why Roger was in prison. I just knew he wasn't coming home for a long time. Belle didn't tell me why he was there, and I was afraid to ask. Somewhere deep down inside, I think I probably knew it had something to do with what happened to my mother, but I never went as far as imagining that he had hurt her. I told myself she fell and that's how she died, but that Roger got in trouble for not calling the ambulance right away. I had another scenario where Roger left the door unlocked, thus endangering her, and that a burglar must have slipped in and killed her while I was sleeping. I went back and forth between the different versions of the story, never casting Roger as a murderer.

Thankfully, life with my grandmother was good. I felt safe in the small extra bedroom at her cozy ranch house. She wasn't much of a cook, but because it was just the two of us, we ate out a lot. She let me eat whatever I wanted to. I was picky, so when we did eat at home, she gave me all my favorite *white* foods—mashed potatoes, apple sauce, bananas, and cheese. Most importantly, Belle never judged me and she supported me completely, which allowed me to grow into a confident young woman, something that seemed unlikely given my past.

I still missed my mother, but I knew that she, like Roger, wasn't coming back. Belle explained to me that my mother had been very sick and had gone to heaven to be with the angels. She said I would see her again someday. I really wanted to believe this, but Belle wasn't that big on church, so my exposure to spirituality was limited. Every so often I would go to church with a friend after a sleepover. I would look around at the beautiful stained glass, the wooden cross hanging above the altar, and the massive organ pipes lining the stone walls in the back, and whisper, "Mommy?" I figured if angels hung out anywhere on Earth, it would be in a church. But I never got a response.

Visits with Roger stopped after a string of incidents where he got into trouble in prison and was thrown into solitary confinement. As a result, he lost his visitation privileges. By the time he got them back, several years had passed and I wasn't interested in seeing him anymore. I was a pre-teen, and I was busy running cross country, writing for the school newspaper, and hanging out with my friends. I was also starting to feel embarrassed about having a father in prison. I had read enough books and seen enough movies to know this wasn't normal. I only told one friend at school—Brandi. The first time Brandi and I got in a fight over a boy at school, Ike Bollinger, she told everyone that my father was in prison. I even considered changing schools, until Debbie Arnold got pregnant after having sex with Keith Preston in the back of the school bus and everyone found out. Once again, my story was yesterday's news.

When I was twelve, I was sent to the judge's chambers to talk to him in person about the situation. The court had appointed me a guardian ad litem named Lucy to help me navigate the case because they said my grandmother couldn't be objective on account of her being Roger's mother. Lucy set up the meeting with the judge when I told her my feelings about Roger. She told me to be calm and simply tell him the truth. We even practiced it in her office. To her credit, Belle did not try to interfere in my discussions with Lucy. She just looked sad when I told her my decision.

"I don't want to see my father," I told the judge without apology. I tried to sound as firm as I could for a twelve-year-old. He looked a lot less intimidating sitting in a shirt and tie behind his desk instead of the black robe he wore in the courtroom in the big chair that looked down on everyone.

"Why is that?" he replied.

"I really don't know him that well. He's been gone for a long time. And the prison is a very scary place. I don't like going there. I'm very happy with my grandmother."

Belle had not been permitted to come into the judge's office. I overheard our attorney tell her that the judge didn't want me to be influenced by her, that it was my decision, and that the judge wanted to speak with me in private. I really didn't think Belle would be upset with me for my decision, but I also knew she still loved Roger despite whatever bad thing he had done to land him in prison. Other kids at school whispered about him killing my mother, but at this point in my life no adult had confirmed this information for me yet.

"Okay, young lady. Seeing that you're twelve, and you seem to have a pretty good head on your shoulders, I'm going to enter an order saying that you do not need to visit your father in prison until you are ready to do so. But in the meantime, I will allow him to send you letters. Is that okay? You have no obligation to write him back."

"Sure, but I don't have to read them if I don't want to, right?"

"Nope, it's entirely up to you. You can do whatever you want with them. If at any time you change your mind and you want to visit him again, let Lucy know, and you and I will have another chat."

I took his words to heart. For twenty-four years I filed Roger's letters away in a box, never opening even one. Though

I didn't read them, I kept them. I wasn't sure why I couldn't bring myself to throw them away. Part of me wondered if I might read them someday.

"Aren't you even curious what he has to say?" Adam used to ask me, every time he saw one of the envelopes perched on top of a stack of mail on the kitchen counter. Of course, I was. By the time I was an adult, I knew the truth. Belle had finally told me what happened. My psychologist told her it was something I needed to know when I was ready. She told me when I was sixteen. She, of course, qualified it with her own personal belief that he was innocent and wrongly convicted on circumstantial evidence by a vindictive, upwardly mobile prosecutor who simply wanted an open-and-shut case.

The information about his conviction, while I secretly suspected it most of my life, sent my sixteen-year-old self into a downward spiral involving alcohol, drugs, and sex. Thankfully my therapist, Dr. Ginette Kincaid, pulled me out of the dark hole and made me realize that I couldn't carry my father's burden around and allow it to ruin my life. Eventually I survived, some would say even *thrived*, rising above my past and trying to live my best possible life in my mother's honor.

Sadly, Belle's insistence of Roger's innocence, which we never spoke of again, drove an untenable wedge between us. It sat there like a poison which infected every strained, civil conversation we had until I went to college. After college, we drifted even further apart. I rarely visited and only called out of obligation for the kindness she had extended to me as a child. I knew my reaction to her was unfair, but I couldn't get over her defending the man who took my mother away from me.

"Not in the least," I would reply to Adam, regarding the letters, without a hint of regret in my voice. I had gotten good at convincing myself that I didn't want to know what Roger had to say. Was it possible that he could have killed my mother but had also been a good father? Was it possible that he did love me, despite this violent act? The day I buried Belle, my last living link to my father, I decided I would never look back.

I wasn't sure how long I had been sitting there in the car in front of the restaurant, Roger's letter in my hand, flooding me with unwanted memories. I saw the door open and a small hand reach out for my business card as it fell from the frame and fluttered to the ground. Maria stepped out onto the sidewalk, her pregnant belly leading the way in a tight black dress, and picked it up. She smoothed her dark sleek hair with her other hand, which was in a long braid slung over her shoulder. She looked nervously up and down the street. I guessed she wanted to see if the person who left the card was still nearby. She then backed into the doorway and closed the door behind her.

Part of me wished I had jumped out of the car and tried to speak with her, but something didn't feel right about the moment. I was pretty sure I would have startled her. So I stayed put. As I watched her retreat into the restaurant with my card, I had a strong feeling I wasn't going to hear from Maria Lopez anytime soon.

7

MULTIPLE MELTDOWNS

"I WOKE UP and there was a pillow over my head. I pushed it off, and I heard him roll over quickly. He pretended to be asleep, but I think he was really trying to smother me."

Suzanne called me, breathless, while I stood in line at Target to return some items. They were outfits for the kids that I had bought on a whim, hoping they would be the right size. But when I got home they were all wrong—wrong size, wrong color, wrong style, according to both of my picky fashion-forward ten-year-olds.

"Seriously, Suzanne, if you really believe he's trying to kill you, that he tried to smother you with a pillow last night, you have to call the police. I can't protect you."

I forgot where I was for a moment and looked around to see the people in front of me in line staring back at me, including the young cashier, who had been sorting through a pile of receipts in front of her, until my much more interesting conversation tore her attention away from the mundane task.

This wasn't what normal moms at Target talked about on the phone.

"Suzanne," I said in a loud whisper, stepping away from the line to a corner of the store near the automatic glass doors. I waited for them to whoosh one time before I continued. "You have to listen to me."

"I know you're right, Maddie, but I'm not ready to leave. Just the other day, I was looking for Winston's passport because I needed to fill out some paperwork for a school chorus trip in the spring, to Costa Rica, and I couldn't find it anywhere. I'm a very careful person. I know where everything is in my house. He's hidden it from me, Maddie. Tanner has done something with Winston's passport. I'm sure of it."

"Okay, don't panic. What about a lawyer? I know several very good family lawyers. That way you could work out the custody of Winston before you leave Tanner. That might ease your mind."

I looked over to see that the line for returns had grown exponentially since I'd walked away. I glanced at my watch and realized I would never get to my next assignment if I waited in the line now. Between work and the kids, I never had a span of more than thirty minutes to run an errand or perform some menial task. I shrugged and left through the automatic doors, heading toward my car.

Suzanne said, her voice changing quickly from somewhat hysterical to calm. "Okay, I'll talk to an attorney. I've got to go. Just text me the information and I'll make an appointment," I was happy that I was able to talk her off the ledge again with a logical solution. It felt good to be helping someone.

"Good plan. And I really think you should try and stay with a friend or in a hotel or something for your own safety."

Should I call the police? I wondered, in the Target parking lot after hanging up. If what she was saying was true, that her life was in danger, and I knew about it and didn't do anything, that would forever weigh on my conscience. Didn't I have an obligation to do something to prevent her from getting hurt or killed?

My mother's blood was smeared on the hardwood floors. It seeped into the cream baseboard that lined the hallway in my grandparents' house. I pictured this scene from a dog-eared, yellowed newspaper article Belle kept in a shoe box in the attic. She didn't know I knew about it, but I had found it one rainy day when I was bored. I could still remember how the old newspaper felt between my fingers, at once stiff and fragile, like it might crumble if I touched it the wrong way. The photo was taken with a bright flash, the dark outline of the stains clearly visible in the decomposing picture.

I still didn't know exactly what I was dealing with, but I knew I didn't want Suzanne's life to end this way.

I was assigned to do a story about a cat they called *Picasso*. Her name came from her amazing aptitude for painting...*yes, painting.* Her owner, Ivanka Picu, displayed Picasso's art in a gallery in the downtown warehouse district, and people were paying more than a thousand dollars to own one. Tonight, was the grand opening of the show. It was another Janie special. The show was naturally titled *Puss N' Painting*. You couldn't make it up.

I suspected Ivanka had some taxidermist stuff a cat, and she dipped the dead cat's paws in paint and then spread them around the canvas. Still, I had to give her credit for her creativity and ability to get Picasso into the limelight. Due to Ivanka's viral videos, the feline had already been on *The Today Show* and several late-night television talk shows, not to mention on the cover of *People* Magazine.

But before I interviewed the genius cat and her master, I decided I had enough time to pay Kojak a quick visit and tell him what was going on with Suzanne. He would surely know what to do. He always did. My gut said he was going to tell me to tell Suzanne to call the police, but I needed to hear this directly from him.

Kojak was meeting me on a corner across the street, about a block away from the art gallery. I circled the block several times to find a parking space. Parallel parking was not my forte. I needed at least two spots to be able pull my massive SUV in and get close to the curb. I had already gotten multiple tickets for violating the city's ordinance that said you had to park no more than twelve inches from the curb. I was ready to get rid of the car since it had 130,000 miles on it, but Adam was always a pragmatist and told me I should wait until we owned the car for at least nine years. I wasn't sure why nine was his magic number, but I wasn't about to question it now.

It was just getting dark as I approached our meeting spot and saw the glow at the tip of Kojak's cigarette. In all the years I had known him, he had never smoked in front of me. As far as I knew, he had quit decades ago, using a nicotine patch at first, and then substituting lollipops for his oral fixation. I met him when he was firmly in the lollipop stage. Those eventually went away, too, when his wife, Marion, put him on a no-sugar diet.

"What's up?" I said as I approached from behind, obviously startling him. He quickly threw the cigarette onto the sidewalk and crushed it with his shoe, a worn, brown leather loafer with a sad-looking tassel. He stiffened his posture like a little boy who had been scolded at the dinner table and told to sit up straight.

"Shit, you weren't supposed to see that. No one is. Fell off the wagon again." He turned to look at me with a sheepish grin that I could barely make out beneath the light of the street lamp. "It's just that the wife has me on this goddamned gluten-free, sugar-free, fun-free diet, and I can't think straight.

I'm craving everything I can't have. I literally want to go into the coffee shop and ask for anything with gluten, extra gluten, gluten as a side dish. Just no more cardboard, *please*."

I smiled to reassure him that his secret was safe with me. Although I was pretty sure gluten was a safer bet than tobacco, it wasn't my place to lecture him. Out of all the secrets I kept for people, this was by no means one of the biggest.

"So what's going on? Sounds like this Suzanne chick is really starting to lose it, huh? Why the hell doesn't she report the guy if he's really doing this stuff? We can protect her."

"Really? You know as well as I do a domestic violence protection order is just a piece of paper. If someone is intent on doing harm to another person, it won't stop him. But at the same time, she's putting all this stuff on my shoulders, and there's really nothing I can do to help her."

"Well, I did a little research. He does have the same initials you saw on the license plate near the running trail the other day TJP. But his last name is not Parker, its Pope. If I'm right, and I'm pretty sure I am, he's in orthopedics, affiliated with Chester Hospital. Definitely a bigwig. He's got a fancy office, expensive house, nice cars. But clean as a whistle from a legal standpoint, as far as I can tell. Still, we both know that means nothing. He could be a bad egg, and not have a record."

"Very interesting. Thanks for getting that information for me. Not sure what I will do with it. But it's always better to know what you're dealing with. So here's what I've been doing. I went to see Maria, but the restaurant was closed. I left her a card in the door, and I was sitting in my car and saw her step out and take it. I probably should have jumped out of the car and rushed over and tried to talk to her. But I kind of froze. I'm not sure what to say to her. Like, *Hey there, are you having an affair with this guy who is threatening his wife, a woman I kind of know?*"

"Do you think that's smart to contact her? You're getting

pretty wrapped up in this mess. Sounds like someone misses the mean streets. Maybe you should give up your pussycat stories and get back to your roots." Kojak slapped me a little too hard on the shoulder.

His lingering tobacco smell wafted over me, making me gag a little.

"No, I'm just trying to help her, that's all. I can't stop thinking about what could happen if I don't. I'm not sure what's actually going on, but I have no doubt she is truly afraid of this guy."

"You're thinking about your mother."

The word *mother* hung in the air between us stronger than any tobacco smell. My heart started pounding so loud I was sure Kojak could hear it, too. My throat was dry and I felt like it might close up. I couldn't get enough air. My palms were sweaty, and I felt throbbing around my temples. I was either having a stroke or an anxiety attack.

"Sit down, kid." Kojak led me to a nearby bench and steered me with both arms onto the seat. "I shouldn't have said that. My bad. Not my place to talk about that."

I hung my head and tried to catch my breath, steadying myself with both arms on the edge of the wooden bench, which was sticky from something I didn't want to imagine. I had panic attacks for many years after seeing my mother's body, but with Dr. Kincaid's help, along with yoga, meditation, and some medication, I had eventually grown out of them. I started running cross country in high school, and they magically disappeared. The last time I remembered having one was when the doctor told me Adam had only a few days to live.

Adam was in the hospital at that point, being kept alive by IV fluids and multiple golden medications that snaked down plastic tubes, into his veins. He didn't hear what the doctor said because he was so out of it, but I did. *It will be soon. Probably a few days.* I ran out of the hospital room and down the hallway toward the nearest public restroom. I was sobbing and trying to catch my breath, when I almost ran right into a female janitor standing in the doorway of the ladies' room.

"The restroom is closed." She put up a hand sheathed in a blue latex glove so close to my face I could have touched it with my tongue.

"Can I just get some tissues and splash a little water on my face?" I pleaded.

"No." She moved the blue latex palm even closer to my face. Her face was stoic, an unmovable mask of nothingness. No empathy.

I ran out of the bathroom and into the first door I could find. It was a linen closet where I fell to the ground in a fetal position and cried myself tearless. All those same symptoms of a panic attack enveloped me at once—the pounding heart, breathlessness, throbbing temples. When I finally calmed down and was able to pick myself up from the floor, I crept out of the closet and tried to regain my composure. I wiped my stinging cheeks with the backs of my hands, pulled my hair back into a tight ponytail with a hairband from my wrist, and tried unsuccessfully to smooth down my wrinkled pants. I bowed my head as I walked back down the hallway towards Adam's room. People who had witnessed my breakdown looked away as I passed, not wanting to make eye contact. I didn't care. Watching someone die disabled your vanity.

"Are you okay, kid?" Kojak asked, bringing me back to the present moment, to the sticky bench on a city street corner.

He was now perched at the far end of the bench, looking at me with concern. In his hand was a bottle of water he must have gotten from a street vendor, although I didn't remember him leaving.

"Here, have some water. Do you want me to call someone?"

"No, I'm good." I straightened and reached for the bottle of water. I still didn't have a person to call. Adam was my person.

Sure, I had some great girlfriends, but I had never been one to rely on my friends the way I relied on Adam. Maybe I was just too proud. I wanted to be that pillar of strength for others in crisis, but never allowed anyone to be that for me. I was paying for that distance I created between myself and other people now that Adam was gone, and my kids were way too young to come to my rescue. Maybe that's why I understood Suzanne so well, her need to share her crisis with a perfect stranger because she had no one else to call, just like me.

I opened the bottle of water, tipped it back, drinking the whole thing in a few gulps. When I was finished, I wiped my cheeks with the back of my hand.

"You have to help me get to the bottom of this. Promise me you will."

"I promise, kid. Now go in there and get your story. There's a cat looking for her fifteen minutes of fame."

Miranda was so confident that sometimes I didn't know what planet she came from. I liked to think that maybe some of this came from me, but when I thought back to the insecure, skinny little girl I had been, I was sure Miranda had some errant strain of DNA from an extraterrestrial.

It was impossible to believe that she and Blake had shared a womb with their divergent personalities. It was if they each got one half of a shared brain. He got the sensitive side and she got the practical side.

Unlike Blake, she preferred that everyone around her have a buck-up attitude, regardless of the situation. Empathy wasn't her strong suit, but she did have a way of always making me feel less sorry for myself with her frank take on life.

So it was no surprise to me when I came home that night feeling down about my silly cat story, about Suzanne's dire situation, and about my inability to be a good single parent, that she put me in my place.

"Help me prop this up." She gingerly raised a clay version of Big Ben off the kitchen counter, into an upright position.

"Bye, Mrs. Arnette. See you tomorrow," our babysitter, Candace, called out from the front hall.

Candace was my savior. She was a local college student who had been with us for two years. I could not have handled Adam's illness without her. Honestly, the summer he was dying, I had no idea where my children were at any given moment. I just knew they were with her and that they were safe.

"Mom, you promised you would help me with this project, so help," Miranda said, with the unbridled indignity of a fifty-year-old woman who didn't care what she sounded like.

"You're right, sweetie. I did promise. And I'm sorry I've been so distracted lately."

I held up my side of Big Ben while she worked on the clock face with a delicate plastic carving tool. For a moment, I forgot about kitty art, Suzanne's mess, and my parental shortcomings. I was just a mom propping up a little bit of history etched in clay.

8

RECKONING

AFTER I MET WITH KOJAK, I had a dream that I was missing something important. It came from something he said, something that reminded me of a piece of information I desperately wanted to remember, but in the fog of early waking it vanished. I was like a scuba diver returning reluctantly to the surface, watching a shell slip from my hands and swirl down into the deep, dark recesses of the ocean. As hard as I tried, I couldn't reach out and grab it. It was something about Tanner Pope. But what was it? I wrestled with it. Maybe if I stayed in bed just a little bit longer, I would remember.

"Mom," Miranda yelled, in an accusatory tone, a tone that seemed to have gained more of an edge every day since Adam's death. I was back at the surface of the water.

"Where is my white shirt? I need to wear it today. I have nothing to wear if you don't find it."

"Laundry basket, foot of my bed," I managed to blurt out, my mouth still partially muffled by my pillow. I didn't open my eyes as she stomped into my room. I could hear her emptying the laundry onto the floor, the zippers and buttons clanking against the hardwoods. When she perceived she had been wronged, she acted out. The psychologist I hired to work with the kids after Adam's death, Dr. Jacobs, said the reason she did these things was because she didn't have the words or the coping skills at her age to deal with the anger she felt about Adam dying. So she expressed it in other ways, like dumping clean laundry all over my bedroom floor.

Dr. Kincaid had been such a help to me after my mother died that I figured a little therapy might help the twins as well. Before Belle hired Dr. Kincaid, she had me meet with a local priest. He promised my grandmother, after only two meetings with me, that I would be fine because I was too young to remember anything. But he was wrong. I had night terrors and unreasonable phobias. Thunderstorms terrified me; I was sure lightning was going to strike the house at any moment and start a huge fire. I couldn't separate the fiction in movies from reality, refusing to go into the swimming pool for an entire summer after I saw a rerun of *Jaws*. After seeing an old documentary about Charles Manson on one of those true crime channels, I was convinced every night that he was going to climb into my window and kill me, even though I knew he was in prison. Eventually Belle realized the priest was wrong, and decided to seek professional help for me.

"Mommy," Blake's sweet voice called. "I can't open the syrup. Can you help me?"

I had no option but to get out of bed. I gingerly placed each foot, one at a time, on the floor next to my bed. Running had taken its toll on my knees and hips, and I never stretched enough. Every morning was like this, but as soon as I got moving, I was fine. There was no time to dwell on pain. There was a white shirt to locate, syrup to open, and a carpool to drive.

"See that blue spot." Miranda shoved the sleeve of her recovered white shirt into my face to show me a microscopic speck of blue on the sleeve. "It's ruined. I can't wear it. I need you to get me a new white shirt right now!"

This was the way so many mornings started with Miranda. Dr. Jacobs told me to be calm in these situations and try to explain to her logically why her demands were unreasonable. I was so tired. I didn't have any energy to fight with a ten-year-old. Part of me considered running to Target to get Miranda another shirt to end her temper tantrum. But I could hear Dr. Jacobs voice inside my head. *Is that really the right thing to do, Maddie? To give in? What do you think will happen if you keep giving in to her? Will she learn anything from always getting her way?*

I convinced her to wear another shirt. Bribing her with the promise of getting her ears pierced. I was pretty sure Dr. Jacobs wouldn't approve of this tactic either, but sometimes parents had to do unsavory things on the battlefield to survive.

It was something Miranda had been begging me to do for months. For some reason I had set the arbitrary age of thirteen as a proper time to pierce her ears, probably because that's when Belle let me get mine pierced.

"Macie Barnes had her ears pierced as a baby," Miranda had said. She had an endless list of friends who'd already had their ears pierced, and constantly invoked them during our ongoing argument on the topic.

I also managed to calm Blake by lightly toasting his waffle and drowning it in syrup. I supervised the making of their beds, threw in a load of laundry, and braided Miranda's thick hair. I picked up dirty pajamas, wet towels, empty water bottles, and shepherded dirty breakfast dishes from the sink into the dishwasher. In between slathering peanut butter and jelly on wheat bread with the crusts cut off, and cutting green apples into thin slices and placing them into two plastic baggies, I remembered what I had lost in my dream.

Five years before his death, Adam ripped the extensor tendon in his middle finger on his right hand. I recalled the moment vividly. We were getting ready for church on Christmas Eve, and he was rushing to force his foot into a tight leather loafer. He stuck his finger into the heel of the shoe to stretch it, and then shoved his foot inside, forgetting to remove his finger. When he went to pull his finger out, the tendon snapped. He cried out in pain and yelled for me, two things he had never done in all the years I knew him. I rushed into the bedroom and he held his hand up for me to see it. The tip of his finger looked disconnected from the rest of the finger. It dangled like a fishing line weighed down by a heavy lure. It made me nauseous. I tried to remain calm and act like it was no big deal.

I wrapped it in a towel with a bag of ice, and we rushed to the emergency room, assuming it was broken. A nurse X-rayed it, and then the doctor came into our little curtained area, where Adam was lying on a gurney, to give us the bad news.

"It's much worse than a break," said the weary, young doctor, who had drawn the short stick on Christmas Eve. He looked down at his clipboard and flipped the page up, shaking his head at whatever was written there. "It's a ripped tendon. A tendon can take a very long time to heal. They're very tricky. For now we'll put a splint on it and hope for the best. If you move it at all, it won't heal. That's the tricky part. You'll need to see an orthopedic doctor after the holidays. Sorry I don't have better news for you."

It wasn't life-threatening. It was more of an inconvenience. But it was *our* inconvenience. The young doctor explained that it was a common injury, one that usually occurred when people were performing the most mundane tasks, like tucking sheets beneath the corners of a heavy mattress. Who knew?

What followed were several unsuccessful months of Adam's

finger encased in a splint. This was then followed by minor outpatient surgery, in which a pin was inserted into his finger to keep the broken tendon straight so it would heal itself. Eventually Adam's body rejected the pin and his finger became infected. Every time he lightly tapped something with it, he told me it sent a shiver of pain down his spine so severe he couldn't speak for a few seconds. When he couldn't stand the pain anymore, they took the pin out, and thankfully his finger was healed by then.

The whole situation was annoying to Adam, especially when it came to simple things he couldn't do, like type, button his shirt, and fasten his belt. But looking back on it and comparing it to his battle with brain cancer, it was really nothing at all. It barely registered on my radar of life events, which is probably why I had forgotten about it.

Last night, sitting under the dim light of the street lamp, Kojak had told me something that jogged my memory. It was before I had my panic attack. When Adam tore his tendon, he was treated by a handsome, affable orthopedic doctor named TJ Pope a.k.a. Tanner Pope.

I didn't know what it meant. Could it be a coincidence that I knew Suzanne's husband? What really confused me was that my vague recollection of the man was positive. He had good energy, from what I remembered. He was open and friendly, not someone who appeared to be hiding a dark side. This memory didn't jive with him being an abuser, an adulterer, or a killer. These weren't things I was looking for when I met him. I just wanted Adam's finger to heal so he could zip his pants, type an email, and unscrew the cap of a water bottle.

"You have no idea how many things you use your middle finger for until you don't have it," Adam told me one day, as he repeatedly failed to buckle his belt. I stopped what I was doing to help him, silently snickering, as I thought about what a lot of people used their middle finger for.

I remember being annoyed as I threaded the two metal prongs into the holes and tugged the leather strap through the belt loops on his pants. Now I longed to do something that simple for him again, to buckle his belt or put toothpaste on his toothbrush.

I recalled talking to Adam about Dr. Pope, about how much we liked him and thought he really knew his stuff, about how lucky we felt to have picked him from a quick Internet search of doctors with available appointments just after Christmas. I struggled to picture Tanner's face now. My memory was fuzzy, but the more I concentrated, an image came to me slowly. His face was angular, youthful, and he sported a well-trimmed, light brown goatee. He looked like a hipster with his heavy tortoise shell glasses and tight pants that tapered at his ankles. I recalled a pastel tie with a small black-checked pattern peeking out of the top of his jacket.

I recalled that he listened with undivided attention to Adam's concerns about not healing quickly enough and how this seemingly small injury had complicated his life so much. He didn't act rushed, like he had to get to the next patient. He put us at ease with his calm demeanor and supportive words. This Tanner Pope, the one that I now remembered, was not at all the man Suzanne had described.

I decided it was time to finally unburden myself with Suzanne, to tell her what I knew about Maria, and ask her more about Tanner. I wouldn't confess right away that I knew him, but I would feel her out and try to figure out once and for all what was really going on.

I worked all this out in my head while I was doing yoga on a mat in my living room, after I had sent the kids off to school, in the carpool. I knew thinking through complex issues was the opposite of what you were supposed to be doing while engaged in a yoga practice. Yoga was about *clearing* your brain, not *filling* it. Yet for me, meditation wasn't about the absence of thoughts, but about having the time and space to unpack them.

I was in child's pose when the phone rang. I looked up and reached for it. The phone was just within arm's reach in front of my yoga mat, not exactly a recipe for relaxation. I could see Janie's picture and number flash on the screen. In the photograph she was dressed like the *Cat in the Hat* from some distant Halloween party complete with black whiskers drawn on her face. In her paw was a beer bottle, and she was winking at the camera. I didn't understand iPhone technology enough to figure out why *this* was the profile picture chosen for her on my phone, nor did I know how to change it.

"Maddie," Janie said, breathlessly. It reminded me of the many times she had called me about breaking news in the past—a missing person, human bones in a dumpster, a murder weapon recovered from a pond, but I had a feeling this time she was calling about another "Amazing Tale."

"Hey, Janie. What's up?" I moved out of my child's pose into giraffe, sitting back on my heels and arching my back with my left hand on one heel while I used my right hand to put the phone on speaker and set it on the coffee table next to me.

"Got a great story for you. This lady, Lucinda Bark, she works at a grocery store on the edge of town, Food Stop, and she's been feeding these ducks. So they basically set up residence on a grassy spot, a little island, in this super-busy shopping center. The owner of the shopping center is trying to have them removed, but this chick, pardon the pun, she started a petition to protect them. Now everyone is feeding them, all the customers. They even built a little habitat for them with a tiny pond, a baby pool. They sent me a picture. It's super-cute. People are going to love this story."

"Wow, that's something," I deadpanned as I felt my prima facia stretching in my feet like a rubber band about to snap.

"And here's the best part. They cross the lane of traffic all the time, holding up cars. So Bark, the grocery store lady, had a local artist put up a sign that says, *Duck Crossing*. His name is Larry Boone. He and Lucinda are willing to go on camera. Best time to go is when the shopping center is busiest, maybe around lunch. The owner is an LLC called Best Practice Properties. Jerome Salinger is listed as the primary person on the LLC. I've emailed the information to you. Just like old times—a controversy! But it's perfect for you because it also includes animals. See how everything comes full circle?"

I sat back down on my mat, with my legs crisscrossed. Without a conflict, most television news stories would not exist. Rarely in these situations was anyone ever happy with the way a news story turned out. Dex always said that if both sides were mad at you after your story aired, then you did your job. By this standard, I was pretty good at my job.

The truth was, I was so exhausted by the conflicts in the hard news stories I covered before my animal beat that I simply didn't care anymore. The negativity had sucked me dry and it was no longer worth my energy. And yet here I was again sticking my foot into the middle of a heated dispute over *ducks*. I knew Janie would not take *no* for an answer. I waved my white flag in my head, like I had done with Miranda earlier that morning over the stained shirt, and agreed to do it.

"Okay, I'll meet Buster at the station around eleven o'clock." I strained to get in twenty more seconds of Zen as I eased into a sleeping pigeon pose with my right leg bent awkwardly beneath me on the mat. *Make peace with your edge*. It was a mantra one of my yoga teachers repeated over and over. Unfortunately I was forced to make peace with my edge just about every day of my life on so many different levels. What if I just wanted to stop short of the edge? What would happen then? I was eager to find out.

Lucinda Bark was a beautiful African American woman with long braids and a slender neck that reminded me of a swan. She looked to be in her late thirties, but I couldn't tell for sure. She had a youthful aura about her, but also a look of despair in her magnetic coffee eyes.

She greeted me at the door of the grocery store, in her green apron with the store's logo on it in large black block print. She wore it over a white flowing hippie dress that matched my pre-image of her as an animal activist. Even though it was a warm day, she wore tall brown suede lace-up boots. What this lovely creature was doing as a cashier in a grocery store, I had no idea.

"Hello." She extended a slender hand with piano player fingers, as she reached behind her back with her other hand to untie the apron. "The store doesn't want me to wear this for the interview. I get it. I am not speaking for them. I am speaking as an individual."

I detected an accent. Like so many people in the Oak City area, she was originally from somewhere else. We had become a rich mixture of cultures in a way that made our quiet southern city much more interesting than it had been when I first moved here from New Jersey years ago.

"Totally understand." I shook her hand as I noticed her exquisitely manicured purple nails.

I stepped back to allow her to pull the apron above her head.

Then walked up a scruffy young man in jeans loosely held up by a black studded belt wearing a faded concert shirt. He was sporting low black, well-worn motorcycle boots and was smoking the end of a cigarette held between his paint-stained fingers adorned by several large silver rings, including one in the shape of a skull. I couldn't see his eyes behind his round multicolor wire-framed John Lennon sunglasses, but I could tell by the specific matting of the hair in the back of his head that he had most likely recently gotten out of bed.

"Larry Boone," he said, in a gravelly voice, tipping his chin upward to me instead of reaching out his hand to shake mine. Unlike Lucinda, I could tell, despite Larry's youthful way of dressing, that he was older than he tried to appear. I placed him in his early to mid-forties. He was clearly still a struggling artist. Janie had explained that he worked at night, stocking shelves for the store in between his artistic endeavors.

"He's very talented. Just biding his time until his big break comes, right Larry?" Lucinda said, without any hint of sarcasm, when she noticed my visual assessment of him.

He again tilted his chin upward in assent. I was beginning to realize this was Larry's go-to gesture.

Lucinda then told me how she had first noticed the ducks when she was on her lunch break, eating at one of the picnic tables reserved for employees on the side of the building. She told me that, at first, she fed them scraps of bread, but then read online that she should be feeding them real duck food instead. That night she stopped by the agriculture supply store and bought a bag of feed she brought with her to work the next day.

One thing led to another, and Lucinda's ducks soon began to multiply and take up residence in a little grassy knoll, a traffic island adorned with one tree, in the middle of the parking lot. Eventually a shopper who knew something about ducks told Lucinda she needed a water source for them. That's when she and Larry decided to place a plastic baby pool on the island for them to bathe in and drink from.

But despite their efforts to keep the ducks on the island with a big bucket fully stocked daily with feed and the blue plastic pool to splash in, the birds insisted on crossing the road to the picnic tables several times a day to the spot where Lucinda had first fed them. That's when Larry got the idea to create the *Duck Crossing* sign.

"I just kept thinking I was going to come out and find some duck pate on the street in front of the store." Larry pantomimed a car flattening a duck with his hands. "People are pretty cool if you allow them to be. Most everyone stops for them. Sure, there are a few angry people, dicks who get a little annoyed and honk because they're in a hurry to get to Pilates or the golf course or some bullshit like that. I'm like, dude, *they're ducks*. They got nowhere to go and all day to get there. Unlike your sorry, stressed-out ass. Chill."

I had to do several takes with Larry to get him to say things again without curse words so I could use his sound bites on the air. Thankfully he seemed to understand my predicament with the FCC guidelines that still prohibited certain language on network television. He was more than happy to oblige me.

"It's important that we allow people and nature to co-exist," Lucinda said, with her dreamy accent, like an ethereal prophet. I wondered if she taught yoga.

"What are we if we can't appreciate God's vulnerable creatures? Then what does that say about us as human beings?"

Janie had contacted Jerome Salinger, whose corporation owned the shopping center, to see if he would be willing to do an interview with us. His assistant referred us to the management company that ran the shopping center, the Howell Management Corporation. As expected, no one from Howell was willing to go on camera and talk about the duck situation, but they did agree to email us a statement. In my opinion, this was always a big mistake. If I were their public relations person, I would have gotten out in front of this mini-crisis immediately and tried to find a solution that made the shoppers and the animal activists comfortable.

Instead of transparency and a solution, we got this: *While we appreciate the efforts of two employees of the anchor store in our shopping center to protect the wildlife, it has caused a major disruption to our patrons, one that we fear will result in an inconvenience and possible negative interactions between drivers and the ducks in our parking lot. As a result, we are asking Ms. Bark and Mr. Boone to remove the food and water source that are keeping the birds in residence on our property. We are also asking them to remove the illegal sign that was erected without our approval and which does not comply with the town's sign ordinance. We hope they will give these requests their immediate attention, or we will be forced to take legal action.*

Howell could have posted positive messages on Facebook, Twitter, and Instagram about their ability to create a peaceful co-existence between wildlife and their customers, but instead they dropped the ball. It would be their loss when the backlash started. And it would start. This I knew for sure, from previous experience.

I shook hands with Lucinda and Larry, thanking them, and gave them business cards so they could keep me posted on the situation. They were both another reminder of why I became a journalist in the first place—to be a passenger on other people's adventures. The characters I met along the way were stitched together in my memory like a patchwork quilt that stayed with me wherever I went. I was constantly adding another square, another story, another rich layer to my interesting life as a reporter. Besides the kids, my work was the one thing that could usually distract me from my grief.

"Suzanne," I said to her voicemail, over my car's Bluetooth as I pulled out of the Food Stop parking lot and headed toward the station. "I am just checking in to see how you are. Also I have a few things we need to discuss. Can we get together?"

Just then, another call clicked in on call waiting. It was Suzanne.

"Maddie." Suzanne's voice was urgent. "Sorry I didn't pick up. I was on the other line, but then I realized it was you."

"It's okay. Just disregard my voicemail. First, how are you?"

"I'm okay, I guess. I just don't know what's going on. Is my mind playing tricks on me? He left in the middle of the night the other night."

"Who left?"

"Tanner. Said he had a medical emergency."

"Well, maybe he did have a medical emergency."

"Maybe, but it was weird. He got a text, looked at it, jumped out of bed, and bolted. The phone was on the table next to the bed. But when he got up, he took it with him into the bathroom while he got ready. It was like he didn't want me to see the text."

"You're probably reading too much into that. Maybe he just didn't want to wake you. Maybe he needed to respond to the text and didn't want to waste any time, so he took the phone to the bathroom. I would hold off on imagining the worst before you know more." I tempered my comments based on my newly recalled memory of Tanner. I was starting to wonder if Suzanne was just paranoid. "Look, I need to see you. Are you free for lunch?"

"Lunch, yes, okay. Where?"

"Oak City Bistro, one o'clock."

"Okay. Maddie, thank you for all you have done for me. You don't know how much I appreciate it. Seriously, you barely know me and you're trying to help me navigate this nightmare. By the way, we never finished our conversation about your mother. I didn't want you to think I didn't remember we were talking about that before all the crap went down with Tanner. I want to be there for you the way you've been there for me. Friendship is a two-way street."

I hung up and placed it back the phone my empty cup holder. I swapped it for a now, lukewarm bottle of water that had been sitting in the car all morning, and took a long unsatisfying sip. *Friendship?* Out of desperation, Suzanne was becoming way too attached to me. We had known each other for just a few weeks. I was not prepared to bare my soul to her.

Speaking to her about my mother would have been a mistake. Suzanne was the vulnerable one who needed my help. I did not need hers. From now on I intended to keep her at arm's length.

9

BREAKING BREAD

Suzanne's mention of my mother had put me on edge. I knew she probably meant well, but it unnerved me. As I sat at the table in the restaurant, dipping a big piece of crusty bread in olive oil, I kept returning to our phone conversation. I knew I was dwelling on my own insecurities when I should be thinking about how to help Suzanne, but I was rattled.

I wasn't even hungry. It was a nervous habit—eating to keep my hands busy and my head occupied. The longer I waited for Suzanne, the more bread I ate, and the more my mind circled back to the moment I mentioned my mother. I was hoping she would forget it.

"Hey, there." Suzanne breezed into the restaurant like a woman who just left the spa.

Her dark hair was a perfectly coiffed cascade of loose waves hanging over her shoulders. Her dark eyeliner and red lipstick made her face stand out like a model in a glossy magazine advertisement. She wore a snug-fitting blue wrap dress and carried her signature large, silver purse over her shoulder, nearly hitting me in the head as she leaned in for an airkiss. She gave my shoulder a quick squeeze.

"You look great," I said after, I swallowed my third mouthful of soggy bread.

"Thanks. It's one thing I learned through crisis PR work. Always look better than your opponent. It psyches them out. And looking better than you feel has a way of creating a positive vibe that hides your internal struggles."

"So Suzanne, the reason I wanted to meet," I said, just as the waiter arrived.

"Ladies, would you like to hear our specials today?"

The waiter was a thin redhead with close cropped hair and lobe expanders—big pieces of round black-plastic that stretched holes in his ears roughly the size of quarters. It was a fashion statement I didn't understand and always had to look away from because it seemed so painful to me. I bowed my head and pretended I was intently studying the menu while waiting for him to go away. Suzanne, on the other hand, engaged him in flirtatious banter about the size of the Cobb salad. Finally, we both settled on salads, Suzanne on the Cobb, and me on the wedge salad with chicken, and the ear-expanding waiter finally left us alone.

"Maddie, I feel like I always talk about myself when we're together. Let's forget about me and my crazy life for a moment and talk about you. What was it that you were going to tell me about your mother, about what happened in Pennsylvania, before we got so rudely interrupted by my creepy husband the other day when we were running?"

I was completely caught off guard by her directness. My brain was racing, trying to figure out what her angle was, what she really wanted from me.

"Well..." I felt the same lump in my throat and redness in my face that I felt anytime I did something scary, like cascading down a zipline in Costa Rica. As I got older, I knew that this was usually a sign I shouldn't do something, even if everyone else was doing it. I was always that person—the person who got bucked off *the sweetest horse*. The person who got sick on the upside-down roller coaster. The person who ran out of air or blew my eardrums on a shallow reef dive. My gut told me this was another one of those situations, that I should not share my dark history with Suzanne Parker.

"Suzanne, I really think we have more pressing things to talk about. Like Tanner," I whispered. Oak City was a small town disguised as a city. Sure, we had tall buildings, crippling traffic, and large concert venues, but the vibe was still small-town. Everyone knew everyone else, either directly or through just a few degrees of separation. I didn't want to risk anyone hearing us talk about Tanner since I had no real proof that he was a bad person.

"It's okay. I'm not scared anymore. Not even after the pillow incident. I made a decision. I am going to leave him. I've got everything lined up a condo downtown, an attorney. I talked to one of the attorneys you recommended, about getting joint custody. I really think this is the best plan. In hindsight, I think I might have been overreacting about everything, all that stuff about him trying to kill me. I might have exaggerated a little bit. Just because a man has an affair doesn't make him a monster. Plenty of men have affairs and never kill their wives. I haven't told him yet that I'm leaving, but I'm going to *very soon*."

Suzanne smiled and then, with her fork, speared a piece of egg from the top of her salad and popped it in her mouth. I sat back in my chair and studied her. Yesterday, she told me her husband was trying to smother her with a pillow, and now she was just going to casually walk out the door and leave him. I was starting to think Buster was right when he said, *The crazies see you coming a mile away*.

I felt like I needed to tell her about Maria being pregnant. I had to get it off my chest. If she found out later that I knew and didn't tell her, she would be devastated. She could do whatever she wanted with the information. I just needed to unburden myself.

I wasn't ready to tell her yet that I knew Tanner, that he had treated Adam's finger. This didn't seem important at the moment. My five-year-old fleeting impression of him, certainly not as important as telling her about Maria. It was hard for me to concentrate on what Suzanne was saying as my inner thoughts competed with her for my attention.

"Suzanne, that's great news. It's wonderful to hear you talking this way. I'm so glad you're moving forward, that you have a plan. I knew you were capable of figuring this out. I just want to make sure you're safe. That's all I've ever wanted."

I tried to sound as enthusiastic as my words, but I was still skeptical that what seemed like such a dire situation could be resolved so easily and peacefully.

"They say the most dangerous time for a woman with an abusive husband is when she leaves. That's when most women get killed. It's a control thing. But I'm not afraid of him anymore." Suzanne picked the onions out of her salad. Mr. Lobe Extenders had forgotten to leave them off, despite her specific instructions. I suspected he was so taken with her that he was too lovestruck to get her order right.

"But I've made up my mind. My lawyer is helping me get everything in place to protect me financially and parent-wise before I drop the bombshell on him that it's over. Honestly, he may be relieved to be rid of me. I think he's wanted out for a long time, too."

My mother told Roger she was done with him on more than one occasion—these were murky memories. But I specifically remembered one time. The look on his face was something between sadness and rage. They were standing in the kitchen.

She was at the sink, wearing yellow rubber gloves, holding a sponge and scrubbing dishes. He was standing at the kitchen table, one hand steadying himself on the edge, swaying. Looking back, I'm sure he was drunk. My mother paused from her dish duty to tell him their marriage was over, like it was an afterthought.

"Roger, I'm leaving you. I'm done. Please pack your things and get out by the end of the day."

Roger stood dumbfounded, like he had no idea what he had done wrong. Even as a little girl who did not understand all the adult words, I was pretty sure he knew he had done something bad, or maybe a lot of somethings.

My mother immediately returned to washing dishes, not waiting for his response, not wanting to engage in any follow-up discussion.

The look on Roger's face was one I had seen only one other time in my life. It had happened when I knocked over a glass vase, spilling the ornamental rocks, water, and flowers all over the carpet in our entry hall. The glass from the vase shattered into tiny pieces that were carried by a tsunami of water in every direction. At the time, I had been standing on my tiptoes at the sideboard, trying to pull the vase closer to me so I could see how the sunlight poured through the small cracks between the rocks. Roger let out a guttural, almost animal-like roar and gave me that look when everything fell crashing to the floor. Time stopped. The droplets of water moved in slow motion through the air, with Roger's terrible distorted face visible through them.

Maybe that's why we went to my grandparents' house in central Pennsylvania, because of the look my mother saw on Roger's face when she told him to get out. She told me we were going on a little vacation, for a quick visit. But looking back, I now know she thought we'd be safer there, that he wouldn't find us.

"Suzanne, just be careful, please. You sound like you're in a good place. I'm happy that you have a lawyer and have been able to come to this decision. But just don't do anything rash. Think everything through one step at a time. And about my mother, I'm sorry, it's just not a story I feel comfortable sharing right now. I hope you understand." I slipped in the last part casually to make it seem less important.

"I understand completely," Suzanne replied with sincerity, and then reached across the table and placed her hand over mine. "You talk about it when you're ready. That's what true friendship is all about. I'm here for you."

I excused myself and went to the bathroom after my soapbox speech, feeling proud that I had nixed her inquiry about my mother. But as I looked in the mirror, I knew there was still one more crucial conversation to be had about Maria. I convinced myself that this should not come as a shock to Suzanne. She already suspected that Tanner and Maria were having an affair, so what if she was pregnant? Sure, it was another complication, but hopefully not something that would implode her exit plan. I returned to the table on a mission.

"Suzanne, there is one thing I need to tell you that may, or may not, be important. Remember I told you I had a cop friend who was helping me figure out who the woman was who texted Tanner, G6? Well I found her. Her name is Maria Lopez. She and her family own a restaurant in town. She works there. And honestly, other than that text you showed me, I have no indication that they're involved. I've not talked to her directly."

Suzanne's face went slack. She went from looking dazzling and cheerful to looking like someone who had been kicked in the stomach. Her downturned lips and sad eyes brought out fine wrinkles in her face.

"And?" She, turned her dark gaze to meet mine. "I know there's more. I can tell by the way you're talking about her, like you know something else you're not telling me."

"She's pregnant," I blurted out without taking a moment to carefully choose my words. "That's what I know. No idea who the father is, but she's definitely pregnant."

Suzanne started crying, burying her face in her napkin. Lobe-extender waiter walked by uncomfortably, looking like he wanted to stop and ask if there was something he could do, but he didn't stop. Instead, he breezed past us awkwardly, trying not to make eye contact.

"Sonofabitch," she murmured, from inside the napkin. "I guess I do need a better plan. This complicates everything. How could that asshole do this to me? I put him through medical school. He wouldn't be anywhere without me." She spit the words out, her head now out of the napkin. Mascara smudges beneath her eyes made her look a little crazy.

"Like I said, Suzanne, I have no idea if he was really involved with this woman, or if it's his baby or not. I just wanted you to know in case she is involved with Tanner. You know, if it is his baby, it has nothing to do with you. People have affairs for all types of reasons, usually based on their own insecurities. It is not a reflection of you as a person."

We both agreed that she would think the situation through longer before she made any quick decisions, that she would re-group with her attorney on the Maria issue, and maybe call the local domestic violence victims' support organization for advice on how to leave the relationship safely. The last thing I wanted was for her to put herself in more danger by leaving. Even though she was now downplaying Tanner's abusive nature, chalking it up to her overreaction, I couldn't get past the possibility that he might be like Roger.

As I walked to my car, I passed the usual homeless people who begged on local street corners. They had always been part of the landscape of downtown Oak City as long as I had lived here, but as downtown became fancier and trendier with the addition of new restaurants, hip boutiques, and luxury high-rise condominiums, they stood out more. It was hard to see them lying in doorways on weathered sleeping bags or cardboard pallets next to shopping carts full of their belongings stuffed haphazardly into plastic bags.

"I just need a dollar for bus money to get home," a man said to me, his dirty palm outstretched in a tattered blue glove that was cut to expose his fingers.

I encountered him about a block from the restaurant. He was one of the regular panhandlers that I recognized. One winter day, I saw him walking around in the cold without shoes. He told me he needed size fourteen sneakers. I went to Walmart that night and bought him some. They sat on the front seat of my car for a month as I drove around every morning looking for him, but he was nowhere to be found. I finally gave up and donated them to Goodwill. And now, here he was again, right in front of me, asking for my help. I looked down and noticed he had on new-looking tennis shoes, which made me feel a little less guilty about not being able to follow through on getting him shoes. I had beaten myself up over not being able to find him, imagining him walking the ice-covered streets with his bare feet all winter long. Now, I felt like I was being given a second chance to help.

I reached into my wallet and took out a five-dollar bill and a handful of change. The man motioned for me to put it in the coffee cup at his feet. It was tucked just behind a metal trashcan.

As I poured the money into the cup, I thought about my sweet Blake. He had such a tender heart that he always asked me for money when he saw a homeless person, whether they were panhandling or not. Sometimes I saw tears welling up in his eyes as he rummaged in my purse for loose change to give them. I couldn't say no. Before Blake, I used to walk right past homeless people on the street, not seeing them, too distracted by my busy life. Now, thanks to him, I saw them everywhere.

My phone rang just as I was putting my wallet away.

"So get this," Kojak jumped in, as usual.

"What? Nothing can possibly surprise me, you know that."

"It's Maria. She had her baby the other night. Tuesday, I think."

"Wow, I didn't realize she was *that* pregnant. How did you find out?"

"Overheard some of the patrol guys talking about it over lunch, taking bets on who the father is."

"Did Tanner's name come up?"

"Nope, not that I could tell."

Part of my conversation with Suzanne came rushing back to me, Tanner had left in the middle of the night for a *medical emergency*. It was all making sense now. He must have left to be with Maria at the hospital while she delivered her child. *Their child?*

"Kojak, this is all adding up. Tanner may have been with Maria the other night. He told Suzanne he had a medical emergency at the hospital, and left in the middle of the night. We need to find out if he was with her at the hospital."

Suzanne was making plans to leave Tanner, mistress or not. News of the baby's arrival would only add to her pain, but it could also possibly get her a better settlement and make her custody of Winston more secure.

"I'm on it. Shouldn't be too hard to figure out."

"You're the best."

"I know. Don't forget..." Kojak hung up before he finished his sentence.

His brain worked too fast for cell phones. Maybe someday the technology would catch up.

It wouldn't be completely crazy to want your dead husband's medical records, would it? I decided this was my *in* to see Tanner Pope again, to find out if he was the sweet, affable guy I remembered him to be or the monster that Suzanne had described.

"I'll just be a minute," I said to Buster, as I hopped out of the news car in the parking lot of the orthopedic clinic where Tanner worked. I thought Buster was so preoccupied with a fight he and Hugh had the night before, about Hugh not spending enough time with Noah, that he wouldn't ask any questions about my little errand.

"Heard that before," Buster said, suddenly paying attention to me as he twirled a toothpick between his lips, a habit he knew I despised. "Your *minute* always has a way of turning into fifteen minutes, thirty minutes, an hour."

"Touché. If I'm not back in twenty, call 911."

"Okay, well I'll be right here answering this litany of ridiculous texts from my husband, who is living it up in a five-star hotel in Dallas right now, while I'm working out of a cramped news car on a sweltering May afternoon, deciding what greasy fast food to have for lunch."

"How do you really feel?" I winked and jumped out of the car. I had made an appointment with Dr. Pope that morning, but I didn't tell the receptionist the real reason I wanted to see him. I figured if I did, she might just give me the records herself and I would never get a chance to see Tanner in person. Luckily someone had just canceled, and there happened to be a rare opening in his schedule. So I told her I was having pain in my hip flexor possibly from running too much. This wasn't too far from the truth.

When I got there, the receptionist asked me to fill out new patient paperwork. I took the clipboard and pen and sat in a large chair with scratchy fabric in the waiting room across from her. At the top of the first page it said: *Describe why you are here to see the doctor today. Give details about where the pain is, the amount of time you have had it and rate the intensity on a scale of one to ten.*

I had never been a very good liar. I immediately brought the clipboard and the blank paperwork back up and slid the pages across the desk to her.

"I'm actually here to see Dr. Pope about a private matter. He treated my husband a few years ago, and my husband passed away." After saying it out loud, I realized how that must sound. "Of a totally unrelated condition obviously, nothing to do with Dr. Pope. But I did have some questions about my husband's medical history, and wondered if I might have a few minutes with the doctor."

"You're that lady from the news." She peered over the top of her red glasses perched on the end of her nose, held around her neck by a thick gold chain.

Her gray hair was pulled back in a bun, and she wore scrubs with tiny colorful cats on them, a sharp contrast to her serious demeanor.

"This is an unusual request. You're telling me the truth right. You're not here for a news story?"

"No, ma'am, I'm not. I promise you. You can look up my husband's name, Adam Arnette."

She clicked around her computer keyboard for a moment, like an airline employee looking for a new flight for a bumped passenger, her gaze darting across the screen. Then she stood without a word and walked into the back of the office through a doorway.

I sat back down in the scratchy fabric chair again to wait. When the woman returned, I watched as she whispered behind the counter with a nurse, most likely about me. After about fifteen minutes, the same nurse appeared at the waiting room door.

"Maddie Arnette," she called too loudly looking over my head to the empty waiting area behind me as if there might be someone else there named Maddie who had stepped out to go to the bathroom.

"Coming," I said eagerly, lest she change her mind and make me lose my one shot at Tanner. I gathered up my purse, phone, and glasses and hurried through the door behind her.

When Tanner entered the room, he was exactly like I remembered him, with the exception of a few more lines around his eyes and mouth. He was wearing skinny, tailored tan dress pants, a yellow tie peeking out of the top of his white lab coat, and a professional expression. He obviously didn't remember me. He reached out to shake my hand with the same gentle, slender fingers I recalled. As he did so I noticed the glint of the matching wedding ring Suzanne had told me about. It was brushed silver with a subtle diamond crisscross pattern that was hard to see unless you looked very closely.

"What can I do for you, Miss Arnette? I understand I treated your husband." He looked at me with a blank stare. "I'm sorry I don't remember him off-hand. I have a lot of patients. But maybe you can refresh my memory."

I was uncharacteristically flustered by his handsome features—his chiseled jawline and tanned face framed by dark slicked back, hair. He looked at me with his twinkling green eyes, giving me an open and engaging smile. I told myself not to be seduced by his outward appearance. I needed to be objective.

"Yes, he had a torn tendon in his middle finger about five years ago. No reason you would remember it," I rambled, realizing I hadn't really thought this through. "Anyway, he died from brain cancer, late last year."

"I'm so sorry to hear that," Tanner replied, his voice and initial hurried demeanor softening.

He leaned back against the exam table and set down his clipboard.

"Yes, thanks. I appreciate it. I am interested in getting his medical records from every doctor he had any contact with over the past ten years. He was part of a study, you know, to try and figure out why people get this horrible disease. And nothing is too insignificant to look at former surgeries, any drugs he may have taken."

This part was true. Adam had been enrolled in a study. He signed the paperwork before he died to allow them to look at his brain tissue and his medical records after he passed. When I didn't hear from the researchers for a month after he died, I called them. They told me their grant money had run out. The study was over.

Tanner, perched on the edge of the exam table, crossed his hands in front of him, nodding at my nervous monologue.

"I wasn't sure if your receptionist would just give them to me, or what, so I made an appointment."

"It's not a problem." His bright green eyes now focused on me with what appeared to be honest concern.

His gaze was so intense I had to look away for a moment.

"You just need to fill out some paperwork to show that you are his spouse requesting the records, and provide the death certificate. As long as he signed a HIPPA waiver allowing you access, it shouldn't be a problem. Again, I am so sorry for your loss. One of my colleagues died from brain cancer several years ago, and I know it's a tough diagnosis. How are you doing?"

I was so taken aback by his seemingly genuine compassion that I stammered again, shaking my hand and standing up to signal that I was ready to leave. Nothing about this man was as Suzanne described. Of course, I knew that people were not always as they seemed, but I was usually a pretty good judge of character, of reading people's nuances, and nothing about this man was giving me bad vibes. In fact, just the opposite.

"Mrs. Arnette, I do remember him now—Adam, your husband," he said, as I was going for the door. He stood up from the edge of the exam table as if he were deep in thought. "He had a terrific sense of humor, told me when I took the pin out of his finger, with the plier-like tool and the blood started spurting everywhere, that I must be a soap opera doctor who snuck into the building, not a real doctor. When I asked him if he wanted a painkiller afterwards, he asked me if I was planning on coming to work with him to handle all his projects for the day since he would be so out of it. A real comedian. Great guy. Really sorry for your loss. I truly am."

My eyes started welling up with tears as soon as I heard Tanner mention Adam's sense of humor. It was a special brand of sarcasm that we had cultivated together. Just picturing Adam joking around made me sad to my core, remembering I no longer had him to share my jokes with.

Tanner pulled out a business card and a pen from the breast coat pocket of his white doctor's coat. With his left hand he wrote a number on the back of the card while his wedding ring glinted as it caught the beam of fluorescent overhead light. I noticed he was a lefty because Adam had been one too.

"Here's my cell number.," He handed me the card. "My nurse will locate those records, and if I can do anything else to help, please don't hesitate to give me a call. I know some pretty good grief counselors."

I grabbed the card and turned without a word and ran out of the exam room. I was trying so hard not to let him see me cry as I hurried down the sterile hallway toward the exit sign. The lights in the waiting room seemed so much brighter than they had been when I first entered the office that I had to shield my eyes. I didn't even stop at the reception desk to continue the ruse of getting the medical records. I ran straight through the double glass doors that led outside.

When I got to Buster's car it was running, but empty. I assumed he must have run inside the building to use the restroom. He always left it running, with the air condition on, and, to my amazement, it never got stolen.

I slipped into the passenger seat, sobbing, and turned up NPR on as loud as it would go so no one could hear me in the parking lot. I was praying Buster wouldn't come back and find me this way. I didn't want to have to explain anything to him. That's when I heard the knock on my window. I looked up and saw Tanner looking down at me with concern.

"Mrs. Arnette, I am so sorry I upset you. It was very insensitive of me to talk about your husband like that so soon after his death. I followed you to give you this." He made a *roll down the window motion*, which in the middle of my sobs made me laugh because no one rolls down a window by hand anymore, but for some reason we still make the motion anyway. It was a funny moment that Adam and I would have shared if he was still alive, dissecting the off-beat humor and reliving the confused look on Tanner's face.

"It's not your fault." I pulled myself together and pushed the button to lower the window. I reached out and took the file from his hand. "Really, it's not." I reached for a tissue with my other hand from the center console and dabbed my swollen eyes. "It just hits me sometimes. I never know what will trigger it."

"Very true, grief can be a long process." He was now leaning over my window and shielding the sun from his eyes with his right hand. "Hang in there. I wish you the best of luck in getting information on brain cancer. Awful disease that needs to be figured out. And by the way, I'm technically not supposed to give you this without the death certificate, but I don't see any reason to make you jump through hoops. I had my nurse go ahead and copy it while we were talking."

He tapped the roof of my car and held up left hand in a goodbye gesture and walked away. In my side mirror, I watched him cross the parking lot and head back through the glass double doors, into his office building. His shoulders were slumped in his white lab coat, as if he were literally carrying the guilt on his shoulders of having upset me. Nothing about this version of Tanner Pope lined up with Suzanne's version.

I blew my nose with a tissue from Buster's center console, and when I looked back again, Tanner had stopped in the hallway of the building. I could see him through the glass doors. He was standing up straight now, with his cell phone to his ear, laughing, as if our sad encounter had never happened. He turned in my direction and smiled at something he must have heard over the phone, but I was sure he couldn't see me looking at him because of the sunlight pouring in through the glass doors. I wondered if Suzanne was right. Maybe Tanner Pope was not the perfect man he seemed to be.

10

REVELATIONS

"SERIOUSLY, IT'S *crazy* this woman survived," Janie rambled on, as I half-listened on the other end of the line.

I had her on speakerphone while I sat in the carpool line waiting to pick up the kids because my sitter, Candace, had come down with the flu. I told her to stay home and get well, that we would manage without her. It wasn't true. I didn't have a contingency plan for when Candace got sick. I had no family around, and while I did have a few other school moms I could call on, I hated to do that. I didn't want to be the helpless widow who was always looking for people to bail me out. So I left work early and told Janie to call me in the car and we would talk about story ideas.

"I still don't understand how a zebra reaches out of an enclosure at a zoo and attacks a woman," I said. "Are zebras really that aggressive? Who knew?"

"Apparently they can be super dangerous. It was like a weird spot in the habitat where the zebra was just close enough to the woman to grab her. She was eating an ice cream cone, not sure if that had anything to do with it." Janie typed as we talked. I could hear the rat-a-tat of her fingers tapping the keys, as well as the muffled static of the police scanner punctuated by sirens in the background. I didn't know much about zebras, but I was pretty sure the ice cream had *something* to do with it.

The attack had happened at a zoo in another state, but the woman was from North Carolina and her family wanted her close to home. So as soon as doctors said it was safe to move her, they flew her to University Hospital in the next town over. The family called us and said she was recovering well and was available to talk. Janie has also lined up a zoologist from one of the local colleges to talk about zebra attacks. The variety of my new reporting beat continued to amaze me. It didn't have the same level of intrigue as crime reporting, but it certainly satisfied my curiosity for all things bizarre.

"Hold on, Janie. I'm pulling up to the curb." The teacher who was monitoring the carpool line opened the back door of my car for the kids to get in. We weren't supposed to talk on the phone in the car while on campus in case a child decided to dart out in front of a vehicle, but everyone broke the rules and then tried to pretend they weren't doing it. Janie knew the drill.

"Hi, Mrs. Millinsky. How are you? Hey, kids, how was your day?"

Four children piled into the car, with their heavy book bags, zippers undone, things hanging out in every direction—sheets of crumpled paper and wadded up jackets. They threw the bags, along with their lunchboxes, on the floor and assumed their regular seats—Miranda behind me, and Blake behind the passenger seat, where he could have a clear view of me. We also drove Sadie and Doug Bradley, our neighbors. They piled into the bench seat in the very back. Their mother, Glenda, reciprocated three afternoons and two mornings a week. It was no trouble because they lived right next door to us. Thankfully they were quiet, well- behaved kids.

"Hi, Mom. I'm so happy you're picking us up. Why can't you do it every day?" Blake made his smile into a dramatic frown, his little lips protruding into a serious pout. His exaggeration made him look like an emoji.

"Sweetie, you know Mommy has to work." I gave Mrs. Millinsky a little wave and pulled away from the curb, waiting until I was well out of her view until I resumed my conversation with Janie.

"Blake, you're such a mama's boy. Who would pay the bills if Mommy didn't work?" Miranda fired in her brother's direction, in her usual acerbic, self-righteous tone.

"Mom, I thought you got life insurance when Daddy died. Why do you need to work?" Blake said with genuine confusion.

I looked in the rearview mirror at Doug and Sadie, who were, as usual, ignoring our family drama. Sadie was reading a book, and Doug was playing a game on his phone. I was always shocked by how aloof they were when chaos was going on inside my car. I guessed they were used to it, which seemed like a bad thing.

"Wow," Janie said, a disembodied voice from the car's speakerphone. "Heavy topics. Want to call me back?"

"Yes. Just let me know when the zebra lady can do the interview. Thanks." I hung up, embarrassed that Janie heard Miranda verbally her brother.

I turned up the radio, rolled down my window and tried to drown out the ugly banter between Miranda and Blake which was still coming from the backseat. It was moments like these when I wondered if I had failed as a parent. I also wondered if it was too late to turn things around. Could I miraculously make Miranda be nice to her brother? I wanted them to have each other's backs. They were twins, after all. Weren't they supposed to be best friends, like all the parenting books told me they would be?

I didn't ruminate on their sibling rivalry for long, as the meeting with Tanner began to creep back into my brain. I still couldn't get over how kindly he had treated me, especially in the parking lot, giving me the records that I asked for and apologizing for upsetting me. But then there was that dramatic shift—from kind, concerned Tanner to joking around on the phone Tanner. Maybe I had misjudged him.

"Mom," Blake screamed with an eardrum-shattering voice. "We have to go back. Miranda threw my math homework out the window!"

I glanced in the rearview mirror and saw Miranda with her arms crossed, a smug expression on her pretty, little round face surrounded by wild, brown curls. I could also see the Bradley kids staring at her. We finally had their attention.

Early Tuesday morning I decided to take a run by myself. It was hotter than I expected, so I ended up sitting down for a moment on a bench next to the paved greenway. I passed benches on my running path all the time and wondered who sat on them way out here in the middle of nowhere. I was not usually a bench-sitter, but I had drained my water bottle already and was feeling light-headed. I decided maybe I *was* a bench-sitter after all.

I squinted in the sunlight to see the screen on my phone. I had forgotten to grab a hat when I left, even though I had a basket of them in the hallway right next to the front door. Since Adam died, I felt like I was always forgetting things—little things like hats, and bigger things like doctors' appointments and friends' birthdays. Grief had chipped away at the part of my brain that managed memory.

I scrolled through the typical unimportant emails from

retailers telling me I had only twenty-four hours to access their online sale, emails from work that didn't pertain to me, and countless emails from school about everything from field trips to new food items in the cafeteria.

My routine was to file or delete emails right away to keep my inbox from getting too cluttered. This was a feeble attempt to prevent myself from feeling overwhelmed. Admittedly, in my haste sometimes I deleted important emails and had to go back and retrieve them from the trash. But for the most part, the system worked and prevented me from becoming panicky at the sight of my inbox.

That's when I noticed the email titled *Body Found*.

Back when crime reporting had been my beat, these emails always made my heart jump. I would immediately click on them, eager to learn as much as I could from the first sketchy details being distributed by our assignment desk editors. Was it an accident, a natural death, a murder? I usually had my own initial theories based on what I had learned over the years. Dead guy in the woods? Probably homeless, natural causes. Dead guy in his house *without* a gunshot wound? Probably a drug overdose. Dead guy in his house *with* a gunshot wound? Probably suicide. Dead guy in a car? Well, it depended.

I willed myself not to read the note. It had gone out to the entire newsroom on an email list called *Update* meant to keep everyone in the loop. It wasn't sent to me directly, so I had no obligation to read it. At least that's what I told myself. This wasn't my beat anymore. Keri Hue was the new crime reporter. She was young, green, and eager. I knew her tenacity would rub some of the old guard in the police department the wrong way, but I also knew she was hungry for a good story, and I could tell by the few moments I had spoken with her that she was bright and would ultimately find her way. I would be there to answer her questions and guide her in the right direction if she needed help, but Keri could now have the dead bodies all to herself.

I closed my email, restarted my exercise app that tracked my mileage, turned up the volume on my music, and then stuck my phone back in the pouch around my waist to continue my run. I was due at University Hospital in an hour-and-a-half to interview the woman who was attacked by the zebra, and I wanted to make sure I had enough time to shower and eat something before I headed out.

Just as I got my stride going again, my phone rang, interrupting my music. Annoyed, I stopped and pulled my phone back out of the pouch. I held one hand up to shield my gaze so I could see the screen and decide if I was going to answer it or not. In my phone I had the numbers of everyone I had ever called, so if a number came up without a name, I had a strict policy of letting it go to voicemail. It was probably a telemarketer. My eyes struggled to adjust in the bright sunlight as I peered at the tiny screen. It read *La Fiesta*.

"Hello," I said, tentatively, stepping back into the shade beneath a large tree that offered a canopy of green leaves to protect my eyes from the sunlight. It *had* to be Maria. *Who else?* While I had never called the restaurant, I had put the name and address in my phone as a contact for future reference while I was investigating Maria's possible link to Tanner.

"Are you the reporter lady?" a man's voice with a Hispanic accent said, as tentatively as I had answered the phone.

"Yes, and you are?"

"Juan Lopez. I am Maria's big brother."

"Yes, I left a card for her at the restaurant," I replied, with hesitation. I wasn't comfortable telling him the real reason I wanted to speak with her. Plus, I assumed Maria was busy with her new baby, and I couldn't imagine why my card would suddenly seem important to her.

"What do you want with her, with my sister?"

"I just wanted to ask her a few questions about a man I thought she might know."

"What man?"

"I'd really rather speak with her directly, if that's okay. I know she just had a baby. Congratulations, by the way, to her and your family. So we can talk another time, when things settle down for her."

I was glad he couldn't see me shifting my weight nervously from one foot to the other on the edge of the paved path. I wished I had never picked up the phone.

"What man? Maria and I are very close. She wouldn't mind if you talked to me."

"His name is Tanner Pope. He's a doctor. Honestly she may not even know him. It really is no big deal. Forget I said anything. Why don't you just have her call me when she can," I replied, instantly regretting mentioning Tanner.

There was a long silence on the other end of the line. I almost thought Juan had hung up, but I could still hear him breathing deeply. I wasn't sure what to make of his silence. Did they know Tanner Pope or not?

"She just had a baby," Juan said, with indignance.

"I know, and that's why I really don't want to bother her right now."

"But you're trying to find him, Dr. Tanner. You're looking for him, too?"

"Too?" Suddenly, I was confused. There was a disconnect. Something was going on here that I wasn't getting. "I never said I was looking for him. I just saw him the other day at his office. I'm not trying to find him. I just have a few questions *about* him that I thought your sister might be able to answer."

With each statement, I could feel myself sinking deeper and deeper into the hole I was digging. What if Tanner found out

I was snooping around, asking questions about him after he had treated me with such compassion in his office? Or even worse, what if he really was the jerk Suzanne described, and he found out I was pressing his mistress for information that was really none of my business. I hadn't thought the situation through at all.

"Dr. Tanner. He disappeared."

"What do you mean?" I tried to keep my voice calm. I thought I misheard him. I wanted to make absolutely sure I understood what Juan was saying.

"He was visiting Maria and the new baby at our apartment Sunday. We live behind the restaurant. He went out to get supplies for the baby, diapers and formula, because she told him we needed some things. He never came back."

"Well, maybe he just went home or something." I was trying to think of how I was going to break it to this man that his sister's lover was married and had another family that Juan probably didn't know about.

"I don't think so. He was coming right back. He wouldn't do that to her."

"Did you report him missing to the police?"

"No police."

"Why not?"

"Because it's not my place. But I found your card in the door, and I thought you might able to help. I don't want no police involved."

A million thoughts started swirling through my head—Juan and Maria might be in the country illegally, which would be a good reason not to want to call the police. Juan might be involved in something shady, something he didn't want his little sister Maria mixed up in. Juan may know about Tanner's other family, or it could be as simple as Juan not trusting the authorities.

"Let me see what I can find out." I wiped sweat from my

brow with my free hand. "Is this the best number where I can reach you?"

"Yes. Please help us find him. He is a good man. You will help us, won't you?"

"I'll do my best." I steadied myself against the trunk of the tree with one hand. Now if only I could steady my thoughts.

My head was spinning when I unlocked my front door and felt the cool air hit my face as I entered the long, dark hallway. I reviewed what I learned from Juan's phone call. Tanner was involved in some type of relationship with Maria. What that relationship entailed was unclear. But they were close enough that he would visit her after the birth of her baby. Another important point—it didn't sound like she was hiding whatever this relationship was from her family, or at least from her brother. So maybe she didn't know about Suzanne? Was that even possible?

And now Tanner was missing. Or was he? Maybe he just ran away from the crazy, messed-up situation he was in, juggling a mistress with a newborn baby and an angry, paranoid wife. Maybe he just needed time to figure it all out. Just because he was missing from Maria's life didn't mean he was really *missing*.

I decided to take a shower to clear my head before I made another move. I would call Kojak and explain what was going on. He would know what to do. Just as I was stepping into the shower, clouds of steam cascading out of the open glass door to meet me, my phone rang again. I looked down and saw it was the station calling. It would have to wait. It seemed like every time I tried to take a second for myself, I was interrupted. Someone always needed something from me—work, kids, strangers. *Breathe, just breathe.*

As soon as I stepped beneath the scalding hot water and felt it pouring down my shoulders and back, I started to feel the tension draining from my body. Adam could never understand why I liked the water so hot. He would always get in after me and scream out in mock pain. How could I explain to him that it was the only way to get rid of all the bad stuff, to let the heat cleanse whatever was weighing on me and allow the water to flush it down the drain?

"You're crazy," he would shout. "How can anyone stand for one second in water this hot."

I closed my eyes and tilted my head back, letting the searing water hit my face as I imagined hearing Adam ranting about the temperature. The phone rang *again*. This time I reached out of the glass door, grabbed the towel hanging on the nearby rack and wiped my eyes. I could see the words *News Desk* glowing on the screen as it vibrated and hopped across the marble surface of my bathroom countertop.

It was obviously important, or at least someone on the assignment desk *thought* it was. I reached behind me, turned off the water and then dried my hands so I could pick up the phone. It had stopped ringing, so I hit the newsroom number stored in my missed calls list. Janie answered on the first ring.

"Oh, thank God. I thought something happened to you when you didn't answer the second time. You're seriously going to kill me. Please don't. But I'm pretty sure that you will want to. Just remember, I'm only the messenger. Okay? So here goes. Keri, well, she's kind of on vacation, and everyone else is already assigned to something. They said to forget the zebra story for now. I mean we're for sure going to do it, just not today. Instead they want you to..."

"Want me to do what?" I said, in a harsher tone than I intended. I knew it wasn't Janie's fault, but I could feel what was coming next. They were assigning me to a crime story because Keri was off. This was exactly what I didn't want to happen.

"It's just that, well, they found a body. A dead body." As if there was another kind of body other than *dead*.

Why was Keri off? My mind wandered. Then I remembered someone saying it was part of her deal when she took the job, that she had a family wedding to attend right after she started, and they allowed her to take the days unpaid since her vacation time had not accrued yet. In Texas? Wyoming? Mississippi? It didn't matter. What mattered was that she was not in town, and I was now on deck for what should have been her assignment.

"As opposed to a live body?" I said with part sarcasm and part passive aggression.

I knew I was being too hard on Janie, but it was like something was breaking inside me. All the reasons why I didn't want to do this were flooding back, and Janie was an easy target. In fact she was the only target available.

"I know. Please don't be mad at me. Dex made me call you. I told him you would freak out. We already sent Buster. You just need to meet him there. I can text you the address."

I silently stewed for a moment and thought about what I should do. This was a turning point for me in my job. I could stand my ground and refuse the assignment and see what happened, or I could suck it up and get on with it. I understood the news business was all about filling holes with available personnel. With so many hours of news to fill a day, we were like assembly line workers stuffing boxes as they rolled along the conveyor belt. There were lots of managers who met to discuss how to fill the boxes, but I was a box-filler, an indispensable part of the assembly line. The managers could disappear and the assembly line would still operate, but without the box-fillers, everything would come to a grinding halt.

"Okay. But *just* today. When is Keri coming back?"

"Thank you, thank you, thank you so much!" Janie's words

flowed out on the tide of a deep exhale. "Dex would have my ass if I couldn't talk you into it. We'll put zebra lady off a day or two. Keri is back tomorrow. At least, I'm pretty sure. Like ninety percent sure. I'll check and let you know for sure."

"She's only been here for a nanosecond. I can't believe she's already off."

North Dakota? Maybe that was it. A long way to go for a wedding.

"I hear you, girl. I'll send you the address of where to meet Buster. And of course you already know this, but you're live in the noon show."

I swallowed hard and felt the old stress flooding back into my body. On my animal beat, I only had to do one story a day, but on the crime beat I could be live in every show without a moment to breathe, let alone a moment to eat or go to the bathroom. It was a level of stress I didn't miss and didn't want to experience for even one day.

"Of course." I hung up as she was still trying to tell me something else. I had inherited Kojak's bad habit of hanging up on people while they were still talking when I was in a hurry. I was in crisis mode again. I could feel every muscle in my body tense. I sped up my getting-ready routine. I then realized that I had not even read the latest *Body Found* email. I scrolled down the email list on my phone and pulled it up.

White male found face down in a ditch, partially covered with brush in the western part of the city. A single gunshot to the head. Foul play is suspected. No one in custody. No identity on the victim yet.

The whole mess with Juan, Tanner, Maria and Suzanne moved down a few spots on my triage list. They would all have to wait, because I had a dead body to attend to.

11

RED CLAY

THE FIRST THING I NOTICED was the thick red mud caked to everyone's shoes. It had rained over the weekend, and because we were on the edge of a farm, there was a lot more soggy churned-up ground under our feet than pavement.

A familiar sea of Oak City uniformed officers milled around, each with their own well-defined roles. Most of them were assigned to keep people from going past the yellow police tape tied from tree-to-tree as a perimeter around the crime scene. There was also a truck from the local CSI unit for Tirey County parked next to the taped-off area. They sent analysts to collect physical evidence for investigators. In a way, it felt surprisingly comfortable to be back in this place, in this role I was so used to. At the same time, it felt wrong to be so comfortable at a murder scene.

"What's up?" I tapped Buster on the shoulder, trying not to startle him.

He was hunched over his camera which was perched on the

tripod next to him. I could tell by his level of concentration that he was shooting something in the distance far beyond the yellow tape.

"Well, look who the cat dragged out here. Miss I'm-done-with-that-crime-bullshit reporter. No rescue dogs or singing parrots here, just muck and murder."

Buster gave me his mischievous smile to let me know he was joking. Still there was always a grain of passive-aggressive truth in everything Buster said. He truly liked the crime beat but had reluctantly transitioned with me to the animal beat, because I think he felt sorry for me after Adam died.

"What's the deal? Do we have an identity on the body yet?"

"Nope. Chief is supposed to have a presser in a few minutes. Just late enough to screw us for noon. I'm going to send it back to the station on the LiveU so they can stream it on the website and the editors can pull a soundbite there. I won't have time to turn it around for noon."

A LiveU was a portable transmission device the size of a backpack that allowed us to do live television anywhere we could get a cellular signal. It meant that we no longer had to work out of cumbersome live-trucks with huge masts that needed a flat surface and a generous amount of room to operate safely. They were also rolling billboards that gave us no anonymity, like our unmarked news cars did.

"This looks like a pretty swanky neighborhood next to this old guy's farm. *Homes starting in the $800,000's.*" I gestured to the stately houses in the distance, behind a big sign near the entrance.

"Yes, even rich people get murdered sometimes. That will make it an even bigger story," Buster said, without looking up from his camera's viewfinder.

"We don't know it's a rich person. Someone could have dumped the body here. He could have been meeting someone here for a drug deal. Don't jump to conclusions."

"Whatever." Buster glanced back at me and then returned to his viewfinder.

I scanned the crowd of police officers for a friendly face, someone I not only knew, but someone who might tell me something. I wished Kojak was here, but I didn't see him. He rarely came to crime scenes anymore since he was a supervisor in the Major Crimes Unit. Instead of coming himself, he sent his detectives to get their hands dirty, and then waited for them to bring back the evidence. I decided I would give it a little while and then call him to see if he knew anything yet. Information had a way of flowing to him quickly after a body was found.

"Folks, the chief is ready to do the press conference. Is it okay to have her right here?" The police department's public information officer, Fred, motioned to a spot at the edge of the crime scene tape.

When no one answered him, he went ahead and ushered Chief Lydia Blankenstock up to the edge on the other side of the tape. Unfortunately, Fred wasn't well-respected by the media because he was often late getting out information to reporters, usually just after their deadlines had passed. When you called him to ask when the information would be released, he could be difficult. He was one of those communications officers who just didn't get it. The media was so easy to manage. If he would just give us *something* in a timely manner, we would all leave him alone. But he always dragged the process out and made it difficult for himself.

The photographers leaned in to clip their wireless microphones on the chief's starched white collar, while Fred stood by her side, looking annoyed, as if he were doing us a big favor by making the her available. Even though it was daylight, photographers turned on their lights to illuminate her because the sun was behind the chief, making her look like a silhouette on camera.

Lydia was a tough talking chief from Pittsburgh, who had landed in North Carolina after an exhaustive search when the previous longtime chief died of a heart attack during the city's annual Christmas parade. He was on a float in a big red armchair, all wrapped up in a heavy blanket, wearing a Santa Claus hat and sunglasses. The rumor was that he was dead for a good mile before anyone realized it.

While the former chief was a tall, lanky good-old-boy, Lydia was a petite fireplug with short blonde hair peeking out beneath her snug blue police cap. She always looked professional in her crisp white uniform shirt, her dark blue pressed pants, and her shiny black combat boots. Many local police chiefs preferred to wear business suits, but Lydia was always in her uniform. I always felt like she was trying to send a message to the rank and file that she was one of them. For this, and other reasons, I had come to respect her. She was a straight talker with the media and usually made herself accessible, despite Fred's consistent interference.

"Okay, we're going to get started, people," the chief said in a baritone voice, far below the registers of most women her size. Fred looked hurt, like he wanted to be the one to start the press conference. One photographer had just pulled up and was frantically setting up his tripod, but the chief was not going to wait for anyone. Buster, as usual, was in place and had been ready to go for several minutes. Lydia looked into the center of the gaggle of cameras and began without referring to the small white piece of paper in her left hand that appeared to contain handwritten notes.

"A woman walking with her baby in a stroller this morning came upon what she thought was possibly a homeless man passed out in a ditch at the edge of Johnson's Farm. She noticed him because there were vultures circling the location." The chief put her right hand up in a stop motion as one of the reporters from the back of the group tried to ask a question.

"Let me finish. Then I will take questions."

"As she got closer, she realized, given the position of the body, it was face down, and because he was partially covered with brush, that the man was most likely deceased. Fearing for her safety and the safety of her child, she immediately turned around and started walking towards her house while calling 911. We will be making a recording of that call available to you later this afternoon."

The reporters were holding their phones up and capturing the press conference live on Facebook. The photographers were also streaming the press conference back to their stations on their LiveUs so it could be used on the air and on their news websites, simultaneously. The news war was no longer confined to the television set. It was twenty-four-seven on every platform. Winning meant owning every battle—on television and online. Today I was back in the fray, fighting for a distracted world's attention just like everyone else.

"Do you have an identity on the person yet?" I said, and raised my hand when the chief took a breath.

I figured it was time to intervene. We had fourteen minutes until the noon news.

"No, we have not identified him at this point. He was not carrying any identification on his person. There are some things on his person we believe will help to identify him fairly quickly. All I can tell you right now is that it is a man. We are having our composite artist draw a picture of him to release to the media to help us with identification and to figure out if anyone witnessed him in this area in the past twenty-four hours. We hope to have that completed later today and to release it to the media."

The chief scanned the group of ten or so journalists for more hands. I raised mine again and jumped in. I wasn't trying to monopolize her, but the clock was ticking.

"Was this a self-inflicted gunshot wound, or are you treating this as a homicide?"

"Based on several factors which I cannot discuss right now because they are part of the ongoing investigation, we are currently treating this as a homicide. If anyone in this neighborhood last night or this morning and heard or saw anything, please call us. Thank you, folks, for your attention. That's all I have for you right now."

With that, Lydia turned and walked into a circle of detectives in suits, who looked like they were waiting impatiently for her undivided attention. During the press conference, they kept looking over at her as if they were willing her to finish. It was no secret that a lot of cops distrusted the media, even *hated* us. I didn't take it personally. I figured they could get in line behind all the other media-haters.

I now watched Lydia lean in with her ear, cupping it with her hand so she could listen more closely to what one of the investigators was whispering to her. She tugged on her police cap with her hand, pulling it tight on her head. Then I saw it, it was imperceptible unless you were watching closely—a small shake of her head. Even from behind I could tell the chief was in disbelief about what she had just been told.

While I was still on the air, answering the anchor's questions, I started thinking about what my next move was going to be.

"Do they have an identity on the person yet?" the anchor, Marti said.

"Not at this point," I said, slightly annoyed.

Was she not listening? I had covered this at the top of my report.

"They plan to put out a composite sketch of the victim later today to see if the public can help identify him."

I needed to find the witness who found the body. That was my logical next step.

"Did they say how the person died?" Marti asked, a little too cheerfully.

"A preliminary report indicates that he was shot, but of course an autopsy will determine the cause definitively."

The witness must live close by if she had a baby. She wouldn't be walking that far.

I had to admit I was energized by the assignment in a way that I hadn't been by my work since Adam's death. Sure, I had a lot of fun with the animal stories and got to be more creative than I did with my crime stories, but they didn't light a fire under me like the one I was experiencing today, the slow-burn that made me want to find answers. It made me feel guilty, like I was going back on a silent promise I had made to myself and to Adam.

I was out of practice, that was for sure. As soon as I got off the air, my head was ticking through the list of things I needed to do to get my job done before my next deadline—the four o'clock news. *Triage, triage, triage*.

Finding the woman with the stroller would be on everyone's agenda. Would she talk to me if she was already scared for her safety? My gut told me probably not, but I had to try to find her. That was my job. My forte was making people talk in difficult situations. I had knocked on many doors over the years, where Buster had told me there was absolutely no way a person was going to talk to me.

"Not going to happen," he would say, as I hopped out of the car.

"Watch me work," I'd say.

After a few minutes, I would come out of the house and motion him to come in and bring the camera. It happened more often than not. It involved a little bit of persuasion and a lot of luck.

In the best-case scenario, I figured the woman who found the body might talk to me on camera, with her identity hidden. We could shoot her from behind and promise not to show her face or reveal her name or where she lived. Since this was an upper-class neighborhood, chances were slim these assurances would provide enough privacy to encourage her to go on camera.

"Buster, there are only six houses on this street. The woman with the stroller must live in one of them. She certainly didn't cross that busy road at the front of this neighborhood to take her baby for a walk."

As usual, Buster rolled his eyes. As much as he loved the crime beat, he hated knocking on *strangers'* doors. Most of the time, he stayed in the car facebooking while I went door to door. I tried to explain to him that if people were willing to go on camera in a compromising situation, they might change their minds in the time it took for him to grab his camera and come inside. When I did get someone to agree to go on camera, I often had to text him repeatedly or call him because his head was buried in his phone.

In this situation, I was also aware that all the reporters would be trying to do the same thing. There was no time to mess around. *Triage.* I started walking toward the houses while Buster got in the car and drove along next to me so he could stay in the air conditioning as long as possible. He reminded me of a parent on Halloween that followed his children from driveway to driveway, waiting for them to return with their candy.

I looked down at my cute black flats and realized they were now coated in the thick red mud from the crime scene. I half-heartedly scraped the bottoms of them on the pavement to no avail. They were caked with the stuff. I decided if I was invited into someone's home, they would have to come off.

Out of the corner of my eye, I saw another reporter behind

me, heading towards the same row of homes. I forgot about the mud and started hustling toward the houses, making sure I was more than a few steps ahead of him.

I rang the bell at each house, listening for footsteps, looking for a rustle of the blinds. It wasn't unusual for people to peer through the blinds at us and then decide not to open the door. There were no cars in any of the driveways, but they all had garages, so it was still possible someone was home. I also listened for dogs. Most of the people whose homes we approached had dogs, dogs that went wild when I rang the doorbell. If the dogs were loud and no one came to the door, it meant either no one was home, or they were ignoring me.

The other reporter was not far behind me now. He was going to each door, one at a time, right after me. He stood back a few feet and patiently waited until I shoved my business card in the door jambs. He then approached with his own card. At least he wasn't trying to jump ahead of me. He probably knew that if I got my proverbial foot in a door, he could probably come in behind me and get an interview as well. I was the warm-up act.

I was getting ready to give up on getting anything, when a door on a large Craftsman home opened just a few inches. I could barely see the young woman through the crack between the frame and the open door. Her dark eyes darted back and forth nervously, looking past me, over my shoulder. Without turning around, I knew she was probably looking at my shadow—the other reporter.

A small dog hopped and yipped at her feet, barred from escaping through the narrow opening, by her legs that were blocking the way.

"No, Rascal, no." She looked down at the dog and then turned her gaze back to me.

"Ma'am, I'm Maddie Arnette from Channel 8 News. I'm looking for—"

"I know what you're looking for, and I know who you are," she replied with more concern than anger. "I can't help you. You need to understand, this is a very scary situation for all of us here in this neighborhood, and I have a baby. I can't risk talking to you."

"I get it. I really do," I said, thinking about how lucky I was that she was still talking to me. She could have easily slammed the door in my face. Many people did slam the door in my face. It came with the job. But when someone kept talking to me, it was always a good sign that I might be invited in.

Out of my peripheral vision, I saw the other reporter loitering at the end of the driveway, just in front of Buster's SUV, waiting to see if the woman would let me in. It was exactly what I would be doing if I were in his situation. I couldn't blame him. Pressure to get *the interview* made us all desperate at times. It was this desperation that often made me feel dirty.

One time I was sent to get an interview with the parents of a woman who had abandoned an infant on the subway in New York City. They lived in a small North Carolina town several hours away from Oak City. We went on a fishing expedition, hoping we might get them on camera. Most of the time, we couldn't afford to gamble on a possible interview, given the need to meet constant deadlines and fill the newscasts. But in this case the network, CNN, and our network affiliates, were also very interested in us getting this interview and sharing it with them. So we went.

When I got there, the woman's family was crammed in the living room of the tiny house, chain smoking, pacing, and taking constant phone calls from friends wanting to know what was going on. I worked on them for an hour, explaining that everyone wanted to know what really happened, and telling them that they had the power to shape the narrative. Again, this was my special talent—convincing people to go on camera. Sometimes it left me with a queasy feeling when I pushed too hard.

Eventually the woman's mother agreed to do an interview with us on her porch if we didn't reveal her identity. We got the interview and headed back to the station after two hours of working to convince her. I was exhausted, but triumphant. We found out later that night, the woman had agreed to do an interview with a competitor full-face, revealing her identity. It rendered what we had done moot. Given this scenario, offering hidden identity interviews was not my go-to. It was a last resort.

I was afraid my colleague waiting in the wings was going to spook the woman with the baby, to make her feel like she was about to be ambushed. So I had to get rid of him.

"Can I come in for a minute and just talk? I won't use your name or address, I promise. I'm just trying to get a handle on how this whole thing unfolded."

She reached down and picked up the little dog and opened the door up just enough to let me squeeze by her. She then closed it and locked it behind us.

I had shed my muddy shoes on her front steps and walked barefoot behind her as she ushered me into a large, modern living room with oversized gray couches facing one another, adorned with huge, square white fur pillows. A monitor with a flashing green light emanating the low rumble of white noise sat on the glass coffee table in between the sofas. As I got closer, I could see a tiny video screen on the monitor that showed the dark outline of a sleeping baby on its stomach. The baby's head was to its side as the baby sucked on a pacifier. There was a yellow blanket draped over the child, and a stuffed lion curled up in the baby's hand.

"I really don't know anything," she said nervously, perched on the edge of one of the massive couches that would have swallowed a normal family's living room.

She reminded me of a suspect who was cornered in an interrogation room. She was twisting her wedding ring in circles. She pulled her hands apart just long enough to gesture for me to sit on the opposite couch.

"I didn't get that close, for obvious reasons." She motioned to the baby monitor, which I took to mean the baby was her main "obvious reason."

"I know stuff like this can happen anywhere, but why here? I mean, it's a very nice, quiet neighborhood. Why here?" she said to no one in particular, looking out the room's expansive bay window revealed a barren field, clear-cut of trees to create another phase of the subdivision.

She was now furiously twisting her wedding ring in circles again. She looked back at me. "But then again, why not here?"

"True," I said, not wanting to interrupt her train of thought.

Most of the time, when I was trying to get someone on camera in a sensitive story, I stayed quiet. What I had learned from many years of interviewing people was that it was better to just let people talk and not to try and fill the silences with your own words just because you might momentarily feel uncomfortable. This was one of the hardest lessons for me to learn. But I realized if I interrupted people in these tense situations, it might break their rhythm and derail their stream of consciousness. Sometimes the slightest interruption gave them a moment to pause and think about what they were doing, often bringing the interview to a screeching and permanent halt.

"There's going to be a black cloud in this neighborhood, you know something you can't ever get over or forget. It changes everything. I don't know if I can stay here. Robert, that's my husband. Robert is not going to understand this, when I tell him I can't stay." She brushed stray wisps of hair away from her weary face. I got the impression that she usually looked more put-together than she did at this moment based on the pristine condition of her den and judging by the beautiful framed family photos around the room. In the photographs, she had perfectly coiffed hair, gleaming white teeth, and color-coordinated outfits with Robert and the baby. Today she looked like a harried, imperfect mother of a young child.

Ultimately, after talking with her for about thirty minutes, she agreed to talk to us on camera if we hid her identity. I reluctantly agreed to this after pitching a full-face interview multiple times. No matter what angle I approached this from she vetoed the idea. She was afraid the killer might still be in the neighborhood. I agreed this was a reasonable fear. I texted Buster and told him to come quickly and bring his equipment.

Once she ushered him into the living room, I assured her that Buster was a pro at shooting anonymous interviews. I always said this in front of him as he set up so that he could then offer his own reassurances.

"So I'll be shooting you from behind. Basically, we'll see Maddie's face listening to you, and just a little bit of your hair. I might shoot your hands on a tight-shot, but nothing else that would identify you." Buster gingerly clipped the wireless microphone on the sagging scoop-necked collar of her tired sweatshirt. "So if you see my camera pointed in your direction, don't worry. I am not shooting your face. I wouldn't do that."

True to his word, Buster shot her from behind so you could only see the slightest outline of part of the back of her head. Most of the frame was filled with my focused face, nodding and reacting to her statements. She repeated what the chief had told us, with a few more details—how the baby had started crying, how the sky was so gray, and that there were vultures. She told me from the distance could see just one article of clothing, a white jacket on the man. Maybe a chef, she thought.

I listened with reverence and sincerity, understanding that for her this was a defining moment in her life, and the least I could do was acknowledge that. So many times I had interviewed people who'd witnessed tragedy. By necessity I had become partially immune to their emotions. I had erected a steel wall around my heart, with a window where I could observe the gritty details of a case without allowing it to penetrate my psyche and poison my soul.

When Adam died, it became harder for me to keep the wall from being breached. After being present for someone's death, I finally understood the gravitas of the moment in a way that was deeply personal. It made me empathize with other people who had experienced death. In a second, without warning, I could be transported back to the moment I realized he was gone. The room got quiet. That's how I knew his breathing had stopped. I jumped up from the couch where I was sleeping, near his hospital bed in our den, and put my hand to his mouth. I felt one last warm exhale of breath. It made the tiniest sound, like the last bit of air leaking out of an almost deflated balloon. He opened his eyes, turned his head, looked at me for a second, and then he was gone.

After Adam's death, my grief counselor told me I could see Thestrals now, the mythical winged horses from Harry Potter that only appeared to people who were present for someone's death. According to the story, it gave them special powers. My new special powers seemed to be a depth that allowed me to connect with someone else's grief at a high rate of speed. I wasn't sure if it was a good power or a bad power.

The woman said her name was Pam—a name I would never use on camera or in the story. So I didn't call her by name because I didn't want to slip it into the story by accident. This was always awkward, not calling someone by her name in an interview. I found myself apologizing multiple times for the omission, even after I had explained why I was doing it.

"What if he comes back, the person who did this? I love walking in this neighborhood. I won't feel safe again, I won't.

I'm so angry that he took that away from us, the man who did this," Pam said, with large, messy tears streaming down her red cheeks. Tears that no one would ever see on camera. They were just for me and Buster.

She grabbed a tissue from a box on a table next to the couch and blotted her face.

I could feel tears welling up in the corners of my eyes, and I reached for my own tissue. My wall had been compromised and there was no going back.

"I got nothing," Kojak said to me, as I cradled the cell phone in the crook of my neck and tried to type on my tablet balanced precariously on my lap in the passenger seat of Buster's news car. "Lydia is shutting this one down hard. No leaks. I don't get it. Something fishy about it. I've been poking the bear but getting nowhere. Sorry, kid. We have a meeting later, where she is supposed to fill in the details to the rest of our team in Major Crimes. But right now it's just her and the investigators from the scene who are on the inside of this one. And they're not talking."

"Maybe they truly just don't know the identity, and because it's in an upper-middle-class neighborhood, they're being cautious. They want to make sure they get it right. Do everything by the book. Rich people are less understanding about screw ups."

"Also because he's white. Let's face it. They think he might be someone important, or at least someone who thought he was important."

"Think you're reading too much into it."

This type of speculation had come to define our relationship. Sometimes when we knew nothing, it was more sport than actual conversation.

"Nope, this is my area of expertise. Tight lips mean

something in the cop world, and it ain't good."

It always cracked me up when Kojak tried to sound like his namesake, like a tough talking cop from a bygone era. But his old-school gumshoe vibe had no effect on me. I was immune to it by now.

"Shit, I lost my Internet connection. Got to go. Got to reboot, on deadline. The dreaded technology curse is hanging over me again."

"Kid, you need to get back to swimming rabbits and runaway cats. You don't need this stress," Kojak said, with a combination of sarcasm and concern.

"You're right, but I am doing this today, and only today. So I need to do my best. Keri will be back tomorrow and take over. At least, that's what I'm told. And by the way, I have not done a story on a runaway cat, not ever. That's so *common.*"

"Whatever. Sure, like you're just going to drop it. Not possible. I know you, remember?"

"Look, really got to go. On deadline."

"Gotcha but real quick, on another note. What's going on with your side gig, your little mystery with the crazy lady, Suzanne?"

"Actually, a whole lot. I don't have time to get into the details right now. Fill you in later. But the most recent development is that the alleged cheating husband is MIA. I still don't know if he was at the hospital the night Maria had the baby, but I do know from a credible source that he was with her shortly after she had her baby. Went out for and errand and never came back.

"So to summarize, he ditched her. Got cold feet after the little bundle of joy came into his complicated life. Makes perfect sense to me. Don't call that missing. Call that *coming to Jesus*."

"Agreed, but it's weird. Her brother made it sound perfectly normal that Tanner was there with Maria, not like he's a cheating husband with a whole other family. And he said it wasn't like Tanner to leave and not come back. Sounds like they know him pretty well."

"He's missing all right. Missing from his other family. Finally came to his senses, crisis of conscience, and went home to his wife and first kid. Guy has a lot on his plate. Don't blame him for being a little confused, a little unpredictable."

Buster leaned in my partially open car window. "What are you doing? Get off the phone and get back to writing. Do I need to crack the whip?"

He hated it when he thought I was lollygagging when I was supposed to be working. He had to wait for me to write my script and record my voice track before he could edit the piece for the show. Meanwhile, he had been hamming it up with a group of cops near the crime scene tape, so he didn't appear to be worried about whether we were going to make deadline.

"My computer crashed." I looked up at him with the most innocent eyes I could muster.

"I doubt you're talking to IT about it. Pretty sure you're jabbering about something else totally unrelated to the task at hand." He tapped the window for good measure and walked back to his circle of officers.

Buster loved cops, and they loved him. It worked in our favor.

"You go deal with your dead guy," Kojak said on the other end of the line, having overheard dozens of similar arguments between me and Buster over the years. He hung up abruptly.

"I will. *Triage, triage, triage* is how I will get through this day," I said into the phone that was now connected to no one.

12

HOT WATER

I WAS THANKFUL when I returned home that night and Miranda and Blake were in their rooms, engaged in homework. I had to credit Candace, my guardian angel, for that and for making them dinner. Thankfully, she was well again and back at work. These days I rarely imposed on her to stay late and help with evening duties, because I was able to organize my feature reporting around the kids' schedules. So an out-of-the blue call to duty for one night was no big deal to her. She had agreed to stay late, and I appreciated her.

I checked in on the kids, gave them quick hugs and pecks on their foreheads while getting a synopsis of their day. It reminded me of a study I read online that said parents on average interacted with their children a total of seven minutes per day. Was I *that* parent? Not anymore. I used to be, before Adam died. Now, most days, my total time with them was much greater than seven minutes. But today was an exception to this new norm. Tomorrow I would do better.

It was time for a hot bath, the place I did most of my thinking, other than on the running trails. It was the one time of the day where I could let go of my angst and sort through things, versus reacting and putting out fires. It was a time for me to examine the hot spots from my day and figure out how to keep them from re-igniting. There was something about submerging my limbs in a bathtub full of scalding water that calmed my monkey brain.

Going to a crime scene always made me feel like I was covered with an invisible film of dirt, like death was something you could catch. I worried I would feel that way about my house after Adam died in the den. On the contrary, I felt at peace in my house because it was the last place we spent time together. It was different when someone was murdered. You could wash away death, but not evil.

In this case, there was some actual truth to my concerns about being dirty. My black flats were caked with a thick layer of red mud from the crime scene. I left them on the front porch, by the front door. I was pretty sure they were going to be a total loss, but I would try to salvage them later when I was less weary. This was a familiar feeling from my crime reporting days that I didn't miss—sheer exhaustion, mental, emotional and physical. I had nothing more to give.

As I sank down into the boiling hot water, I pictured the silhouette of Adam standing over the tub, trying to talk to me. It had always annoyed me at the end of a long day, when he tried to invade my sacred space with his talk of carpool logistics and grocery lists.

"A little privacy," I would say, without opening my eyes, and he would go away, quietly shutting the bathroom door behind him with a tiny click.

How I longed to call him back again now, to talk to him about who was picking up which kid and when, and who would run out to the store and get milk so we would have it for breakfast the next morning.

I wondered if the man in the ditch was a husband or a father. I wondered if someone was missing him tonight. Surely if he was loved, someone would be looking for him.

As hard as I tried to block it out of my mind, it was the white coat I kept coming back to. It was a strange thing for someone to be wearing. Maybe it was a uniform of some kind? I had to put it aside. I had spent too many sleepless nights going over the details of a crime in my head, hoping the next time I went down the list something new would come to me.

It would be Keri's problem tomorrow. I would be back on my animal beat, and I could leave all this gooey red clay behind me for someone else to clean up.

~

When Janie called me the next morning and told me a small town outside the city had a missing *town peacock*. I couldn't help but smile. The kids were at the kitchen table happily eating scrambled eggs with cheese and multi-grain toast—a new habit I had gotten into, trying to make them a healthy, protein-infused breakfast. They still preferred sugary cereal to my basic culinary delights, but they were getting used to it. Plus, they liked us all being together in the kitchen.

"What's so funny?" Janie sounded miffed by my laughter at her story suggestion.

"Nothing, I just had someone tell me yesterday that I should *get back to missing cat stories*. Here I am about to do a missing peacock story. Ironic, don't you think?"

"Not really. A missing-peacock story has so much more depth than a missing-cat story. Those are, like, a dime a dozen. But sure, spin it however you need to. Anyway, Piper was a fixture in the Pinnacle town square. One family fed him, but he belonged to no one in particular, just the town. People used to always see him walking down the sidewalk, crossing the street, strutting his peacock stuff. He was like the town mascot. Then poof, he vanished. No ransom note yet."

I was thinking that if Piper was kidnapped he was probably a long way from Pinnacle by now. I assumed they were expensive birds and probably could be sold for quite a bit of money. The other, more distasteful option—Piper was roadkill. Crossing the street didn't seem like a good plan for a peacock, especially on a busy four-lane road like the one that bordered Pinnacle. Traffic was always heavy as drivers navigated rush hour in and out of the burgeoning Oak City suburb.

"Okay, so I'll head to the police department since they sent out the missing peacock bulletin. I've got to get the kids to school first. I can just meet Buster there."

"Actually," Janie hesitated.

Her hesitation wasn't good. It never was. "So he's going to be with Keri today since he knows the dead-guy-found story, because he was on it yesterday. We thought it would be easier to keep him working on that case so he can help her, since she's new and all." Janie paused, waiting for my reaction.

I knew this day would eventually come, the day Buster would be fed up with my animal stories and want to get back into the game, back to the sketchy, hardscrabble world of crime reporting. I couldn't blame him. He had been a good sport for so many months, putting up with my quirky, often silly stories that had a surprising amount of humanity, but little edge. It was about time for him to jump back into the fire. I would be able to survive without him.

"It's just for today," Janie said, filling the silent gaping hole in our conversation. "And maybe tomorrow, well, you know, until we get an identity on the guy and stuff. Dex just thinks it makes sense. I put you with Jeremy."

Jeremy was a young, affable photographer who was pleasant enough and did whatever I asked him to do. He was also just young enough and just green enough to still care about the artistry of video, which made every story just a little bit better. Older photographers had that desire squeezed out of them by an industry that prided itself on lauding speed over creativity.

I was happy to work with Jeremy. Also because we had no emotional ties like I did with Buster, it would be an easy, breezy day with no head games. Just what I needed.

"Great, tell him I will see him there at ten o'clock."

"Will do," Janie said, her voice dripping with palpable relief that I had not imploded.

She was used to dealing with lots of difficult personalities. Reporters didn't get to be good journalists by being agreeable.

I looked at the kids, happily eating their breakfast. Miranda was reviewing for her science test, her laptop open on the table next to her. Blake was looking at his phone, playing some video game that beeped constantly. My steaming hot coffee sat on the counter in front of me, inviting me to sip it slowly, maybe in the chair by the window where I could see the magnolia trees, which surrounded my back porch, in full springtime bloom.

For just a moment, all was right with the world. But I was knew it wasn't going to last.

⁓

As I was pulling out of the driveway, I heard my phone vibrate. I wanted to ignore it, but I was afraid it was the newsroom reaching out to tell me something had changed. I stopped the car, put it in park, and clicked on the new email on my phone. It was from Janie, telling me that before I went to the peacock story, she needed me to "swing by" a press conference about human trafficking. *Swing by* was a euphemism used by newsroom managers to make it seem like we were just picking up a gallon of milk on our way to another story. It insinuated that our job was so easy we barely had to stop the car, let alone slow down, to cover an event. In reality every story, even a press conference, required more than just a *swing by*. It required setting up equipment—the camera, the tripod, lights, microphones. It required listening, getting information, gathering facts, and understanding those facts. It also required talking to people, getting their names and titles, asking them questions, keeping them on topic, and doing it all quickly and diplomatically.

"Sure," I fired back at Janie, knowing it wasn't the hill I wanted to die on today.

Triage, triage, triage, I said to myself, repeating my calming mantra. I was pretty sure Deepak Chopra never said *triage* in his head while meditating.

I put the address of the press conference in my GPS and backed out of my driveway. It would be a slight detour in my day, but I was calmed that affable Jeremy would meet me at the event.

As I pulled onto the highway, my phone rang again. I hit the answer button on the screen on my dashboard.

"Maddie, its Suzanne," she said, urgently

"Suzanne, I am sorry I haven't been in touch. Work has been crazy, but I haven't forgotten about you."

"It's okay. I totally understand. I just wanted you to know that it's finally over. He's gone."

"Wow, that's good, right? What happened? How are you?"

"He just up and left me before I could tell him I was leaving him. So it's finally over for real. For good. Such a relief. You don't even know."

"Did he say anything?"

"Yes, he just told me it was over and that there was someone else. I'm assuming it's that slut, Maria. The one who he probably got pregnant. Don't know, don't care. He didn't say who it was. He was in the doorway with a suitcase when I got home night before last. It was very civil, to tell you the truth. No yelling. No anger. We both handled it like adults."

"Wow, that's amazing. Are you okay?"

"Surprisingly, I am. I'm just so relieved. He didn't tell me where he was going, but he said his lawyer would be in touch and that he would make sure I was taken care of. He told me Winston was better off with me, and that he did want to be a part of his life, but that Winston needed his mother more than he needed Tanner."

"Wow, it sounds like an almost perfect parting of ways," I said, barely able to hide my confusion and surprise.

This didn't make any sense if Tanner was really the awful man she had described. But it did make sense if he was the kind man I had met in the doctor's office. My guess was that the truth lived in the gray area. He was some combination of these two Tanners.

"I was really scared when I saw him holding the suitcase. I mean, so many things went through my mind. I was like, this is it, he's going to take me down on his way out the door. But it was as if all the anger inside him just disappeared in an instant. He suddenly seemed very reasonable, even happy for the first time in a long time. Maybe he's in love with the other woman, whoever she is, I don't know. Maybe it's enough to change him."

If he left Suzanne and he left Maria, where was he? Where did he go? Was there another woman? A third woman? It was a mystery, but at least he had left Suzanne without incident. That was the important thing. And if the parting was as amicable as she described it, he no longer sounded like a threat to her, which meant all the angst I had been feeling about her situation could now fade away. I could stop worrying about her.

"Suzanne, that's great. I'm so happy for you. I really am."

"Thanks, Maddie. I want you to know I really appreciate everything you did for me—coming to the hospital after the race, listening to me without judgment, trying to help me extricate myself from this awful marriage. You've been an amazing friend. I will never forget your kindness."

"I really didn't do anything, seriously. I'm just glad he's gone and that you are safe. That's the important thing."

It was turning out to be a better day than I could have ever imagined. Over the years, I had covered horror stories that involved crumbling marriages and poorly executed exit strategies. Often these involved wives throwing their wedding albums into a fire or keying their husband's fancy midlife-crisis sports cars. It sounded like Suzanne and Tanner had no such drama. Her parting was the rarest of all, one rooted in mutual respect for their shared history and the love of their child.

"No, that's not true. I can never thank you enough. I can finally breathe again. He even said Winston and I can stay in the house. He isn't going to fight me on that. It's a miracle. I'm so happy that I even made a new goal today. I'm going to run my first full marathon. Training starts today!"

"Wow, that's amazing. What a great goal. I'm happy for you. I really am."

After we hung up, the Australian male voice on my GPS informed me that I had passed my exit and it was rerouting me. I was trying to focus on where I was going, but I couldn't get the conversation with Suzanne out of my head. She was *free*. It was unbelievable. I was cautiously optimistic that she was out of danger, but there was still a nagging feeling in the pit of my stomach, something I couldn't identify. It was the same feeling I got when I thought back to the night my mother was killed. It was an unsettled feeling, and I didn't like it one bit.

Jeremy was already set up at the press conference when I arrived. He had put the microphone on the podium and carved out a spot for his camera and tripod in between two other photographers a few feet from where the speaker would stand. As I walked through the door, a young woman in a sleek black business suit handed me a press packet and gestured for me to sit in the front row of chairs with the other reporters.

"Here's some information about our organization, plus some statistics about human trafficking in our area and across the state. We're going to get started in just a moment," she said, with a beaming smile beneath bright blue hipster glasses.

Her light brown hair was pulled back into a severe bun. I could tell she was trying to look older and perhaps more serious than her smattering of freckles and youthful smile indicated. She gestured with a wide sweep of her arm for me to sit in the first row of metal folding chairs near the podium.

I followed her directions and sat down in the front row, making brief eye contact with Jeremy, who smiled and nodded back at me. I opened the packet and started to leaf through it. I simply needed the basics—a few numbers I could use to make a graphic, a definition of human trafficking that our viewers could understand, and a soundbite from a speaker at the podium, explaining the scope of the problem in our area.

I hadn't covered the issue extensively, but I knew enough to ask the right questions. Human trafficking is defined as anytime people are forced to perform services against their will for no compensation. The most common form of labor trafficking involved migrant workers on farms across the state, being forced to work in the fields for little or no money. But human trafficking in the city mostly involved the sex trade. Women were being sold for sex in online platforms. Their captors held them by force or fear in local hotel rooms where the women performed sexual acts for money, money that went right into their captors' pockets. This looked like prostitution, but the women were the victims of these men, not criminals. Sometimes the victims were children who were being sold by their parents for money or drugs.

The organization holding the press conference was called *Stop Human Trafficking in its Tracks*. Their goal was to educate people about human trafficking so they would know what to look for and report it to police when they spotted it.

As various people walked up to the podium to speak about their roles in helping to combat human trafficking, I glanced at the information sheet for the group, scanning their mission statement for key facts I could use in my brief story. I ran my finger down the page, reading the impressive list of board members—movers and shakers in the community who had admirably taken on this cause. Most of the names rang a bell, but one jumped off the page—*Tanner Pope*. I surveyed the room, looking for his face, but I realized he wasn't there. This once again confirmed my belief that he seemed like a good man, considering he was involved in such a worthy cause. But what did his absence mean? Where in the world was Tanner Pope?

"They spotted him." Janie said excitedly.

It took me a minute to realize she was talking about the peacock and not Tanner. Obviously she knew nothing about Tanner, and was talking about Piper the peacock. My overworked brain was getting so mixed up. The other day I told Buster I needed to stop and get gas in my car, and he said, "But we're in my car. How is that going to work?"

"Piper, he's stopping traffic up on the 510. It's crazy." Janie finally exhaled. "We've got the helicopter flying over it. Need you and Jeremy to break away from that presser and get up there as fast as you can."

Human trafficking, the missing Tanner Pope, a peacock on the run. My head was spinning. Little fires everywhere. There was no room for inflexibility. I had to shift gears. It wasn't easy for a planner like myself to handle these abrupt transitions, but I had learned how to cope after many years of walking through hot coals.

"Okay, we'll head that way." I replied, having learned a long time ago that griping about the constantly changing landscape of television news assignments meant you needed to find another job.

"Great. Thanks so much." Janie replied with appreciation for not having to stroke a reporter's fragile ego.

"My pleasure."

I decided to leave my car in the parking lot of the building where the press conference was and jump in Jeremy's news car so we could get to Piper faster. As we got closer to the spot on the highway that was blocked off, it became clear that we might miss the entire event while stuck in traffic. Without discussing it, Jeremy jerked the steering wheel hard to the left and drove into the median and parked. He did exactly what I was thinking we should do. We jumped out, put on our yellow safety vests, and started walking past the traffic barricades. I just had my phone and notepad, but Jeremy slung his camera over one shoulder and balanced his tripod on the other as we carefully moved along the narrow side of the road.

I heard the peacock before I saw him. He made a high-pitched squawk which took me off guard because I didn't know peacocks made any sounds. I also didn't know they flew until I saw Piper, with his massive wingspan, glide above four lanes of traffic and land on the median about fifty feet from us. Jeremy had quickly set up his camera and was now quietly shooting video of Piper's dramatic approach. I stopped and froze, trying not to spook the bird.

"Don't move," Jeremy whisper, behind me.

"I'm not," I whispered back.

While the cars were behind a line of police vehicles, drivers were leaning out of their windows with their phones, trying to get their own video of the magnificent Piper. A woman in a brown uniform with *Animal Control* written on the back was inching toward the peacock. She had a large padded glove on one hand and a long stick with a crook on the end in the other hand. She looked very professional, like she knew what she was doing, but at the same time I didn't think local animal control officers were used to wrangling peacocks.

As the officer crept closer, Piper stared at her with what appeared to be more curiosity than fear. Behind the female officer, another animal control officer was also tiptoeing, carrying a metal cage and trying not to rattle it. When the pair got within a few feet of Piper, the peacock turned right and scurried across the lanes of traffic on the other side of the median and into the woods. We lost sight of him.

For the story, it didn't matter if Piper was caught or not; what mattered was that we got the video of a peacock shutting down a highway. Video that would no doubt go viral on social media as soon as we posted it. Jeremy and I turned around and I started putting the microphone into the windows of the drivers behind us, asking them if they were annoyed by the inconvenience, or amazed by the show.

"I have never seen anything like that," said a man in a shiny, white Lexus. "Amazing, just amazing. Better than the Discovery Channel."

"Seriously shutting down the highway for a damn bird," said a woman in a brown sedan with dents in the side. She threw her cigarette butt past me, onto the pavement, the bright red ember still glowing after it hit the ground. "Some of us got to work."

The animal control officers admitted in their interviews that this was a first for them—peacock chasing. The highway was reopened a few minutes after Piper disappeared into the woods. The officers told us the one thing they did know about wild birds was that if they didn't want to be captured, it was almost impossible to bring them in. As long as Piper wasn't causing a public nuisance, there was no need to capture him.

"We had these bird gloves mostly to deal with injured owls, hawks, and the occasional eagle..." said the female animal control officer. "...But peacocks are rare, not what we're used to. Did our best. Fast bird. We really didn't have a chance." She shook her head in a display of defeat.

I could still detect longing in her voice since she had been so close to catching Piper.

Not unlike Piper, Tanner had pulled his own disappearing act, and just like a wild bird, it was obvious that he did not want to be found.

"Thanks for meeting with me," Keri said, as I slid into the chair at the small rickety table in front of the coffee shop, next to the television station. I moved the full ashtray from the middle of our table to another table next to us. She had texted me during the peacock fiasco and asked me if I would meet with her for a few minutes after work.

"No problem. Happy to help. What's going on?"

"Well, there's this weirdness about identifying the body of the man they found the other day."

I could tell Keri was nervous about talking to me. It was as if she were trying to figure out whether I might be envious of her taking over my beat. What she didn't understand was that it was my choice to change assignments, and that I wanted nothing but for her to be successful. I was more than happy to help her and hoped I could put her mind at ease.

"Well, by now, they may know who it is," I said. "But if that's the case, there must be a reason why they aren't releasing the information."

"That's what I think, too!" Keri said, with the excitement of a teenager.

"So you have to figure out why they won't release it. Usually they hide behind the excuse that they haven't been able to locate and notify next of kin. Have they said anything like that?"

"Nope total silence, nothing. We're still waiting on that composite they promised us, the one they said they were going to use to ask for the public's help in identifying him."

"Okay, well keep asking for that, because they did promise that yesterday. I can make some calls and see if I can find out anything."

"That would be great!" Keri exclaimed with too much enthusiasm and then covered her mouth quickly out of embarrassment.

She looked around. Nobody was paying attention to us. They had their eyes buried in their cell phones.

Keri had shoulder-length brown hair and a kind, open face with twinkling green eyes. She always dressed professionally. She had the kind of girl-next-door look that women and men both found approachable. She was the type of woman you would want to hang out with or go on a date with.

"My pleasure. I'll let you know what I find out."

Keri thanked me profusely, grabbed her bag, and trotted back toward the station. In that moment, I realized that I did care about the outcome of the murder case, but that I no longer had an emotional connection to it like I did when it was my beat. I was finally free of my addiction. It was time for someone else, someone younger, someone with more fuel, like Keri, to take over. For the first time since Adam's death, I realized I was ready to move on in more ways than one.

13

REUNITED

I WAS STILL WORRIED about Suzanne. Despite her cheerful phone call, I wasn't convinced that she was out of danger or that she was truly okay with her husband leaving. I decided I would reach out to her and see if she wanted to have breakfast the next morning. She agreed, and we met at a hotel near Blake and Miranda's school that had a nice outdoor seating area.

I arrived a few minutes late, and she was already seated, sipping coffee and eyeing the menu through large black sunglasses, her long black, wavy hair cascading around her face, her large silver bag slung over the back of her chair, as usual. I often wondered what she carried in that oversized bag, as it always seemed to be bulging. She looked up and gave me a princess-in-a-parade wave as I approached.

"You look great!" I pulled the heavy wooden chair out and scooted myself into the table. She reached across the table to give me a little hug and an air kiss.

"I feel great, like a big weight has been lifted off my

shoulders. It's seriously amazing. Everything looks different now, better. The trees swaying in the breeze, the birds chirping, the sunshine dancing across the pavement. It's like when you cry, and suddenly everything in your field of vision gets sharper and comes into focus." Suzanne gestured to the manicured lawn beneath the patio, where the first vestiges of the southern spring were blooming. The whole scene was bathed in a golden sunlight, which glistened on the surface of the nearby pool.

"Wow, that's terrific. I was worried about you. That's why I wanted to touch base. To check in."

The waiter poured me a cup of coffee, and I reached for the cream as I waited for Suzanne to respond.

"Worried?" She cocked her head and put her coffee cup down on the saucer in front of her.

"Well, after all you have been through, even though you got the result you wanted, the end of a marriage is never easy. I hear it's like a death, grieving the end of the relationship."

"Well, not in my case. I feel free as a bird for the first time in years. Anyone who has been in an abusive relationship can relate to how I'm feeling now. I'm just so happy to be rid of him. I really am. I had no idea it would feel this good. I might even make one of those online dating profiles." She chuckled.

I imagined her posting a sexy photo with a side profile shot, looking coquettishly into the camera. I was pretty sure she would immediately get responses on just about any dating site she chose. But it seemed kind of strange to be even joking about dating so soon after splitting with your husband. I wasn't sure if *I* would ever think about dating again.

I sat back and studied Suzanne for a moment. She looked so happy, almost *too* happy. But I couldn't see her eyes behind the big jet-black sunglasses. Maybe she was just putting on a good show of strength for me because she didn't want me to feel sorry for her. She was right about one thing—I had never walked in her shoes. Sure, Adam and I had our moments, but it wasn't the same thing. I had never been emotionally abused by a man, so what did I know?

"I'm sorry, Suzanne. I didn't mean to be critical of your feelings. I'm honestly very happy for you. I'm so glad things turned out the way they did. And I hope, moving forward, you guys can stay amicable and agree on Winston's custody."

"Sure, when I find him. I filled my lawyer in on the latest developments, but there's nothing we can do until Tanner surfaces again, which is fine. I'm willing to wait, as long as I don't have to deal with him in my house every single day."

"So no word from him. No word on where he went?"

"None. My guess is that he's with that woman, the one he said he was leaving me for, the pregnant one. Frankly I don't really care where he is. He can stay away forever if he wants. Good riddance."

For some reason I felt hesitant to share with Suzanne what Juan had told me—that Tanner was missing from Maria's life, too.

As I sat in my home office, I could hear the laundry in the nearby dryer rolling around a zipper, or perhaps a button, or a coin, slamming against the metal of drum with each rotation. I could hear the whir of my space heater that kept the basement cozy even in the spring and summer when the air condition was too cold for my taste.

If I concentrated hard, I could also hear a television upstairs, with an audience laugh track playing in the background behind the actors' up-tempo dialogue. Chances are it was a television left on, not one being watched. Above me, I also heard footsteps on the kitchen floor. I knew they were Miranda's because they were clicking and clacking, hard-sole shoes, one lazy foot dragging—her trademark walk.

Isolating these sounds made me think about just how important listening was. I needed to take a moment and really listen to what Suzanne was telling me. It wasn't just about her words, but about everything else—the way she looked and acted, her body language. What was she telling me without saying anything at all?

Something wasn't adding up in the cavalier way she had eliminated Tanner from her life. He was simply gone, vanished, and she was no longer worried about whether he posed a danger. She didn't seem at all concerned about whether he might try to take their son away from her. She also didn't seem to care or be even the least bit curious about where he was.

Let it go, let it go, let it go, said the voice inside my head. Something about Tanner taking off didn't seem plausible. And he wasn't with Maria, so *who* was he with? Maybe he was just so fed up with both women that he left the country. *Good riddance.* This was one of the rare times when my radar about a person was shut off. There must be another side to this man that I hadn't seen.

I started thinking about every possible scenario. Maybe he didn't take off at all. Maybe something had happened to him. I knew nothing about Juan. Maybe he was trying to protect his sister from certain heartache and something had happened between the two men, something violent. Maybe his call to me and pleas for help were well-constructed attempts at covering his tracks. There was only one way to find out. It was time for me to find Juan.

"The reason it's so easy to get injured in a situation like this is that you naturally assume it can't happen. You assume you're safe," Clare, the woman who was attacked by a zebra, said to me through the uninjured side of her mouth.

The other side of her face was covered in a thick white

bandage with gauze peeking out, the edges of it stained pink from blood. Her arm on the same side was also wrapped in a thick layer of tape and gauze from her wrist almost to her shoulder.

"Because it's a zoo?" I followed up. I was perched on a hard plastic chair next to her hospital bed.

Buster was over my left shoulder with his camera.

"Yes, because it's a zoo." Clare motioned to her sister on the other side of the bed, to bring the cup of ice water to her from the bedside table.

The sister hopped up quickly and brought the straw to Clare's lips. Clare tried unsuccessfully, to lift her head to reach the straw. Her sister motioned for her to stay put as she patiently held the cup just below the woman's chin.

"You just think you're safe in a zoo. I mean, children go to zoos. If there's a risk, kids are going to take it, dangling their arms or legs over the fence of an exhibit. I wasn't doing anything like that. I was just leaning on the fence, eating an ice cream cone and digging in my purse for my phone to take a picture, when it happened."

I sat quietly, not wanting to interrupt Clare's train of thought. There was nothing worse than re-watching the interview on my computer, only to find out that I had broken someone's stride during the best part of the interview. She was silent for a minute, and I nodded for her to continue. No matter what kind of pressure I was under, it was important not to make her feel rushed. Our deadline was not her concern.

"I saw something like a flash out of the corner of my eye—a rush of black and white, black hair flying, and then *big* teeth grabbing my arm, pulling me in. A sound, like gnawing, pain in my face, my arm, pain like I've never experienced. I can't adequately explain it. Worse than childbirth. Surreal. It was like it was happening to someone else and I was watching it outside of my body."

Clare exhaled and closed her eyes, like explaining the experience required such an abundance of energy that it became too much for her to speak.

"Do you need a moment?" I whispered after the silence had lasted for a minute.

"No, I'm good. Let's just finish. The next thing I remember, I was on the ground. There were lots of people standing over me, yelling for help, looking down at me. I will never forget the looks in their eyes. It was the kind of look you get when you see something horrible, something that can't be fixed. People were also kneeling next to me, shouting. The sun was so bright in my eyes, and I could feel the blood trickling down, sticky and thick on my face. But my arm, I couldn't feel it at all. It was like it wasn't there. I tried to scream, *Where's my arm, where's my arm*? but nothing came out. And that was that. Then I woke up in the hospital."

"That's an unbelievable story." I wondered immediately if I should have kept this commentary to myself.

"Yes, it is. Unbelievable that it happened, unbelievable that I survived. I was so lucky to be life-flighted here, to come home to University Hospital. There was a plastic surgeon waiting for me when I arrived. It was like all the pieces came together to give me the best possible chance of recovery."

"So what is it that you want people to know?"

"I want people to know that safety is an illusion. That's it's just a thing we tell ourselves so we can function, because if we walked around worried all the time about all the bad things that *might* happen to us, we would never be able to handle it. We would be paralyzed. But it's precisely in those situations where we feel too safe, in situations where we're taking a calculated risk, that we need to be on guard. This zebra was not supposed to be able to get that close to the fence. He was supposed to be on the other side of the ditch that separated the grass from the fence. It was usually filled with water and rocks, but it had been dry. Somehow he made his way across it. They're not supposed to be that aggressive, but I was told later that there were some baby zebras on the other side of the ditch. A zoologist called me and said the zebra must have thought the babies were in danger when he attacked me."

"That is crazy." I scribbled notes on my pad out of habit, even though I would watch the interview in full later. It kept my hands busy.

"It is. I'm tired now. I think I'm done."

I thanked Clare, stood and softly squeezed her good hand. I looked back at Buster to make sure he had all the shots he needed before we left. He nodded. He was good about getting his shots while we were chitchatting in the beginning of an interview so he wouldn't have to do it at the end and make the person wait.

As we walked down the hallway, I kept thinking about what Clare had said. *Danger always lurked where you least suspected it.* I thought about Suzanne and how I had jumped into her situation without investigating it or questioning it. I was vulnerable in her presence because she knew I had my own story about my mother and domestic violence. Then it hit me—one of the details my mind had been trying to locate. She said Pennsylvania when she asked me about my mother during our recent lunch. *Pennsylvania.* How could she have known that? I didn't remember telling her about Pennsylvania. What did it mean? I didn't know. I filed it away for another day.

I called Juan and left him a voice message when I left Clare's hospital room that night. I didn't hear back from him, so I busied myself with logging the tape from Clare's interview and writing her story on my laptop, at home. I tried not to work at night at home, but the kids were already asleep. Candace had stayed late again so I could work. It seemed like I was falling back into my old bad habits, but I told myself it was just a night here and there, that I was still present for my children. I was doing what I had to do to provide for them.

I worked because I couldn't sleep. The second I lay down, my mind would begin jumping from one topic to another—*I need to make a dentist appointment for the twins. We're almost out of coffee. Where is Tanner?*

After a restless night, I noticed I had a missed call from Juan, but there was no message. I decided to try to reach him again. He picked up on the first ring and said he wanted to talk about Tanner. We agreed to meet me at a local coffee shop.

Juan was short, stout, and older than I expected him to be. He had jet-black hair, a small mustache, and a belly that protruded slightly between the overextended buttons of his light blue work shirt. There was a name embroidered in red on the right breast pocket. It said *Skip*, but I was pretty sure it was either a joke, a nickname, or maybe a co-worker's shirt. He caught me staring at it.

"I ran out of work shirts. Belongs to a guy who used to work for us. Fired. Boss gave me his shirts in case I needed some extras."

Juan didn't smile at the end of his explanation. He stated it matter-of-factly as if to clear the air before our conversation so that I wouldn't be focusing on some unnecessary detail instead of on what he had say. He had an accent, but his words were clear as a bell.

Juan extended a small, weathered hand across the table with a firmness that surprised me, and then turned to the waitress and ordered a black coffee before sitting down.

"Thank you for meeting me. We've been so worried about the doctor. Makes no sense." Juan shook his round head and looked down into the steaming hot cup of black coffee the waitress had just placed in front of him.

But didn't make a move to pick it up. He looked back up at

me with warm brown eyes that appeared to have tears in the corners.

"My pleasure. I could tell you were very upset. First, let me ask you a few questions so I can fully understand the situation."

Juan nodded and appeared to be hanging on my every word. He didn't come across as a man with something to hide. It occurred to me that he probably had no idea that Tanner had a wife and a son, that he must have thought Tanner and his sister were in a monogamous relationship.

"Anything, anything at all," said Juan.

"How long had she known Tanner? The doctor?"

"For at least a year. He was a very good man. Very good to her. Very good to us."

"In what way?"

"He brought us food, clothes, got Maria's car fixed. When our water heater broke, he gave us money to replace it. He said he would help with things the baby needed."

That's big of him. He was going to help with his own child.

"He helped Maria settle down, get away from bad men, people that treated her with no respect. She has been through a lot. But thanks to him, she's in a better place now. We were all so relieved when he came into our lives. He was a blessing to us. That's why we worry now."

Juan reached across the table and squeezed my hand. He held it just long enough to make it a little awkward, but his intentions appeared to be genuine. So I sat there in uncomfortable silence until he finally pulled his hand away.

"He sounds like he means a lot to you and your whole family. Do you know anything else about him? About what he did when he wasn't with you, wasn't with Maria?"

"Oh, sure. The doctor is a very important man. He works a lot. He also has a wife and a son named Winston. He showed us picture of them. He is a very proud man, a family man."

I was stunned.

"And Maria doesn't mind? It doesn't bother her that Tanner has a wife and son?"

"Why should it?"

"I don't know. I mean, I would think she would be jealous or something."

Now, Juan was the one looking confused. He cocked his head to the side as if he were listening for some special frequency that might explain what I was talking about.

"Did you think the doctor and Maria were together?"

"I assumed."

"No, no, absolutely not." Juan shook his head and pushed back his chair from the table as if he needed to put more space between us after what I said. "He is our friend. The doctor is our friend. That's all. He helps us."

I was trying to make sense of what Juan was telling me when I felt my phone vibrate on my lap. I looked down and saw the goofy picture of Kojak flash across my screen.

"Juan, if you will excuse me for a moment. I need to take this."

I stood from the table and stepped outside onto the sidewalk to take Kojak's call.

"Maddie Arnette," I chimed out of habit.

"Kid, are you sitting down?"

"No, I'm standing. Why?"

"We had our meeting with the chief. Get ready to have your mind blown. The stiff from the fancy neighborhood. They identified him."

I had a sinking feeling in the pit of my stomach. My biggest fear was finding out that a dead person was someone I knew. The way Kojak was drum-rolling the information, I felt like this might be that moment.

"Who is it?"

"It's the guy, the guy you've been investigating, the guy who disappeared, the doc, the Pope guy."

Everything was starting to make sense. Tanner wasn't missing—he was *dead*. But who would want him dead? Suzanne? Maria? Juan? Or maybe he was just the victim of a random crime? Unlikely, but possible. Yet none of the possibilities seemed to fit. Being angry enough to kill someone was an enormous leap.

"Any working theories of the case yet?"

"Not really, but he was wearing his white coat you know, the one doctors wear, so he must have been leaving work when he got popped. Looks like he was killed somewhere else and then dumped like a bucket of old garbage in this swanky hood. Someone haphazardly tried to cover him up with that brush, but it was a half-assed attempt to hide him. My guess is that they had no time, or no means to bury him. So they just dumped him and hoped for the best. Most likely two people involved. A grown male stiff is heavy, would be hard for anyone to move alone."

"That's insane. I mean, whoever did it certainly wasn't trying to cover it up, leaving his doctor's coat on, dumping him in a public place. They obviously wanted him to be found."

"That's not the craziest thing. You're not going to believe this next part."

I was pacing the sidewalk, occasionally glancing through the window into the restaurant where Juan was still drinking his coffee and staring at his phone.

"I'm not sure I want to know."

"He's missing a hand."

"A what?" I thought maybe I had heard him incorrectly. "Say that again, please. I though you said *hand. Missing a hand*."

"That's what I said, kid. A hand, like the kind you write with, eat with, brush your teeth with. Whoever killed the dude cut off his left hand after they shot him. Or at least, let's hope it was *after* he was shot and not before."

"That's crazy. What does that even mean?"

"One of two things. It could be a serial killer who keeps trophies, or it was a drug cartel hit, sending a message about what happens to people who cross them."

"Both of those seem pretty far-fetched, if you ask me. I mean, what would a serial killer want with Tanner Pope? Don't they usually go after women? And drug cartels, that's just bizarre. He's a doctor. He can get drugs all day long on his own good drugs, opiates. Why would he be involved with a drug cartel?"

"Don't know. Good question. Maybe he was selling, not buying, and something went wrong."

"This is starting to sound like the plot of a horror movie."

"People don't get murdered for no reason. The part about the hand is way off the record, not for public consumption. If it gets out, I'm screwed. It will come right back and hit me in the damn face, so don't burn me."

"I won't. You know I won't. But the whole thing is so unbelievable. I'm trying to process it. Shoot. I need to go. I'm meeting with someone right now, someone who was looking for Tanner. I guess I need to let him know what's going on. Is it public yet?"

"Soon."

"Does Suzanne know?"

"Yes, they sent a cop to her door. She apparently took the news very hard according, to my guys."

"Wow, okay. I will call her. I mean, he was still the father of her son, and the separation was new. It's still got to be devastating."

I leaned up against the brick wall of the restaurant and peered through the large picture window, back at my table, looking for Juan. Two abandoned cups of coffee sat in the middle of the table, and Juan's chair was empty. To me, he just became suspect number one.

14

ON THE RECORD

KERI CAME BY MY DESK in the newsroom that afternoon to tell me the great news—Fred had sent out a press release identifying the dead man as a local doctor named Tanner Pope. I could tell she was about to burst because she was so happy about finally learning the dead man's identity. It made me pause and think about what an odd job this was, that the name of a dead person elicited joy.

"That's great, Keri. I know you've been working hard on this case, waiting for a break." I tried to act like the information was news to me.

She was so excited I doubted she would pick up on anything in my voice or expression that might give me away. While I knew the information before anyone else, I couldn't tell a soul in the newsroom until the police confirmed it on the record. Otherwise I would have been breaching Kojak's confidence.

"Yes, I still don't know what took them so long. I guess because he's a semi-important person, *a doctor*, they wanted to make sure they notified the family first."

"That makes sense." I powered down my laptop and started to load it into my computer bag. Keri was standing at the edge of my desk, shifting awkwardly from foot to foot like a boxer warming up.

"So I should go there, to his family's house? Try and talk to his wife? Knock on her door? I have the address. It was in the press release."

It struck me that she knew the answers to her questions before she asked them, but just wanted confirmation from me that this horrible thing she was about to do—knock on the door of a murder victim's wife—was, in fact, what she was supposed to do.

I stopped loading my computer bag and turned to give Keri my full attention. Obviously she needed to try to talk to Suzanne. That's what journalists did in these situations. Because I knew Suzanne, the professional thing for me to do was to introduce her to Keri. But I still felt protective of Suzanne and wanted to shield her from the onslaught of media that was surely already descending upon her house. My boundaries were blurry. I decided not to let Keri know that I knew Suzanne. If Suzanne was going to talk to anyone, maintaining her trust was the only way to make that happen. I might be able to facilitate something between her and Keri in the coming days.

"You can try that. It's unlikely she will talk. After all, her husband was just murdered. But you never know. Dex is going to want you to at least *try*." My head was bent over my computer bag, trying not to make eye contact with Keri. I felt guilty for misleading her.

"But if they don't know who killed him, it might help for her to go on camera and plead for the public's help, asking people to call the police if they have any information about the crime. That would be very powerful coming from the widow."

"True. But my gut tells me this is not a case where that might happen. Let me think about it a little more. I'll make a few calls and see what I can learn about the case first before you do the drive-by. Give me about thirty minutes. I'll call you or text you. Okay?"

Keri looked like she was about to hug me. She gave me a toothy smile and bounced off toward her desk.

I dreaded what I had to do next. I knew it was time for me to call Suzanne, to give her my condolences, to warn her about the media tidal wave that was about to cascade on her. I wasn't sure how Suzanne was reacting to Tanner's death given, their rocky relationship and the way it had all ended. That's what friends did—lend support in difficult times. I had finally come to the conclusion that what Suzanne and I had formed, albeit under tragic circumstances, an unusual friendship.

At first I wanted to go to Suzanne's house and speak with her in person, but I decided against it, figuring there might be lots of reporters staking it out. Plus, there could be police questioning her or even guarding her house if they believed she might be in danger from the person who killed Tanner. I didn't want to risk being seen by anyone else. So I called her.

"Hello, Maddie, oh, thank God it's you. So you've heard. I'm sure you've heard." Suzanne's voice trailed off into tears. "I just can't believe it. How am I going to tell Winston? He'll be home from school any minute."

"You haven't told him yet? You didn't pick him up at school? Suzanne, everyone just sent out breaking news alerts. It's all over social media. What if someone says something to him?"

"Oh, God, you're right. What kind of mother am I? I need to go get him. Shit, he's probably already in the carpool line."

All I could hear was muffled crying through the phone. I immediately felt bad that I hadn't gone to her house. I felt helpless listening to her sobbing on the other end of the line and not being able to do anything. I wanted to reach through the phone and give her a big hug.

"Suzanne is anyone with you. Can I call someone for you?"

"My sister. My sister, Jessie, is on her way from Chicago. I called her. She's getting the first flight out. I'm just in such shock. I don't even know what to do or where to begin. I need to call Tanner's parents. I don't know if I can do this, Maddie."

I was surprised by the depth of Suzanne's grief, but then I realized that relationships are complicated. On the one hand, her marriage was over, but on the other hand, she had a long history with this man, and a child. You don't just stop loving someone overnight, even if that someone doesn't treat you well. Plus, she also had to be thinking about what a tragedy it was for her son to lose his father.

"Suzanne, listen to me. You do need to call Tanner's family, but you don't need to talk to anyone else. Don't answer the door. Don't answer the phone unless it's a number you recognize and it's someone you really want to talk to. Your house is soon going to be *crawling* with media. A reporter from my station included. You have no obligation to speak with anyone."

I felt overwhelmed with a great amount of concern for Suzanne. It was like I was transported back to the day we returned to our house in New Jersey after my mother's murder, before Roger was arrested. Even though I was just a little girl, I clearly remember the news media camping out in the street in front of our house. We had left my grandparent's house in Pennsylvania the day of the crime because it was swarming with cops. It was also surrounded by yellow tape. My grandparents went to a hotel, and we went to stay with Belle at her house in New Jersey. But soon Roger decided it was time for us to go home to *our* house.

Their bright television lights bathed our front yard in a

soft yellow glow as the reporters stood in a line in front of their cameras along the curb. I remember peeking through the beige blinds when Roger left the room, pulling them back just enough so I could see them but they couldn't see me. Sometimes they would catch me peeking at them and point at me. I would duck down into the couch and giggle, like it was a game.

I guess Roger wanted to show everyone that he was not afraid of their speculation that he had something to do with my mother's death. Belle later told me that he had freely done interviews with police without a lawyer present to help them eliminate him as a suspect and find the real killer.

Those days with Roger after my mother's death were fuzzy, but I clearly remembered the doorbell ringing again and again and Roger peering through the blinds to see who it was.

"Damn reporters," he'd mumble. "Maddie, stay away from the window. I don't want them trying to get a picture of you. And definitely don't answer the door."

The phone rang off the hook. Roger would let the answering machine pick it up. We would sit at the kitchen table and listen to the messages.

"Sir, I'm sorry to bother you at a time like this, but I'm calling from the Tribune. I'd like to speak with you about your wife. Maybe talking about her would help bring some closure to your tragedy. It might jog someone's memory in the community maybe someone saw something and would come forward to the police. Please call me back and we'll set up a time to get together."

Even though I was very young, I couldn't forget the look on Roger's face when he heard those calls. He looked lost. Thinking back on it from an adult perspective, I now realized he truly was lost. He had lost his wife and was about to lose his child and his freedom. The buzzards were circling around him. It was only a matter of time. When a woman was murdered, it was almost always the husband. The reporters knew it and Roger knew it. When the police finally knew it, they would come for him. And they did. One day there was a knock on the door, and it wasn't a reporter.

"Suzanne, what can I do to help?" I heard myself say after I pulled myself out of the reverie.

"Maddie, can you come over, as a friend? Not as a reporter. I just don't have anyone else to turn to until Jessie gets here. You deal with stuff like this in your job all the time. You will know how to handle it."

I was silent as I let the gravity of her plea sink in. For the first time in my career, I had no idea what to do.

When Adam was dying, I used to cry alone in my car at stoplights. People would look over at me and stare. I'm sure they thought I was crazy. But something about being alone in my car felt safe despite that it was a fish bowl on wheels.

My car had always been my safe haven, especially when the kids were babies. After sleepless nights when one twin would wake up as soon as I got the other one back to sleep, I couldn't wait to wrap myself in the solitude of my car. In the morning I would leave them in the strong, capable hands of our nanny at the time, Daisy, and skip to my car. I set my travel coffee mug in the cupholder, put down the windows, and turned up the radio just enough to feel celebratory, but not enough to distract me from my, peaceful respite. Other than the shower or the running trail, the car was the only place I was ever truly alone with my thoughts.

Now I wasn't so sure I wanted to be alone with my thoughts. My head was swirling with so much information. I kept replaying the facts in a loop, hoping I might get some new understanding each time I reran the timeline.

The facts—I met Suzanne after her accident at the road race.

She told me she thought her husband, Tanner, had poisoned her and was trying to kill her. She was afraid to leave him because she was concerned that he would try to take their son away from her. She also suspected him of having an affair with a mystery woman nicknamed G6, a woman I thought might be a prostitute, and who had just given birth. The woman, Maria Lopez, has a brother named Juan. Juan told me Tanner was *not* romantically involved with his sister, and that Tanner was missing. Suzanne told me Tanner had left her. Tanner wound up dead. What was I missing?

The man behind me, in a shiny silver Audi, laid on his horn as I daydreamed at the green light. It wasn't a gentle reminder to go, but a self-important long beep that annoyed me enough to want to remain sitting there for a few more seconds.

"Chill out," I said. "I'm sure you're not in that big of a hurry."

My phone was vibrating in the cup holder. I tried hard to set a good example for the kids by not texting and driving. This meant ignoring the texts even when the children weren't in the car. I had to be consistent. As a runner, I had watched drivers swerve and almost hit me while texting, many times.

When I first met Adam, texting was just starting to become a thing. I had a flip phone, and each key had three letters on it. So in order to text you had to hit each key multiple times until it got to the correct letter. It was tedious and time-consuming. But this meant when you received a text, you knew the person had worked for it. Oh, how I loved those early texts from Adam, about how I looked that day or how he couldn't wait to see me that night. Now my text messages were almost always a source of angst because they generally involved someone needing something from me.

I turned up the radio and tried to ignore the incessant vibration.

You're giving me a million reasons to let you go. You're giving me a million reasons to quit the show, Lady Gaga crooned in her hipster, country pop tune.

I sang along with the song, not caring that people could probably hear my crappy voice through my open window as traffic crawled. I wasn't sure where I was going. I had told Suzanne I was coming over, but there were so many reasons why this was a bad idea. The number one reason was that I was a journalist and I didn't need to insert myself in the middle of a murder investigation. I was already in too deep with Suzanne as it was. If the investigators thought I knew any information that might help solve the case, they had every right to call me in for questioning. That wouldn't look good for me or the station.

I finally glanced down at my phone as I sat stationary in a never-ending traffic jam. I clicked on the most recent text. It was from Juan.

The doctor is dead. We are very sad. Do you know what happened? —Juan

I had forgotten to circle back with Juan after he left the restaurant. Maybe he was telling the truth. Maybe Tanner had just been a friend to Maria and his family. Or, maybe Juan had fooled me. Maybe he was using his concern for Tanner's disappearance to cover up that he was involved in his death.

And then there was the missing hand. I couldn't get my mind off that bizarre detail. I wondered if Suzanne knew about it.

At the next exit, I pulled off the highway. I texted Suzanne and told her I would be there as soon as I could, but that I needed to make a stop first. I figured the later I got to her house, the better. Under the cloak of darkness, I would be less likely to be noticed by the reporters and photographers camping out in the street in front of her house.

I also texted Keri and told her I had learned that the family wasn't talking to the media right now, so there was no need to go by the house, but that I would keep her posted. If at some point there was an opportunity to interview Suzanne, I would make sure it was with Keri. But until I knew more about what was going on, I wanted Suzanne to stay out of the spotlight.

Keri texted back and said that Dex was making her go to Suzanne's house anyway, just in case she changed her mind and decided to talk. I knew Keri had no choice but to do what Dex asked her to do. I was just glad I wouldn't be the reporter feeling desperate tonight.

On instinct I decided instead of heading to Suzanne's I would pay Juan a visit at La Fiesta. When I finally pulled up to the restaurant after making my way back across town in the insufferable rush hour traffic, it was crawling with police. The parking lot was cordoned off with yellow tape that read *police line, do not cross* in bold black letters. Crime scene investigators from the Tirey County CSI team were coming and going from the building with large brown paper bags and boxes of items labeled *evidence* in large red letters. They wore blue plastic gloves as they loaded the boxes and bags into unmarked white vans. Knowing it often took several hours to get a search warrant, I realized that the focus on Maria and her family must have started immediately after Tanner's body was identified.

I parked across the street and sat in my car, watching the commotion. Nobody noticed me amidst the frenzy of activity. What now? I wasn't there in my official capacity as a journalist, but everyone would assume otherwise. I knew I should call Keri and let her know what was going on so she and her photographer could come get video of the search, but there were so many ethical entanglements for me in this case that I had no idea how to unravel them.

Out my driver's side window, I saw Kojak leaning up against the brick wall in the back of the restaurant, sucking on a lollipop and staring down at his phone. I wanted to get his attention, but he was facing in the other direction, and he was too far away for me to yell at him without getting other people's attention. So I took advantage of his phone-centered gaze and texted him. He jerked his head up and swiveled his neck in both directions until he spotted me in my silver SUV wedged in between two unmarked cop cars across the street. He put his phone in his pocket and started toward me.

Kojak opened the passenger door and slid into the seat, glancing around. I could see the sweat pouring in droplets from his forehead onto the black frames of his Wayfarers. I guessed he must have been standing outside for a while.

"This is too fresh right now. You don't need to be here," he said, with a nervous catch in his voice that I had never heard before. "I'm trying to keep you out of this whole thing. But you need to work with me here. You need to get out of here before someone spots you."

"I get it. I know. And I appreciate what you're trying to do for me but I need to know what the hell is going on. Why are they here? Do they really think Maria had something to do with Tanner's murder?"

"Apparently Major Crimes got a call earlier today from a dude out in the country. He and his wife bought an old freezer from the restaurant two days ago. They told him they were replacing all their old freezers with new models. Bought it on Craigslist. Came to Oak City and loaded it up in his old pickup truck and hauled it home. Anyway, got the thing to his house, plugged it in in his garage. A few days later, his wife decides to put some stuff in it. Opens it up, and its real small inside, smaller than he expected from looking at it on the outside. But then he thinks about the great deal he got, and decides to let it go. Still something ain't right. The bottom is uneven, and everything is sitting kind of funny inside the thing. So he pries up the white panel at the bottom of the freezer and finds something in a bloody plastic bag. At first, he thinks it's some leftover meat that somehow got caught underneath the panel. But it's *not*, guess what it is.

"I've got no idea. A gun? Money?"

"Nope, better than that."

"No frigging idea. Just tell me. I don't have time for jokes today."

"No joke. Just about the strongest piece of evidence I've ever seen in a murder case. It was a hand—a hand they think belongs to one Tanner Pope."

15

THE HUM

I FELT OLD AND TIRED as I drove through the city streets across town to get to Suzanne's house. I looked in the rearview mirror and could see the short, curly broken hairs surrounding my face from years of harsh ponytail wearing. They used to look charming, even endearing. Now they just made me look weary.

I lost a lot of weight when Adam was dying, and it wasn't flattering. It made my cheeks hollow and my eyes sink into my skull. My skin, once elastic and healthy, sagged because it had nowhere to go. I eventually gained the weight back, but the formerly youthful, ruddy glow that used to define my face was replaced by an unbecoming grayish pallor. I had neglected my health, and it was time to get back to taking care of myself.

It occurred to me that maybe I needed some sun, a vacation with the kids, in a tropical paradise where I could put my phone down and just look at the water. Water had always been my go-to for healing. How long had it been since I took the kids to the beach? Too long. Not since Adam died. I made a mental note to look at our calendar and schedule a beach trip for the kids' summer break.

I still didn't know what I was going to say to Suzanne. I also didn't know how I was going to slip into her house undetected, past the throngs of media people outside. Part of me wanted to advise her to just speak to them, and then they would go away. But with so many unanswered questions, it felt prudent as her friend to tell her to hold off. I knew how easily people's intentions could be manipulated by an unfortunate placement of words during in an interview. Throughout my career I had tried hard to discern people's intentions during interviews. I tried to honor those intentions by making sure their words matched them. I often asked people to repeat their statements when I didn't think this match was achieved. I wanted to give them another chance to say what they really meant.

When I pulled onto Suzanne's street, I slowed to avoid hitting the cars parked haphazardly on both sides. When I got closer to her house, I could hear the hum of the news vans, their generators powering the huge transmitting masts that reached high into the night sky. They were parked near Suzanne's driveway, and blocked my view of the front of her house. I decided to pass the house and try to find a parking spot away from the fray.

I glanced over at Suzanne's well-lit, white brick home. It looked like every light in the house was on, like she was preparing for a party rather than a press invasion. Reporters and photographers gathered in a U-shape around the front steps of the home. It confused me for a second. Why they were all on her private property without her permission. Normally we stood in the street so no one could accuse us of trespassing. But then I noticed someone at the top of the steps, on the edge of the porch. It was Suzanne. I could barely make her out behind the large bouquet of microphones attached to the top of a metal stand in front of her. I couldn't believe my eyes. Suzanne Parker was holding a press conference.

I finally found a parking space about a quarter mile from the home, and pulled into it. I was lucky to find two spots where I could glide in. It was a long walk, but I figured the cover of darkness would give me anonymity as I approached the house. If my media colleagues saw me go inside, they would assume I was scooping them—getting what we called *a sit-down* or *one-on-one* interview with Suzanne. This was always better than interviewing someone at a press conference and getting the same sound bites everyone else was getting.

I crept down the street, the distant glow of the photographers' lights looking like a constellation of stars that had fallen to earth and wound up at the foot of Suzanne's steps. As I got closer, I could see she was reading from a small yellow legal pad, and then looking up. Next to her was a slighter woman, also brunette, who had her hand on the middle of Suzanne's back. I assumed this was Suzanne's sister, Jessie, from Chicago.

As I approached the sidewalk, I saw the petite woman I assumed was the sister put her hand up in a stop motion to the crowd. She grabbed Suzanne's shoulder, spun her around, and steered her back inside the house like a robot. The group began to disperse towards their news vans. I spotted Keri in the distance, with a photographer named Marcus. They headed toward their van, which was parked in the street, right next to Suzanne's mailbox. I was glad had Keri ignored my suggestion to stay away. I would have felt horrible if she had missed the press conference.

I could only imagine what Suzanne's neighbors must be thinking of the chaos on their street. People always threatened to call the police on us, telling us we had no right to be camped out in front of their homes. Under the law, we did have the right to be on a public street and shoot what we could see from that vantage point. But even though we had the legal right, it didn't always feel right.

I decided to text Suzanne and tell her I was there, hoping she could tell me how to get into her house without coming in through the front door.

"I'm here. Don't want to run into other media. Do you have a back door?"

I sat there in the shadows, wondering why in the world Suzanne would have held a press conference after I had advised her not to talk to the media. My pride was dented, because I expected her to follow my advice. On the other hand, I guessed she felt like she had nothing to lose. Maybe it was cathartic for her to talk about it.

Side flagstone path, right side of the house if you're facing it. Hug house. Winds to back door. Meet you there, Suzanne's text read.

I replied "K," and then, crossed a neighbor's lawn to stay away from her well-lit driveway, which looked more like a tarmac waiting for a plane to land. I scurried with my head down, trying not to be spotted by anyone I knew. Just as I rounded the back corner of Suzanne's house, a door that led onto a back porch swung open. In a thin shaft of light from the open door, I could see the woman from the press conference, a diminutive brunette with high cheekbones—the woman I assumed was Suzanne's sister even though they looked nothing alike. She was wearing black leggings, an oversized gray shirt, and black sandals. She reached down the porch steps and extended a hand to me as she held the door open with the other.

"You must be Maddie.," She smiled. "I've heard a lot about you, that you've been very helpful to Suzanne."

"You must be her sister." I managed a smile that I wasn't

sure she could see in the darkness.

I grabbed her left hand in an awkward fingertip shake.

"No." She chuckled, as she ushered me up the stairs and into the screened porch. "I could see why you might think that, though. Jessie, her sister, is still on her way here from Chicago. Her plane lands in about an hour. I'm Suzanne's lawyer."

"Lawyer?" I said, with more surprise than I intended, mostly because the woman was dressed so casually and seemed so comfortable in Suzanne's home more like a close friend than an attorney. "Why does she need a lawyer?"

We were still standing in the near pitch darkness of the back porch. Even though I was closer to her now, we had moved away from the shaft of light, and I could barely distinguish her outline. I strained to see her eyes as they caught the light coming from behind the ajar porch door.

"I'm pretty sure you know the answer to that one," the woman replied, smugly, her formerly friendly tone morphing into battle mode. "Her husband is dead. They don't have a suspect. She was in the process of leaving him. Not a good scenario. She needs to protect herself."

I stood there quietly, thinking about how this tiny lamb of a woman appeared to be more of a wolf. I could picture her in the courtroom, her stature tricking people into thinking she was not a formidable opponent. And then, without warning, she would pounce, bringing her fury to the unsuspecting person on the witness stand before he or she even knew what was going on. She was here to protect Suzanne, and no one was getting by her if she had anything to say about it. Even me.

"Come on in," the little lamb said, too cheerfully. "Suzanne has been waiting for you. You didn't bring a camera or any kind of recording device with you, did you? I know you're a journalist. Can't be too careful," the wolf said.

"No, nothing like that. I am here as a friend, not as a reporter." I tried my best not to sound insulted by her question.

People like this woman really pushed my buttons. People who casually wielded passive aggression like a machete. I was used to handling arrogant gatekeepers. I knew better than to let her see my hand. I had to remain cool and try to win her over.

I followed her into a posh den that looked like something out of a Restoration Hardware catalog. Suzanne was sitting on the biggest wraparound white couch I had ever seen. In front of her was a massive, distressed wooden coffee table that held nothing on it but a large octagonal silver bowl. Above the table hung a modern light fixture with about a thousand tiny glass crystals dangling from it.

Suzanne looked like she came with the Restoration Hardware showroom. Her long jet-black hair was flat ironed and cascaded across her shoulders. Her eyes were accented with black liner, and she wore her trademark bright red lipstick. She was wearing a tight-fitting, black jersey dress cinched with a simple back belt with a silver clasp. She stood to hug me when I walked into the room, reaching out as I approached. Her face looked genuinely relieved.

"Maddie, you're really here, in person!"

"Well, I didn't want you to be alone until your sister arrived, but I guess you already have company." I nodded at the wolf, trying not to sound too annoyed, and then gave Suzanne a sincere hug.

I sat on the couch, feeling frumpier than ever in my conservative black dress pants, modest flowy white blouse, and black flats.

"Oh, you mean Shandra?" Suzanne gestured grandly to the wolf, who had perched herself at the far end of the couch.

Shandra was staring at her phone like she wasn't listening to us, even though I knew she most certainly was.

"She's an old friend from college. She's done a bunch of legal work for me. She was in the process of working on my divorce settlement. She felt like it would be prudent to get out ahead of this thing. So we just released a statement."

"What did it say, if you don't mind me asking?"

"You know, the usual stuff people say in situations like this. *I want to find out who murdered my husband, the father of my son. Justice needs to be served in this case. We need the public's help to catch the killer. Blah, blah, blah.*"

Blah, blah, blah? Who says that when they're talking about a murder? I was starting to feel uncomfortable, between Suzanne's flippant tone and Shandra's scrutiny.

"Shandra said it would make them go away, the reporters. They've been camping out here since Tanner's name went public this afternoon, leaving their water bottles and fast food wrappers in the street, shining their bright lights in everyone's faces, and taking up all the parking. My neighbors must be furious." Suzanne waved her hand in an exaggerated gesture toward the street.

Again I found it strange that her perception about the media's disrespect for her neighborhood was anywhere near the top of her list of concerns

"How is Winston?"

"Devastated. Poor little guy. I sent him to his friend's house. I didn't want him to be in the middle of this chaos."

"He's not here! Don't you think he needs you right now?"

"You know how resilient kids are. He'll get through this. I'll get him counseling if he needs it."

I didn't like how this visit was going. I went to Suzanne's house expecting to comfort someone who was grieving, but instead I found someone who seemed inconvenienced by the whole thing. I knew Suzanne had no love lost for Tanner, but her son had lost his father. Her misplaced flippancy sent a chill down my spine. Had I misjudged this woman completely? Was she secretly happy that someone had taken care of her problem by getting rid of Tanner? I decided I couldn't be there one more minute.

"Well, it looks like you and Shandra have everything under control here. And your sister is on the way, so I think you're in good hands. I just wanted to stop by and make sure you were okay.," I stood from the couch.

"You don't have to go. Stay, have a drink. You will love my sister. She's a trip."

I was already walking toward the back door, her voice trailing after me. I had no interest in making this a girls' night. Nothing about this situation felt right.

"No, really, I can't stay. My babysitter agreed to stay late again with the kids. I really need to get home and relieve her."

Suzanne spun me around and pulled me in for another hug, holding on tightly this time. It lasted about three seconds too long. I was starting to feel like I might scream if she didn't pull away soon. She finally let go and backed away from me.

"You have been so helpful to me in so many ways. I don't know how I can ever repay you," she said, pretending not to notice my awkwardness.

She put her hands on my shoulders.

"I didn't do anything. Just listened."

"Listening is just what I needed. It's so important. Few people know how to do it well. I guess that's why you're a good journalist. You are a good listener. It's your job," Suzanne chuckled, manically.

I left the way I came in, through the back porch and into the dark night. I zigzagged across the neighbor's yard, wanting to get as much distance between myself and Suzanne as I could.

I was a good listener, that was true, but I had a growing feeling that there was something I wasn't hearing.

"So this giraffe gave birth at a zoo somewhere in the

Midwest. It was all caught on tape—the birth, the pregnancy. The whole thing went viral. People became obsessed with it. So Dex wants you to use the video and find some psychologist to talk about why it was such a phenomenon, why people are so hooked on this. Are they looking for something to distract them from all the horrible things going on in the world?"

"Really?" I sat on my screened-in porch, sipping coffee and looking out at my neighbor's free-range chickens walking up and down an embankment right on the edge of my property line. I could never understand how they just stayed in her yard and didn't wander off into the street, but she explained to me that they stayed where the food was, not unlike human beings.

"It's either that, or the lady trying to save some eagles in a nest near Griffin Lake. The Wildlife Commission is about to do a controlled burn to get rid of underbrush, decrease the wildfire risk. The eaglets can't fly Yet so they'll be collateral damage. While they're not on the endangered species list, they have something called *protected status.* But apparently state wildlife officials can override that for the burn."

I watched the chickens pecking at the ground, looking for food, I assumed. Maybe my neighbor wasn't feeding them like she should. They hung around with one duck that we all called *Chuck* because he thought he was a chicken. The chicken-duck lost his duck family to a hungry fox, so our neighbors put Chuck in with the chickens and he never looked back.

Janie said, "But I think Dex really wants the giraffe thing since she just gave birth today. We can do the eagle story tomorrow."

I wondered how it had come to this. How had I wound up covering such inane stories? It was a redundant question. I knew the answer. I made a choice to change. Now it was up to me to embrace this change. People loved animal stories. *Give them what they want,* I remembered a news director in one of my earlier jobs saying to me. After all, who was I to judge what information people really needed to have?

"Okay, I'll do the giraffe thing. Do you have a psychologist in mind?"

"Funny you should ask. I do. She's a social psychology professor at N.C. State. I already spoke with her. I think she will be great on camera. Her name is Dr. Wanda Partridge. I'll email you her contact info. She's available at eleven, so I already set it up."

"Before you talked to me?" I said, with feigned anger.

"I knew you'd do it." She laughed.

And she was right. I was nothing, if not a team player.

"By the way, what's going on with the murder case?" I hadn't spoken with Suzanne, Kojak or Keri in a few days. On the one hand, I was trying to keep my distance from it, but on the other hand, I couldn't help being curious.

"You didn't hear?"

"No, that's why I'm asking you."

"Oh, I just figured you got news alerts on your phone."

"I used to, but I turned them off. Too much distraction. Overwhelming."

"Well they made an arrest a few hours ago. Some woman. Isn't that weird? A lady killer, a black widow. She's on her way to the jail right now to be processed. Turned herself in at the police department."

"A woman? What's her name?" My heart started racing. My vision started to blur. I couldn't see the details on the chickens anymore, just blobs of orange and white waddling around in front of me. I felt nauseous. It couldn't be, but it had to be. *Suzanne.* She shouldn't have done that press conference. I should have stopped her from talking. It was all my fault.

"Let me look."

I could hear Janie tapping on her keyboard, looking for the press release from the police department, which was likely buried in the thousands of emails in her inbox. I started focusing on the ambient noise of the newsroom in the background—people talking, phones ringing, scanners chattering.

"Lopez, Maria. Maria Lopez. I don't know what the connection is yet. Investigators haven't said much."

"Thanks," I said, sounding a little too shocked.

It was like being on a train that jumped the tracks. My brain couldn't wrap around the fact that I was going from Suzanne to Maria in a split second. It didn't make any sense to me that a *woman* was behind such a gruesome act. From what I had learned from Juan, Maria didn't have a motive to hurt Tanner. The hand they found in the freezer from the restaurant must have been Tanner's. It was too much of a coincidence. But did that mean *she* was responsible for his death?

"You okay?" Janie finally interrupted my stunned silence.

"Sure, got to go. Tell Buster I will meet him at the professor's office on campus at eleven."

"Will do. You sure you're okay?"

"I'm sure."

But I wasn't sure.

Dr. Wanda Partridge explained. "So it's a collective experience shared by everyone, and gives people a sense of hope. In the not-so-distant past, people gathered around the television set and shared important events, like the first moonwalk or a high-profile trial, for example. Today, the Internet is the collective force that brings people together. The only difference is that because there's so much noise on the Internet, it's very difficult for something to stand out, to take hold, to get people's attention."

I wasn't going to need to ask the professor many questions. I just had to prompt her here and there with head nods and positive murmurs to keep her rolling. I was trying to pay attention to what she was saying, but I kept thinking about Maria being arrested. It was so incongruous. She just had a baby. How would she have had the strength to move his body and cut off his hand? The only thing I could think of was that someone must have helped her, someone like Juan. Just thinking about being in such proximity to him made me shiver. I remembered how he held my hand too tightly for too long when we had coffee.

"The shared experience of the giraffe birth is almost like a rebirthing of hope for everyone who watches it, separately on their computers, on their phones, on their iPads. Alone, with others, it doesn't matter, because the experience is still a shared one through the collective connectivity of the Internet."

It took me a minute to realize Dr. Partridge had stopped talking. I was so lost in my own thoughts.

"Can I ask you a question off-topic, not on camera?" I turned around to look at Buster. He nodded and pointed the lens down to make it obvious we weren't recording.

"Sure. Shoot."

Dr. Partridge sat waiting for me to ask my question. Her curly red hair was barely contained by a multi-colored scrunchy. She peered at me over the rims of her bright blue glasses perched on the tip of her nose. She looked like a middle-aged hipster who had made a wrong turn and ended up in a professor's office instead of at a coffee house.

"What kind of woman murders someone? I mean, it's very unusual, correct?"

"Well, I'm not a forensic psychologist, and I really haven't done any profiling, but I can tell you that women are less likely to be violent. Generally, if a woman kills someone, it's in self-defense."

"But what if it's not in self-defense? I mean, what kind of person, what kind of woman is capable of doing that?"

"Well, in general, and this is a big generalization, women,

like I said, tend to be less physically violent. They are more likely to be emotionally abusive if anything. But if you mean cold, calculating, planning someone's murder, in general, a woman would have to be a sociopath. The most likely scenario is that the victim is in her way, for whatever reason, and she wants to get rid of that person. Again, this is a sweeping generalization based on what I have read over the years. I am by no means an expert in this area."

"What about postpartum depression? Is a woman who is suffering from this more likely to lash out, to be violent?"

"Postpartum depression can manifest itself in many ways. Women are often so sad and desperate that they can harm their newborns."

"Could it cause a woman to want to do harm to someone else, like the baby's father, perhaps?"

"Sure, in extreme circumstances, I think so. Although, I am not aware of any documented cases of this."

Buster cleared his throat behind me. He knew exactly why I was asking these questions, and I anticipated a tongue lashing from him once we got in the car.

Why do you care? he would ask. I wished I didn't care. I decided that as soon as I was done with this interview, I had to talk to Kojak and find out what they had on Maria.

"So back to the main topic. Are we good? Was I clear on the collective hope issue? I don't mean to be rude, but I have a class to teach in about fifteen minutes, so I really need to wrap this up."

"Absolutely I really appreciate your time. Thanks again for agreeing to speak with us. I will shoot you a text and let you know when the story will air."

As we got up to leave, all I could think about was that hope was something I could use a lot more of at this moment.

"What in the world?" I said for the fifth time.

"I know it's crazy. I agree, but it's strong."

Kojak leaned back in his tired office chair. The blue material on the armrests were faded from the sun and frayed from years of overuse. His old wooden desk was scarred with ink stains, coffee mug rings, and cigarette burns from the days when they allowed smoking in offices. I was pretty sure Kojak had continued to smoke in here well after that law was passed, until he quit. He was not one to follow rules when they didn't suit him.

"But it makes no sense. What about cutting off the hand? I can't imagine a woman doing that."

"They think she had help, for sure. Probably one of her brothers. But she's not talking. Her lawyer shut us down. So she's going down alone."

"But she just had a baby. There is absolutely no way she did this alone and for what reason?"

"I agree. It's crazy. Pretty sure one of the brothers did the deed and then cut the hand off for good measure, to make it look like a drug thing."

"If they did it under some misguided belief that they were protecting her honor, why would they let her take the rap for it?"

"Because they think a jury is less likely to convict a woman, especially one who just had a baby."

"What else do they have on her?"

"Besides the hand in the freezer? Pretty sure that's enough."

"But it doesn't specifically tie Maria to anything. It could have been any person in her family, anyone who had access to that restaurant."

"Precisely. But the physical evidence is airtight, let me tell you. My guys found the gun in a vat of salsa in the walk-in refrigerator. No prints, wiped clean. Well, not clean. It was covered in hot peppers, but there were no prints to be found.

Still the ballistics matched the slug we found in the doctor."

"Okay, still strong against someone in that family, but why focus on her specifically?"

"They got a tip, anonymous caller, saw her at a grocery store with him the night before he disappeared. They were getting into a car in the parking lot of a Food Stop. Woman caller didn't want to be identified, didn't want to get involved, but it checked out with the guy who rolls the carts in. Showed him her picture, and he positively identified Maria."

"Okay, I guess it is pretty strong. But maybe she just led him to the spot where her brothers killed him."

"Possible, but that still makes her an accessory. If she knew about what they were going to do in advance, it makes her just as guilty under the law as the person who pulled the trigger."

I looked out the window streaked with yellow lines of pollen. It looked like someone had tried to wash it off and then gave up. Kojak's office was on the seventh floor of an ancient building that desperately needed some attention. Around his office were piles of abandoned files stacked on top of battered metal filing cabinets. There were dogeared yellow labels in the square metal brackets on the front of each drawer written in fading blue ink: *Open Files*, *Closed Files*, *Homicide*, *Sexual Assault*.

"Face it, they got her. And in record time. We got no choice but to move forward with this prosecution. There's a lot of pressure from Madame District Attorney to get this show on the road. You going to the doctor's funeral?"

"Yes. I haven't spoken to Suzanne since that first night. She lawyered-up. It got weird. I had to extricate myself from the whole thing."

"She lawyered-up?"

"Yes I thought it was odd, too. But she's an educated, professional woman. I guess she decided it was the prudent thing to do."

"That's one way to look at it."

We sat in silence for a minute. I knew we were thinking the same thing. Was Tanner Pope's murder really solved?

Tanner's funeral could not take place until Maria's arrest because his body was being held at the state medical examiner's morgue as evidence until the case was officially closed. Following Maria's arrest, his body was released to Suzanne and she had him cremated.

The day before the service, Suzanne emailed me about Tanner's wishes to be cremated. *Maddie, it would mean so much to me if you came to the service tomorrow. I don't want to put you in an uncomfortable situation professionally, but I would love to have you there for support. You've been so good to me. Think about it.*

It felt awkward having this kind of personal communication with Suzanne. We had shared a lot in a short period of time, but after seeing the callous way she acted that night after Tanner's death, I realized I really didn't know her at all. She was a stranger whose path had crossed mine, but we had little to nothing in common. Still I felt obligated to do the right thing and go to Tanner's funeral despite my discomfort.

I finally revealed to Dex that I was friends with Suzanne. He appreciated my candor and I could not cover the story from here on out because it would be a conflict of interest, but he also urged me to stay on top of it from the background and feed Keri anything I could to help our coverage. It was the classic conundrum of the news business: don't report about people you know personally unless they happen to have a good story.

I agreed to Dex's terms and took them with a grain of salt. If there was anything that I could give Keri that wouldn't compromise what Suzanne had said to me in confidence, I would do it. Otherwise, I was going to the funeral as a private citizen, not as a reporter.

Tanner's funeral was being held at a stately old Episcopalian church in the heart of Oak City. Despite the floor-to-ceiling stained glass windows, the stone building was dark and cold inside. The ancient organ droned through the sanctuary, bouncing off the cathedral ceiling to produce an eerie, somber dirge.

Suzanne fit the role of the grieving wife elegantly in her snug, chic black dress, with a tight wad of tissues balled up in her hand. She stood at the back of the church and greeted people as they walked in, with quick hugs and mournful nods, as gentle tears cascaded down her cheeks. I was confused by what appeared to be her genuine grief in the face of the flippancy I had witnessed at her house.

A little boy, I assumed was Winston, stood in between Suzanne and the woman I now understood was her sister, Jessie. There was no doubt they were sisters, with their shared porcelain skin and jet-black locks. The boy extended his hand to visitors, looking every bit the uncomfortable young son of a dead man.

I felt sorry for Winston as I stood in line, knowing a child his age had no real capacity to understand mortality, especially the murder of his father. I knew how hard my own children, especially Blake, had taken Adam's death. I also knew it was not a loss a child would ever get over.

"You came." Suzanne's face lit up when she saw me. I still couldn't figure out why she was so drawn to me. She pulled me in for a real hug, unlike the limp air hugs she had given the people in line in front of me. "Thank you."

Out of the corner of my eye I could see that the people behind me wore curious looks. They were wondering what our relationship was. Winston shuffled his feet and then looked up at me with a questioning gaze. I pulled away from

Suzanne and extended my hand to the little boy.

"I'm so sorry young man."

"Thanks. Me too." He glanced up at his mom with a concerned look, as if he might have said something wrong.

"I just can't believe he's really gone." Suzanne put her hands on Winston's shoulders.

Instead of gentle tears, large tears were now pouring down her red cheeks. "And for what? An affair? A jealous woman's rage." She bowed her head and touched her forehead to the top of Winston's head, burying it in his hair.

I was shocked that she was talking so openly about the murder case in front of Winston. She had lowered her voice so others couldn't hear her, but there was no way he didn't.

I almost believed that she really missed Tanner. *Almost.* Then I watched Suzanne center the clasp of her thin silver belt on her dress. It was askew from all the hugging. Then she smoothed the right side of her hair down and pulled it forward over her ear. They were almost imperceptible, but deliberate movements. They were not the movements of a woman consumed and distracted by grief. I knew grief, and I was not witnessing it.

16

JURY OF HER PEERS

KERI WAS ASSIGNED to cover Maria's trial, but she had scheduled a vacation months before the trial date was set. It included nonrefundable plane tickets, so I had to fill in for several days until she returned. Dex suddenly decided it *wasn't* a conflict of interest for me to cover the case because I didn't know Tanner personally, just Suzanne. I vehemently disagreed with his logic, explaining that in an unrelated capacity, Tanner had been Adam's doctor at one time. Despite my strong protests, I lost the battle because we simply didn't have enough people to cover it. I was stuck in the courtroom for a week.

Suzanne sat stoically in the front row, on a wooden pew just behind the prosecutor. She was always pulling tissues out of her big silver bag, and her sister, Jessie, sat nestled next to her, leaning against her like a baby bird. It looked like they were propping one another up. While they weren't twins, they looked like clones of one another, with their long dark hair, creamy white skin, and bright red lipstick.

Suzanne was tight-lipped once the trial started, nodding at me from across the courtroom when I walked in every morning, but never stopping to chat in the hallway during the breaks. I wasn't sure why she was keeping her distance from me. We had talked a few times between the funeral and the trial, mostly through emails and texts. I had gone to her house one time for coffee to pay my condolences, but that was the last time we spoke face-to-face. It was fair to say our friendship, or whatever it was, had run its course. I was relieved that it was over.

I still couldn't shake the creepy feeling she gave me at Tanner's funeral—the little signs that made me question her grief. But as time passed, I started to question my observations from that day. Maybe I was being too hard on her? After all, it was normal for her to have had mixed feelings about a man she thought was trying to kill her in the weeks leading up to his death. Maybe her grief was for Winston's sake.

After Keri returned from vacation and started covering the trial again, I remained a voyeur, watching excerpts of her coverage in between my *snake-on-the-loose* story in an elementary school, and the monkey at one of the local university research laboratories who could do fifth grade math. I did a deep dive into the online coverage of the trial every day on my phone while I waited for the kids in the carpool line.

It looked like the state's case was falling apart. The defense had done a good job of punching holes in the Maria and Tanner relationship theory. They revealed that Tanner was on the board of the local human trafficking organization *Stop Human Trafficking in its Tracks*. His lawyers said that in that role, he had reached out to Maria and helped her get away from an unhealthy relationship where the boyfriend was advertising her on a website for sex and setting up *dates* in local hotel rooms. Maria's defense attorneys said Tanner learned of her situation from a counselor affiliated with the group. He was passionate about the issue and was eager to do more than just sit on the board. Tanner was the kind of person who wanted to get his hands dirty, not just sit around a table and talk about the annual fundraiser at the local country club.

The boyfriend who pimped Maria, Raymond Fischer, was arrested after Tanner went to the police and showed them Fischer's postings online advertising her services. An undercover officer did a sting where he pretended he was meeting Maria for sex, and when Raymond asked the officer for the money, they arrested him on the spot. After this incident, Tanner stayed involved with Maria and her family, visiting her frequently. He connected her with good prenatal medical care once she found out she was pregnant with a child that was presumably Raymond's.

One thing that still stumped me was the alleged text Maria had sent to Tanner under the name G6. I recalled Suzanne taking a screen shot of it and showing it to me. I also remembered that the text Suzanne showed me was followed by several heart emojis. That did not seem like the text of someone who was just friends with Tanner. But the prosecution never presented any illicit texts between the two during the trial, even though Maria's phone and text records were subpoenaed.

The Raymond Fischer story negated the state's entire case, which was based on the narrative that Maria and Tanner were romantically involved, that he left her right after she had the baby, and that she became so angry, she killed him, or had him killed. The state kept this last part vague on purpose, I suspected because it was unlikely that she could have done it by herself.

The only evidence linking Maria to Tanner the night he disappeared was a female witness at a Food Stop grocery store, who believed she saw Tanner and Maria get into a car together in the parking lot. She told investigators what she saw, but she had recently left the country to take care of her sick mother and was not available to testify. Another grocery store employee, Claude Roper, who was bringing the carts inside that night from the parking lot, corroborated this sighting after he was shown a photograph of Maria. He did take the stand.

"Yes, that's her." Claude nodded as the prosecutor asked him to identify Maria in the courtroom by pointing at her.

Maria looked down at her hands folded in her lap when the Claude's finger zeroed in on her from the stand. He quickly pulled his hand back and nervously readjusted his thick, brown glasses, which tilted awkwardly on his nose during his testimony.

Claude wore a plaid shirt buttoned all the way up to his neck. His pimply face was framed by a tangled mass of brown curls that looked like they had never seen a comb.

"I remember her long black hair. It was shiny. I could see it under the light in the parking lot."

Defense attorneys said the sighting was not credible because Claude was only shown *one* photo, a photo of Maria, not a lineup containing photos of Maria along with other people. Prosecutors admitted this was not an ideal way to make an identification, but that the officer in charge of meeting with Claude was a rookie and didn't know the proper procedure. Normally a gaff like this would cause the judge to throw the evidence out, saying it was obtained improperly, but Judge Wemberly allowed it after questioning Claude. The judge did this out of the presence of the jury to determine if Claude was improperly influenced to identify Maria by the photograph.

"No, sir. I knew it was her immediately when I saw that photo. There's no doubt in my mind it was the same woman."

This sighting would have been sometime in the evening, after Juan claimed Tanner had come for a visit, run out to pick some things up, and never returned. When Juan took the stand, he said Maria never left the family's residence behind the restaurant that night. She stayed there with her newborn baby, and therefore could not have been at the grocery store.

"No way. She never left the baby's side, not for a minute," Juan looked directly at the jurors as he made this statement.

He was all cleaned up in a starched white dress shirt. His jet-black hair was slicked back behind his ears. I still wondered if Juan was the real killer. He came across as a combination of a loving brother who would defend his sister to the end of the world, and a gritty hustler who may have acted on that desire.

While it was up for debate whether Maria was at the Food Stop, there was no doubt that Tanner was at the grocery store that night. Or at least his car was. Both Claude and the female tipster noticed a personalized license plate on the car with the letters TJP. This could not be a coincidence.

My gut told me that Maria was not going to be convicted of Tanner's murder. It was a circumstantial case with no direct forensic evidence pointing to her. Sure, they had the gun and the severed hand connected to the restaurant, but one could argue, as defense attorneys did, that hundreds of people had access to that restaurant and could have planted the evidence. With all the traffic in and out of La Fiesta daily, anyone could have stolen the gun and then hid it in the salsa. Hiding Tanner's hand in the freezer was more problematic to explain for Maria's team, but they threw out the possibility that Maria's brothers may have been involved in his death without her knowledge. It was enough of a red herring to raise reasonable doubt.

The other problem with the state's case was that they gave the jury no plausible motive for Maria wanting Tanner dead. Even if she was upset with him, even if they were romantically involved, it made no sense that she would want to kill him, especially if he *was* the father of her child. To date, no DNA test had been done on the child to determine who the father was. It could have been the child of any one of the number of men Maria was forced to sleep with before Tanner intervened in her life. I guessed she didn't want anyone else laying a legal claim to her baby. So she preferred not to know.

The jury deliberated for four days before telling the judge they had done their best, but they were hopelessly deadlocked. I learned about this from a breaking news alert on my phone. I had opted out of them for several months, preferring to be blissfully unaware of the gloom and doom. But I had recently turned them back on when I felt like I was missing too much. The headline on my phone read: *Judge declares mistrial in case of murdered doctor after jurors tell him they cannot reach a unanimous decision.*

As I sat in the parking lot outside the drycleaner, I watched the live courtroom reactions to the judge's decision. I could hear the sound through my car speakers thanks to the magic of Bluetooth. Maria shrieked and then turned to one of her attorneys, a pale redheaded woman, who hugged her and then whispered in her ear. The camera then panned to the other side of the courtroom and zoomed in on Suzanne. The angle was from the side. I could barely see her face, but I could tell her lips were pursed and she was shaking her head. Jessie rubbed her back and laid her head on Suzanne's shoulder. I couldn't see Suzanne's expression. Was it anger? Despair? Disappointment? Finally she turned and looked right into the camera lens, and I saw it. Disgust. She obviously wanted someone to pay for Tanner's murder, but Maria was not going to be that person.

In the days following the trial, I decided it was time to let go of my grief. I realized I was still living in a suspended state of reality where I expected Adam to walk through the door at any moment. It was time to let the pain go.

I sorted through his clothes and gave most of them to charity. I packed up his memorabilia—photos, awards, favorite books, and put them in boxes in the attic for the kids to have someday. I threw away his ratty flip-flops, his razor, and his threadbare robe.

Right after Adam died, I held onto the most bizarre reminders of him—the last towel he showered with, his favorite orange juice, a tinfoil-wrapped piece of used gum discarded at the foot of our bed. It wasn't until I noticed that the bloated container of juice in the refrigerator was full of mold that I threw it away. I continued to smell that shower towel, to bury my face in it every time I needed a good cry in my closet. Finally, the familiar comforting smell of Adam on the towel gave way to the stench of mildew. So I pitched it. Every time I walked by the gum wrapper on the floor, I ignored it against all my obsessive-compulsive inclinations, like it was a literal shrine to my dead husband. One day, I reached down, scooped it up, and threw it in the trashcan like it meant nothing.

Once I moved Adam's belongings out, the house felt lighter, and so did I. I knew he would not want our house to be an altar dedicated to his memory. He wanted to be remembered, of course, but he wanted us to go on living.

He told me when he was dying not to feel obligated to visit his grave.

"I won't be there," he said, on more than one occasion. "I will be with you wherever you are."

"That sounds a little creepy," I replied, through smiling tears and squeezed his hand as I sat in a recliner at his bedside, in our den, where I slept most nights.

Shortly after the trial, I decided it was time to pay Adam's grave a visit for the first time since his death. The lush green canopy of the North Carolina springtime was just beginning to pop. It took over the landscape like a plush blanket in every direction as I drove on the windy country road to the little cemetery.

When I pulled in, the sun was just beginning to dip its pink and orange hues casting a gentle glow across the shiny gray and white granite headstones. To my surprise, someone had put fresh flowers on Adam's grave, a bouquet of white lilies. They were slightly wilted and carefully tied together with a bright purple ribbon.

I got down on my knees and ran my hand across the smooth, damp gravestone, feeling the grooves of the words etched in it with the edges of my fingers. The engraving came from *Gone Girl* by Gillian Flynn, a book I read when Adam was dying: *A rocket science brain with a rodeo spirit*. It perfectly explained my nerdy husband with his throw-caution-to-the-wind tendencies. It was an unconventional grave marker, but I'm sure he would have liked it.

"I'm okay now. We're okay. All three of us. You can get on with whatever you're doing, wherever you are. You don't have to worry about us."

I closed my eyes, and for just a moment, I could smell Adam's scent. For a second he was there with me again. And then—just as quickly, he was gone.

One of the jobs I had Miranda do to earn her allowance was to sort my pictures into photo boxes for everyone, as keepsakes. I was so paranoid about technology changing and losing all my pictures in the damn iCloud, that I still printed them, just to be on the safe side. As the self-proclaimed historian of the family, I wanted to not only preserve our family's history, but I also wanted to make sure that my kids knew I was a good mother, as supported by ample photographic evidence. They went on vacations, they had birthday parties, they had a mother who documented their activities and attended their special events. This would be their visual legacy of my love for them long after I was gone.

I had eschewed real cameras when I discovered the iPhone's built-in camera was good enough to compliment my mediocre photography skills. To save time, I uploaded all my photos to a photo printing website. Often I failed to take the time to sort them and delete the work photos from the mix.

"Mom," Miranda would say, "what do you want me to do with all the pictures of bad guys and pictures of where they did bad stuff?"

"Just throw them away, honey," I would call, from a twisted yoga position on my mat in the den, my voice muffled as my head was facedown. *Mother of the year*, allowing my ten-year-old to view mug shots and crime scene photos. This was life growing up with a crime reporter for a mother.

Like many other tasks, this one often got away from me. Months would go by where I would forget to get my pictures developed, and then I would upload whatever was in my phone, hundreds of photos, mugshots and all, and a big box would arrive a few days later, ready for Miranda to sort.

Shortly after Maria's trial, I uploaded a bunch of photos from the case. Many of them were pictures I had taken in the courtroom during my short stint—Maria sitting stoically at the defendant's table with her attorneys; Juan and the rest of her family sitting in the audience; Suzanne sitting on the other side of the courtroom just behind the prosecutor, nestling with her sister, Jessie.

Some of the photos were of the state's evidence presented in the courtroom during the trial: the clothing Tanner was wearing when he was found, including his white doctor's jacket; the gun police found hidden in the bin of salsa; the freezer with the grisly discovery inside—Tanner's hand.

I also took pictures of the photographic exhibits: photos of the crime scene, of places investigators searched, like the restaurant, Maria's apartment, and Tanner and Suzanne's home. Most of these pictures, I uploaded to my social media posts during the trial to augment people's interest in the case, and to push them to our television coverage. Not everyone could be in the courtroom during a trial, but we knew how to make them feel like they were there.

During the trial, prosecutors showed the jury autopsy photos with Tanner's missing left hand, his arm with a clean cut to the wrist—something defense attorneys pointed out would be a difficult thing for anyone, especially a woman, to achieve with a hand saw. It had to have been done with a power saw, and there was no evidence Maria had ever owned one or had access to one.

The state explained this away by saying that Maria's brothers probably did this after she killed him, as a symbolic gesture, taking away the surgeon's dominant hand to remove his power once and for all. He was a lefty just like Adam. I remembered that from the day he put his cell phone number on his business card and handed it to me.

After the testimony about Maria's ties to Raymond Fischer seemed to negate the prosecutors' theory of a romance between Maria and Tanner, the defense threw another red herring into the mix, saying maybe the killing was in some way connected to a drug cartel that Maria's brothers had ties to, and that cutting off his hand was part of their signature because they believed he was about to sell them out. I had looked up Juan's criminal record, and his brothers'. While there were some minor drug possession infractions, misdemeanor charges for having drugs for personal use, there was no evidence any of them had ever trafficked drugs. For the defense, this strategy was all about creating reasonable doubt.

It was all so far-fetched, like a movie script. It was an impossible leap of faith for the jury to convict Maria on such circumstantial evidence. For two weeks after the trial, the district attorney, Joan Starr, waffled about whether to try Maria a second time. If she did take the case to trial again, it would not be double jeopardy because the first trial had ended in a hung jury, not a decision. I learned from one of my sources in the district attorney's office that Starr and her team had done exit interviews with several of the jurors. Jurors told her the group was split eight to four in favor of acquittal. Armed with this information, Starr thought it would be a bad gamble to try Maria again. She dismissed the charge against her.

Miranda threw the discarded work photos in a trash bag and left them in the corner of the kitchen for me to take outside to the garbage can. Instinctively, I reached in and grabbed a handful. It was probably my last trial, and despite my best intentions, I had more than a little nostalgia for the process.

I thumbed through the photos of the players in the courtroom—Maria with her long black hair neatly braided to the side, looking exhausted at the defense table; Suzanne with her long, black curly mane, looking predictably pulled together, except for the pained expression on her face. Even now, with the chance to study the fine details of Suzanne's face captured in the photos, I still couldn't figure her out. Every time I thought about her, the funeral replayed in my head on a loop. There was her over-the-top warmth towards me and her visible grief—but then I pictured her adjusting her belt and smoothing down her hair. While these seemed like insignificant details, to me, they symbolized an inappropriate attention to self at a time when most people would be drowning in grief.

Tanner's best friend and fellow doctor, Tim Horde, delivered the eulogy at the funeral. He spoke about Tanner's charity work and what a great father he was. The two had attended medical school together and then practiced together briefly. Tim told funny stories about their late nights in medical school, fueled by Mountain Dew, and their first office with its ugly mint-green walls and hand-me-down furniture from Tim's parents in the lobby. His words brought Tanner to life.

"Tanner was a man who wore his integrity quietly, but visibly. He made connections everywhere he went, even with the employees at Taco Bonanza, his favorite vice. Don't judge." Tim chuckled.

A ripple of laughter spread across the audience.

"In fact, the Taco Bonanza employees are here." Tim gestured to several people sitting in the back row of the stately church.

They were still in their brown polyester uniforms with their nametags on them. They gave shy waves when Tim pointed them out and bowed in their direction.

None of this gelled with the heartless philanderer Suzanne had portrayed Tanner to be. The man obviously had many layers. I understood that it was possible for Tanner to be nice to the Taco Bonanza employees and *also* to be an ass to his wife. But it was still a puzzling contradiction that gnawed at me.

And that wasn't the only thing gnawing at me. Soon after his father's death, Winston had made a cement handprint decorated with brightly colored mosaic stones inlaid around the edge of the mold. Etched in his childish handwriting in the stone were the words, *My dad is an angel who watches over my garden*.

I saw Suzanne briefly one time after the funeral and before the trial. She had invited me to her house for coffee. She made it a point to show me the stone in the pristine garden behind her house.

"I can see it from the kitchen window when I'm doing dishes. It just gives me a strange sense of peace. I really can't explain it. It's like there's still a part of him there in the garden. It's like we're still a family, the way it used to be." She stirred her coffee with a silver spoon, absentmindedly, and looked through the window, out into the garden. "You know what I mean, don't you, Maddie?"

I bristled at her suggestion that her grief could be equated to mine. I truly loved my husband, so in my mind, there was no comparison. Not once during this visit did she ever mention the bad things that had happened between her and Tanner. It was like his death had erased his sins. But I knew the truth. The marriage was over and she wanted out.

I shook my head, trying to erase this flashback of my visit with Suzanne. I returned my attention to the pile of photos that were now spread out across my kitchen table in front of me.

There were several photos, from multiple angles, of the large, metal vat of salsa where the gun was found. The photographs showed the industrial-sized can tipped on its side, the muzzle of the gun peeking out from the red chunky liquid.

There were also photos of the gun inside a large plastic evidence bag laid on a white towel. Red, sticky sauce with bits of onions and peppers stuck to the plastic inside the bag.

Defense attorneys argued during the trial that the gun was kept beneath the register at the restaurant for security reasons, but that shortly before Tanner's murder, it disappeared, only to show up later in the salsa container, during the search of the restaurant.

There were a few gruesome photos of Tanner's hand, in the plastic bag at the bottom of the freezer. There were also a few photos of the hand by itself on a white towel on a table, dark red and shriveled like a fake hand you might see as a Halloween decoration.

I cringed thinking about Miranda looking at these. This was definitely not my finest parenting moment. I was hoping maybe she thought the hand was fake. Or maybe it had gone right over her head. I made a mental note to explore this with her later to see if she understood what she saw.

There were routine photos of Tanner and Suzanne's home, during a standard search. Most of the shots were mundane—garage, kitchen, den, bedroom—normal scenes of life in anyone's home, which only stopped being normal when someone was murdered.

There were several shots of Tanner's dresser. The top of it was a jumble of loose change, golf tees, and crumpled receipts. It didn't look like the dresser of a man who had packed his belongings and left his wife. In the middle of what appeared to be a pile of junk, something caught my eye. There was a Rolex watch—not something anyone would leave behind. Right next to the watch, I spotted something else. It was small, silver, and shiny. I grabbed my magnifying glass from the kitchen drawer so I could examine it to more closely. A wave of clarity washed over me as I confirmed that the object was Tanner's custom-made wedding ring with the crisscross pattern of tiny diamonds. There was the ring he never took off, the one that should have been on his missing left hand. Yet it was right there in the pile of discarded stuff, hidden in plain sight.

17

SILVER LININGS

I SAT SNUGGLED on the couch in the den, wrapped in a furry throw blanket even though the heat was cranked up as a defense against the cool early fall breeze nipping at the windows' edges. The photograph was on my lap. The shiny ring was a beacon calling to me in the middle of what anyone else would see as just a pile of stuff. I was itching to call Kojak and tell him what I had discovered in the picture, but he was out of town on a well-deserved vacation in Florida, with his wife. I didn't want to bother him, especially because I didn't know exactly what seeing the wedding ring on Tanner's bureau meant. I knew for sure his wedding ring was never presented as evidence at trial. I remembered the district attorney, Joan Starr, telling the jury in her closing statement that his *missing ring* was one of the many mysteries of this case that would probably never be solved. Police must have missed it when they searched the house. Where was it now?

My gut told me it meant that Suzanne had kept her

husband's wedding ring, kept it from police, kept it for herself. But how did she have access to it if his left hand was missing and he never took it off, except for surgery? My mind wasn't ready to accept what this could mean.

In my experience, once you truly hated someone the way Suzanne had appeared to hate Tanner, it was hard to imagine loving that person enough to publicly grieve for him. I couldn't imagine even pretending to love a man if he had done half of what Suzanne claimed Tanner had done to her. Had he really done those things to her? Or had she made them up to make herself look like a victim?

I studied the photograph again. There was no doubt it was *the ring* I saw Tanner wearing that day in his office, the ring that should have been on his missing left hand when he died. Instead it was discarded on his bureau in a pile of junk like it didn't mean anything at all. Maybe he took it off when he left, as a symbolic gesture of the dissolution of their marriage. "They cost a small fortune." I recalled Suzanne telling me the day we went running. "He never takes it off, even to sleep. He is paranoid about someone stealing it. It is a symbol of our lifetime union."

If Suzanne had something to do with Tanner's death, but wanted to keep the expensive ring, or maybe sell it, she couldn't have put it with her things; that would have been too obvious. In case investigators found it, she would need to make it look like Tanner had just taken it off and left it on his bureau among his other belongings. It was reckless, but smart. When police didn't zone in on the ring during the search, maybe she figured she was home free and it was hers to do with what she wanted.

I realized my new theory was as crazy as the drug cartel cutting off Tanner's hand. His left hand was his surgery hand, his golden hand, but it all seemed so far-fetched. In my mind, either the killer wanted investigators to *think* a deranged person had killed Tanner, or the killer *was* a deranged person. My brain was racing with so many disjointed thoughts that I almost didn't hear my phone ring.

"This is Maddie, Maddie Arnette."

"Mrs. Arnette, I'm not sure if you will remember me. My name is Lucinda, Lucinda Bark."

The name sounded familiar. It was an unusual name, not one you were likely to forget. I scanned my photographic memory for an image. A vision of a beautiful black woman with dreadlocks and a peasant shirt came to mind, but I couldn't place her.

"A while back I did a story with you about ducks, saving ducks in the Food Stop parking lot."

"Yes, yes, of course I remember you."

The last thing I wanted to think about at that moment was a story about saving ducks, but I also realized I had chosen to answer the phone. I could have let it go to voicemail. So I needed to be polite, but my energy and attention for the mundane were waning.

"Well, I'm not sure if you know this or not, but I was interviewed by the police about a murder case I think you covered. The doctor, the one they found in the ditch, the one with the missing hand?"

She had my full attention. It was like two disparate worlds colliding, creating an explosion of confusion. I couldn't imagine what the duck lady would have to do with Tanner's murder case.

"I didn't testify at the trial because I was back in Haiti. My mother was dying of cancer, and I went home to take care of her until she passed."

"I'm so sorry."

"M, too. Thank you. She was an amazing woman. And as far as the case went, I just didn't want to be on display in a courtroom. I'm sure you hear this all the time, but with what I was going through with my mom, I really didn't want to be involved. I know it sounds weak, like I didn't care about the truth, about doing the right thing, but I did, I really did, in my own way. It just wasn't a battle I had the energy to deal with at that time. The police assured me they had another eyewitness from that night, another employee who saw the same thing I did. He was willing and available to testify. So they really didn't need me. Anyway, they took a statement from me about what I saw. I told them I saw the doctor, Tanner Pope, and the woman who was charged, Maria Lopez, with the long dark hair, getting into his car at the grocery store the night he disappeared. Of course, I didn't know his name at the time, but I remembered the fancy car and the personalized license plate."

While I hadn't covered much of the trial, on a personal level, I had followed it closely. I remembered how important this detail was to the state's case. There was no physical evidence connecting Maria to Tanner the night he was killed. This eyewitness sighting was the only thing that put them in the same place.

"Anyway, I really need to speak with you, because I think I may have been wrong, and I don't know what to do about it now. I've got to make it right. I can't sleep at night. It's been consuming me. I didn't know who else to talk to. You were so fair and kind that day I met you. I thought you might be able to help steer me in the right direction."

I sat there holding the photo of Tanner's wedding ring on his bureau with one hand and cradling the phone in the other hand as Lucinda rambled on nervously. At that moment my discovery and what Lucinda was about to tell me seemed of equal importance.

"What makes you so sure you were wrong?"

"It's been tugging at me for a long time, back there in the deep in my brain. I kept trying to ignore it, but I just can't do that anymore. I was so caught up in what was going on with my mother that I couldn't process it. When I saw them that night in the parking lot, the woman, well she turned and looked at me, maybe for just a fraction of a second, but I could see her face clearly under the bright light in the parking lot. You'd be surprised how bright those lights are when you stand directly beneath one. I just caught a glimpse, but she looked very different than the woman they arrested. I watched the trial online. And I studied that woman's face, Maria's face. I really don't think it was her that night in the parking lot. I've thought about it a lot, and I'm sure I was wrong."

"Well, as you know, she was never convicted. So thankfully, your misidentification, if it was wrong, didn't cause an innocent woman to go to prison. But it's an important detail, one that you need to share with police. Because if it wasn't her, then there is a killer still out there, and that person needs to be caught. Plus, Maria could always potentially be retried on this charge, although I don't think it will happen. But she does deserve to have her name properly cleared, after what she's been through."

"I agree one hundred percent. I knew it was the right thing to give you a call. I knew you would know what to do. And one more thing, I don't know if this means anything, but I never mentioned it to police because I didn't think it was important at the time, but maybe it is. The woman I saw that night, she had a purse, a big silver purse over her shoulder. I'm absolutely *positive* about that."

Lucinda's call unnerved me. There had been so many signs pointing to Suzanne's involvement in Tanner's murder, but I had ignored them. *A woman could never do this alone.* Kojak and I had repeated a hundred times to each other. *So she had help. She's a beautiful woman. It's not crazy to think someone would be willing to help her.*

I had a fitful sleep where I wrestled with my covers and eventually threw them off because I was burning up despite the whirring ceiling fan. When I finally awoke, something else jumped into my mind. She said *Pennsylvania.* The day I met Suzanne at the Oak City Bistro for lunch and she told me Tanner had left, she referred to Pennsylvania during our conversation, the place where my mother had been killed at my grandparents' house. When I first realized it, it bothered me. But I shrugged it off, thinking I must have mentioned it to her. But now I was *positive* that I had never mentioned Pennsylvania to her in any of our previous conversations. I had remembered this detail earlier and dismissed it, thinking I must have heard her wrong. But I hadn't. She knew this detail before I told her, which meant she must have researched me. She must have known my family's history all along. She targeted me, used me in her scheme to play the victimized wife because she knew I would be more likely to believe her. Plus I was the former crime reporter at the station, so I had sources within the police department. I had influence within the newsroom. What better ally to have in her master plan than someone like me?

There was no doubt that I had been duped. Suzanne knew exactly who I was the day she must have faked her accident and accused her husband of trying to kill her. She made me believe her, made me worry about her, and used me to make a case against Maria. I set Maria up by sharing information with Kojak, who in turn shared it with homicide detectives when Tanner turned up dead.

After the mistrial, the detectives continued to work on the case, acknowledging behind the scenes that they may have been wrong. They focused primarily on Maria's brothers. But

Kojak told me they worked on it halfheartedly, knowing the district attorney, Joan Starr, was unlikely to give them another shot at a new suspect after the time and money she had spent trying Maria.

Still when I told Kojak about the ring, about Lucinda's recanting of her eyewitness identification, and about the silver purse, he couldn't help but get excited. He didn't even mind that I was interrupting his vacation. Like me, he had always been skeptical of Maria being the killer. At most he believed maybe one of her brothers or cousins had killed Tanner in a misguided attempt to protect her honor, but even that theory never sat well with him.

"And she knew about me, about my personal story, details I never told her," I said to Kojak, with embarrassment in my voice.

"About your mom?"

"Yes, about my mom."

That was the moment he went from *considering* I was on the right track, to *believing* I was on the right track.

Kojak always told me that every case had one irrefutable piece of evidence, and that if you found it, you had your man, or in this case, *your woman*.

Detectives worked quietly with the new information I had given them, all the while digging deeper into Suzanne's background. They learned she had cashed in on a major life insurance policy after Tanner's death. They also learned from her ex-husband, Clint Stamos, that she had been diagnosed with narcissistic personality disorder during their marriage, a condition that ultimately tore them apart after she refused to go to therapy.

In their divorce filings, Stamos said Parker was "full of delusions of self-grandeur, paranoid, devoid of empathy, sometimes terrifying to be around." He said she frequently lied and often made up horrible stories about him to her friends to get attention. He also said she had a twisted fascination with symbolism that included keeping a lock of hair from a girl she had once fought in junior high, as a trophy in an old scrapbook. He said when he asked her about it, she told him she had ripped the girl's hair out behind the bleachers during a football game because the girl had made a pass at her boyfriend. Rather than being embarrassed by the incident, Stamos said Suzanne appeared to be proud.

In a new official photo lineup, which included pictures of Maria, Suzanne, and others, Food Stop employees Claude Roper and Lucinda Bark identified *Suzanne* as the woman in the parking lot with Tanner that night, *not* Maria. Claude profusely apologized to investigators, telling them he never meant to lie on the stand, but he had only been shown one photo originally—a photo of Maria.

While the new identifications were groundbreaking evidence, it would be problematic for the state if the case went to trial and the witnesses had to explain to the jury why they had changed their opinions. And these revelations were not enough on their own to make a case for murder. Investigators needed the smoking gun, or in this case, something to link Suzanne to Tanner's missing hand. It was also going to be hard to convince the district attorney that Suzanne did this by herself—cut off a man's hand and dumped a body. Kojak and I were sure she had help, but who that help came from we would probably never know.

I decided to do a little investigative work of my own. I knew detectives had already gone down this road and that Kojak would be furious if he found out what I was up to, but I decided it was time to pay a visit to the person who bought the freezer with Tanner's hand inside.

The heavyset woman said, "We bought it from a restaurant

in Oak City off Craigslist. They were replacing all their freezers, getting modern ones." She adjusted her purple scoop neck t-shirt and swayed back and forth on the balls of her feet.

She said her name was Rose, and her husband, Bud, and she had driven to Oak City to pick up the freezer. Bud wasn't home now, but Rose had opened her door to me, a perfect stranger, and now we were chatting in front of her house.

"But I really don't think I need to be talking to you. I already talked to the cops. You a lawyer?"

"No, nothing like that. Just a writer trying to figure some things out."

"A writer. Wow. I been writing a book for a long time now. It's pretty good, I think. Do you think you could look at it? I'd love a *professional* to read it."

A small white cat walked in between us and nuzzled my ankle.

"That's Snowball. My neighbor died and now I have her. She's a real sweetheart, but the problem is, I don't have the money to get her fixed, get her shots, feed her, buy litter. Already have two dogs. Nothing against cats. Need to find a home for her. I really need to go now. Bud wouldn't like me talking to you."

The woman dropped her cigarette in the dirt and crushed it with the toe of her faded yellow Croc. She turned to go back inside her tiny brick ranch house that had nothing but dirt for a front yard. Piles of old stuff—cans, broken clay pots, wooden planks—were stacked up on the porch near the front door. As she opened the screen door, I tried to think about what I might offer her, anything that would keep her talking to me.

"I may be able to help you find a home for your cat. I have so many followers on social media. We'll post a picture of her, with your contact information."

"You would do that for me?" The woman peered back at me through the screen door, suspiciously. I was anxious to make the deal because I was pretty sure Bud would shut her down if he came home and found me there.

"Sure, if you'll talk to me."

She stared at me, surveying me up and down. I regretted wearing heels and a fitted red dress. I was coming across as a city girl—not the best way to approach a country girl.

"Okay, first you post the cat online. Then we'll talk."

I did as she asked, luring Snowball to me with some high-pitched baby talk while I followed her with my iPhone to get her on video.

"I got good pictures of her that I can send you if you give me your phone number. I love to take pictures. Take pictures of her all the time." Rose followed me closely as if she didn't trust me with Snowball.

I posted the video and the pictures on Facebook, Twitter, and Instagram, along with a note that she needed a good home. I also included Rose's name and contact information, although I was starting to think Rose had given me a fake name, because when I called out to her, it took a few seconds for her to realize I was speaking to her each time.

The lady I knew as Rose then invited me into her den to talk, scooping a pile of laundry off the tattered, stained couch, and brushing ashes off the faded green seat cushion as she ushered me to sit down.

"Met us in a gravel parking lot up in Oak City somewhere, not sure where. Don't know the city that well. Woman had the freezer on a little dolly, used a pull-out ramp to roll the freezer up into the truck. Real friendly gal. She was with a guy, messy hair, lots of tattoos, skull rings. You know, like a motorcycle dude. *She had help,* I thought. *But who?*

"I stayed in the truck, but Bud got out and dealt with them. He's good that way with people. I'm on the shy side. The guy said nothing at all, just helped Bud load it up. But then that lady came over to the passenger window in the truck where I was sitting, and she told me to make sure I kept it plugged in from the minute we got home. Said these freezers lost their ability to cool if they stayed unplugged for too long. The top was wrapped in duct tape, she said to keep it stable on the ride. Didn't open it for a few days, until I did my big shopping at the Cost Mart and needed the space for the big packs of meat and whatnot."

I listened intently, not leaving her gaze. It was true that the restaurant had recently sold some of its freezers and replaced them with new ones. But they were all sold directly from the restaurant. Buyers pulled up, and Maria's brothers loaded the freezers into their trucks and vans. There was no mention of any being sold offsite, in a random gravel parking lot in Oak City. I was amazed that this detail had slipped through the cracks of the original investigation. Or maybe detectives discarded it because it didn't gel with their narrative of the case. *And who was the mystery man, the helper?*

"When I did open it, it was smaller than I expected. Bud didn't even think the food from my one shopping trip was going to fit. I was pissed. About to tell Bud we got gipped. But we crammed the food in. Was a white panel in the bottom of the thing. It was uneven. When I put my groceries in there, they was lopsided. Wouldn't stand up straight. About drove me crazy. We took everything out and I pried up the panel with my nails. Couldn't believe my eyes, like something out of a scary movie. Plain as day. It was a hand, a bloody hand in a plastic bag. Thought it was some kind a sick joke. Closed it and we called my neighbor Earl to come take a looksee. Earl has seen some rough stuff in his days. Said it was real. So we called 911 right away. I didn't want to get caught with that thing up in my house. I knew it had to belong to somebody. Somebody was missing it."

"The woman, the one who sold you the freezer. What did she look like? Do you recall?"

"Sure, I do. Long black hair, real plain, no makeup. Baseball hat, jeans. But pretty. Said her name was Maria, and that the freezer was from a Mexican restaurant her family owned. Funny thing is she wasn't no Mexican. She was a white girl."

"Did you or Bud tell the police this?"

"Nope. They didn't ask us. We don't tell cops more than we need to. I already done told you way more than I should, but it's for a good cause, for Snowball's sake."

"If I showed you a picture of the woman I think it might be, do you think you would recognize her?"

"Sure, I could. But you don't need to do that. I got a picture of her and him, the guy she was with."

"What?"

"She was in the background while the motorcycle dude and Bud were unloading the freezer. I was taking pictures of Snowball prancing around the parking lot. We take her with us everywhere, and when a cat's been cooped up in the cab of a truck for forty minutes, Lord knows she's got to roam."

I looked down at her phone as she handed it to me. There was a picture of Snowball, larger than life, in the foreground. In the background, an older man in overalls—who I assumed was Bud—was strapping down the freezer with bungee cords in the back of the truck, with the help of a forty-something messy haired, hard-living *motorcycle dude* as Rose had called him. A pretty, dark-haired woman was standing in the background, to the right of the truck, with her work-gloved clad hands on her hips. It didn't take long for me to figure out that the woman was not Maria—it was Suzanne. It took me longer to identify the man. But after staring at the photo for another minute I recognized him. It was Larry Boone, the artist who had made the duck crossing sign at the Food Stop, Lucinda's co-worker.

I took a photo of Rose's screen with my phone, and then texted the picture to Kojak, with an explanation of what he was looking at. He sent me back an emoji of a smoking gun.

It was race day again. The anniversary of the day my world first collided with Suzanne's. I could still recall my intense energy that morning, jumping around, stretching, trying to shake off the nerves. A damp mist had wrapped around us in the dark as we waited not-so-patiently for the sunrise start. If I had known what was about to happen, I might not have left the starting line that day.

This was my first time watching a race instead of participating. I couldn't help but feel a pang of disappointment that I wasn't part of it. But today I had a greater purpose.

It was chillier than it had been last year. I was bundled up in a medium-weight zip-up down coat, a hat and gloves. The runners started with layers, many of them from the thrift shop, and shed them along the way as they got hot. The street was littered with old oversized sweatshirts, ripped sweatpants, and cheap mittens and hats most likely purchased from the Cost Mart dollar bins. Just looking at the runners stripped down to their tank tops and tiny running shorts gave me a secondhand shiver.

I had parked my car a few blocks away, tucked into one of the many unknown secret spots in the city that only true locals knew about, and walked towards the finish line. I was waiting for Kojak's call. He promised me I would be the first person to know after he got the go-ahead from the district attorney.

As I watched the exhausted runners slog toward the end of the 26.2 miles, I noticed that most of them, despite their obvious fatigue, were smiling. And why not? They could see the finish line now. For most of the race they could only imagine it. But now it was there, glowing in the distance, not a mirage, but a tangible thing, a beacon of hope, a reward for all their hard work over the past few months. I recalled this moment vividly, the visceral exhilaration in a race I felt when the end was in sight.

One more important piece of information had surfaced in Tanner's murder case. After I gave investigators the photo of Tanner's wedding ring, they interviewed his nurses and desk staff about whether he was wearing the ring when he left his office the day he disappeared. They said that he was. He was also still wearing his white doctor's jacket. Police re-interviewed Maria and her family, too, although they were reluctant to speak with investigators after what they had put her through. But her lawyer gave her the go-head to answer a limited number of questions. They, too, said Tanner was wearing the ring and his white jacket when he left to pick up diapers and formula for her.

I marveled at the variety of runners who were almost at the finish line. They all had unique stories that had brought them here. There was an older man with a white beard and a headband decorated like a rainbow. He was staggering towards the finish with a huge grin on his face despite his obvious pain. There was a young woman with a freckled face, dressed head-to-toe in purple, with her hair in French braids, bopping her head to her music. There was a middle-aged man dressed in a US Navy t-shirt, running with a prosthetic leg.

My observations were interrupted by the annoyingly loud ringing of my phone, which Miranda had secretly changed to "I Want You Back" by her favorite band, 5 Seconds of Summer. I fumbled with the phone, embarrassed to be interrupting everyone.

"We got it," Kojak said, in a loud whisper. "The arrest warrant. We got it."

"Wow. I don't know what to say."

"It's all you, kid. You made this possible. You wouldn't give up. You're an honorary detective now. Larry Boone talked. Spilled the beans. Met him at the grocery store. Said she paid him a bunch of money and also gave him a little roll in the hay in return for his help and silence. Said he thought they were *in love,* if you can believe that shit. He's getting a deal in return for his testimony."

"Wow, that's amazing," I said, noticing myself using Janie's catch phrase. But this time it fit. "My pleasure. But keep my name out of this."

"What name? I don't even know who I'm talking to," Kojak chuckled softly.

"Did they find the wedding ring?"

"Just where you said it would be. In the garden, under Winston's palm print stone. Very creepy place to hide it."

It had been a guess, but it was a good guess.

"Thanks for the call."

"You bet."

As I put my phone back into my pocket, I watched more runners zoom by me with their it's-almost-over smiles. Some were limping, some were crying, others scanned the crowd for their family and friends. Finally, I spotted her. She was triumphant. Her shiny black ponytail bounced high atop her head. She was dressed all hot pink—a tight tank top and capri leggings decorated with purple swirls. She wore black, wraparound sunglasses. White Airpods protruded from her ears and connected to her iPhone in a clear plastic case on her upper right arm. As she passed, she noticed me on the sidelines for just a split second and gave me a frantic little wave. I almost felt guilty. *Almost.*

It might have been the wireless earbuds, or the roar of the cheering crowd that blocked out the sirens. Seconds before Suzanne's feet would have touched the finish line, two Oak City police officers pulled up in a patrol car across the street, blue lights blazing. They jumped out, hopped over the orange webbed safety fence, and grabbed her by her elbows. She looked from one to the other. At first her face looked surprised, then resigned. She looked like she might collapse as they escorted her to the waiting patrol car. The crowd of runners swallowed the trio, and I lost sight of them.

By the time I crossed the road, dodging the finishers, the patrol car was already pulling away. I looked down at the ground where the car had been. It was littered with runners' numbers, empty water bottles, and confetti. Race waste. But one thing caught my eye—a bright pink hairband emblazoned with purple smiley faces. I had never seen another one like it. It was mine, the one Miranda had given me for good luck at my first race, the one I had given Suzanne the day we ran together in the park. I reached down, scooped up the hairband and shoved it into my jacket pocket.

I turned and headed toward my car. Over my shoulder, in the distance, people were struggling to finish the race. I remembered that feeling, when I was close to the end of a race and wasn't sure if I could make it. The truth was that no matter how many runners started the race, someone always had to be last. Today that person was Suzanne Parker.

PREVIEW OF "LIES THAT BIND"

THAT SINGLE SENTENCE unraveled all the good in just a few seconds. The good vanished like an exhale on a cold day, that floats away immediately after you take a breath.

It wasn't really an admission. It was just four simple words. You couldn't help yourself. My questions put you on the defensive.

"What's it to you?"

They came on the heels of my inquiry, indirect, but subtle words with a subtext we both understood to be an accusation. It wasn't what you did. It was about what it symbolized—the darkness of a person I didn't know, didn't want to know.

"You know what you did," I said.

To my surprise, I said it without anger, or even despair. It just came out. I hadn't planned to say it, but there it was, out in the open. And once it was out there, you only had two choices—lie, or admit to it.

I'm pretty sure that you knew me well enough to know

your admission changed everything. It undermined any positive narrative I had spun about you over the years. My naïve heart was broken, shattered under the weight of your ugly truth.

"What's it to you?"

The flippant way you said it, your inflection, made me realize you were not the man I had fantasized about. You were a stranger, a vain interloper preying on my vulnerable spirit. How could I be so wrong about a person? I've been beating myself up every single day since that moment, wondering where I went off course.

No, you didn't do it to me. Frankly it had little to do with me. But your admission finally made me see the real you. It also did something else, something brilliant. It set me free.

—Tilly

"Maddie, Maddie Arnette?" The unfamiliar woman tugged at my sleeve. I was used to people coming up to me in public places because I was a local television news reporter, but this was something different. This felt personal.

I scanned the grocery store and surveyed the dozens of people milling around the produce, examining the tomatoes, avocados, and heads of lettuce for imperfections and then putting them into their carts once they had passed the eyeball test. I was safe. I was not alone. Nothing bad could happen to me here. At least that's what I told myself.

"Yes," I replied, after a long pause. "That's me."

"I've been trying to get in touch with you for a while. This is going to sound weird, but I have some important information for you. I know something that you need to know."

"I'm listening," I finally got a grip on the thin plastic bag, and peeled it open to put bananas inside.

It took me three tries to open the bag, one less than usually. I was silently applauding myself.

I was half-listening. People routinely approached me with story ideas. Most of the time, their pitches were like the diverging roots of a tree—long and bending, curling down into the soil in a million directions with no real focus. Stories I could never corral into a minute-and-a-half television segment. But I always tried to be polite.

"It's about your father, Roger."

"What about Roger?"

My heart started beating faster. I chose not to think about him most days, because when I did, I spiraled into a panic attack. We had been estranged so long—decades—that it was easy for me not to think about him.

"I know this is going to sound crazy, but I know Roger didn't kill your mother."

The other shoppers in the brightly lit grocery store vanished, and it was just me and the woman in the red puffy winter coat, standing between the apples and the oranges.

"How do you know that?" I whispered, as I leaned closer to her.

"Because my son is the one. He killed your mother. The wrong man went to prison."

ACKNOWLEDGEMENTS

I WOULD LIKE TO THANK all the characters I have met along the way, in the television news business and in the field, who served as muses for my first work of fiction. Any perceived connection to real people or real news stories I have covered is coincidental. All my characters and scenarios are fictional. I would also like to thank my cousin Leslie for originally editing the book, and my favorite unpaid assistant, Kelly, for giving me important notes. And special thanks to Light Messages Publishing and my editor Elizabeth Turnbull for all their hard work in making my first novel something of which I can be truly proud.

ABOUT THE AUTHOR

AMANDA LAMB is a television reporter with three decades of experience. She covers the crime beat for an award-winning NBC affiliate in the southeast. She is also the author of nine published books—three true crimes, four memoirs, and two children's books.

Amanda makes her home in North Carolina with her husband, two daughters, and her poodle, Dolly Parton.

IF YOU LIKED DEAD LAST YOU'LL LOVE THESE BOOKS

The Nicole Graves Mysteries

The *Nicole Graves Mysteries* have been compared to the mysteries of Mary Higgins Clark and praised for **contributing to the "women-driven mystery field with panache"** (*Foreword Reviews*) as well as for their "hold-onto-the-bar roller coaster" plots (*RT Book Reviews*). *Kirkus Reviews* concluded, "Boyarsky's weightless complications expertly combine menace with bling, making the heroine's adventures both nightmarish and dreamy."

Saving Tuna Street

(*The Blanche Murninghan Mysteries*, Book 1)

Blanche "Bang" Murninghan is a part-time journalist with writer's block and a penchant for walking the beach on her beloved Santa Maria Island. When her dear friend is found murdered in the parking lot of the marina, Blanche begins digging to find who's behind his death. The deeper she goes, the more it seems like she's digging her own grave.